Blessed Transgression

Lois Jean Thomas

Seventh Child Publishing, LLC

All scripture verses are taken from the King James Version of the Holy Bible.

Cover design by Allen Thomas and Lois Jean Thomas

ISBN: 978-0-9910749-8-3

Library of Congress Control Number: 2015911364

Lois Jean Thomas, Saint Joseph, Michigan

This book is fondly dedicated to my siblings: Stan, Ron, Gary, Charlie, Esther, Rachel, Mark, and Janet, who all shared with me the experience of growing up Mennonite.

CONTENTS

CHAPTER 1 1

CHAPTER 2 10

CHAPTER 3 20

CHAPTER 4 28

CHAPTER 5 34

CHAPTER 6 42

CHAPTER 7 58

CHAPTER 8 71

CHAPTER 9 78

CHAPTER 10 86

CHAPTER 11 95

Chapter 12 106

CHAPTER 13 112

CHAPTER 14 123

CHAPTER 15 138

CHAPTER 16 150

CHAPTER 17 162

CHAPTER 18 177

CHAPTER 19 192

CHAPTER 20 206

CHAPTER 21 215

CHAPTER 22 225

CHAPTER 23 241

CHAPTER 24 250

CHAPTER 25 257

CHAPTER 26 268

CHAPTER 27 278

CHAPTER 28 287

ACKNOWLEDGMENTS

As always, I'd like to express my deepest gratitude to my husband Allen, for his endless patience and kind support in helping me format this book.

A special thanks to my sister Rachel Roberts who provided some of the details used in the story.

And a big thank you to the members of Writers' Bloc: Marnie, Judy, Anne, Sue, Isabel, Richard, and Mike. Your feedback helped make this a better story.

Most of all, I am indebted to my dreamtime muse, who kindly offered me the inspiration for this novel.

Blessed Transgression

Lois Jean Thomas

CHAPTER 1

"Train up a child in the way [she] should go . . . ."
Proverbs 22:6

No one ever said my father, Herman Unruh III, was a handsome man. But I didn't mind that, not in the least. I wasn't at all concerned about his lack of good looks, because he was everything I ever needed him to be.

People did, however, say my father looked a lot like Spencer Tracy. As a Mennonite child, I wasn't allowed to watch movies, and I had no context for this comparison. But later on, I could attest to their physical similarities. I've seen my father in his 1942 wedding photo, standing in his wide-lapelled, pinstriped suit next to my mother in her unadorned white dress, and I've known him as a dear old man. Like Spencer Tracy, my father's pleasant, youthful face became craggy in mature adulthood, and his stocky frame grew heavy. But while his look-alike movie star sported a head of white hair in his older years, my father ended up bald, with the perfect dome of his large cranium encircled by a fringe of faded red hair. And my father never shared Mr. Tracy's problem with alcohol, as being a Mennonite, he never touched a drop of intoxicating drink.

My father's kindly nature and unpretentious manner made him easy to be with. It seemed that he was loved by everyone, although I had to wonder how my mother felt about him. When he'd wrap his beefy arms around her and kiss her cheek, she'd wince. If she thought no one was watching, she'd pull away and say, "Don't!"

My mother, Ada Hochstedler Unruh, could have been a beautiful woman, as lovely as Hedy Lamarr, if she'd only tended to her looks. But by the time I came along, she'd let go of all such efforts. Each morning, she'd hastily twist her long, gray-streaked hair into a bun, the same style worn by other Mennonite women in our community. Throughout the day, wisps of hair would escape the bun, springing out in every which direction, giving her a harried look. She always appeared frail and thin, except for the sloppy little roll of fat she'd grown around her once-waspish waist.

My mother was nervous, her movements sharp and angry. She seldom laughed, and despair clouded her dark brown eyes. Being around her made me feel agitated.

I much preferred the company of my father, whose calm demeanor invariably soothed my wounded feelings or smoothed my ruffled feathers. I've seen pictures of me as a baby curled up on the broad expanse of his chest, thumb in my mouth, lulled to sleep by the slow, deep rhythm of his breathing.

I continued to find refuge in my father's lap for years to come, until my long, skinny legs hung all the way to the floor. I loved laying my head against the warmth of his heart, listening to the reassuring thump-thump, thump-thump. The fingers of my left hand had a habit of reaching around to the nape of his neck, searching for a lock of curly hair to twist while I sucked the thumb of my right hand. Afterwards, the twisted lock would stick out at an odd angle. My mother would swat at it with a testy hand and say, "Herman, you need to get your hair cut."

I was born late in my parents' lives, in May 1960, when my mother was thirty-nine and my father was forty-three. Because I was so much younger than my three siblings, my childhood bore little resemblance to theirs.

I had little involvement with relatives. My mother had one sister, Myrtle, who never married. Their widowed mother lived with Myrtle in Archbold, Ohio. I dreaded our annual Ohio trips, and tried my parents' patience with the repeated question of every fretful child on a long road trip: "Are we almost there?" I found my aunt and grandmother, both nervous, finicky women like my mother, neither interesting nor engaging.

My father's family lived in Kansas, and he maintained little contact with them. Once when I was five, I was sitting on his lap entertaining myself with a shoebox of old photographs from the shelf in my mother's closet. He pointed to dog-eared picture of a man and woman standing in front of a farmhouse. "See this, Vickie?" he said. "This is where I grew up. These people are my mom and dad."

I peered closely at the sturdily built man with suspenders holding up his rough work pants, standing next to a heavy-set woman in a dark, ankle-length dress. Both stared at the camera, haggard and grim-faced. "Why don't I know them?" I asked.

My father took the photo from my hand and gazed at it for a long moment. "Because they're dead, Vickie. They died before you were born."

"Why?"

Another silence ensued before he said, "I guess life in Kansas wore 'em plumb out."

I barely even knew my own brothers. Michael and Robert, both dark-haired and dark-eyed like my mother's side of the family, were seventeen and sixteen when I was born. I have no memory of them living with the rest of us in our farmhouse on the outskirts of Goshen, Indiana. Following their high school graduations, each of the boys left to attend Eastern Mennonite College in Harrisonburg, Virginia. Both of them married girls from Virginia, and they settled down and raised their families in that part of the country.

Once every couple of years, my brothers would come for a brief visit, and for a day or two, I'd play with nieces and nephews just a few years younger than me. For some reason, my brothers seemed ill at ease around us, as if they were reluctant to expose their newly formed families to the family they came from. Little did I know there was a story, carried along in the memories of my parents and siblings, an underground river of silent shame that, years later, would become a torrent when it converged with the stream of my own life.

However, my sister Lucinda, nine-and-a-half years my senior, was ever-present in my life, a red-headed bundle of turbulence. Once, a woman in our church said to me, "We all thought Lucy was your parents' last baby. Then, almost ten years later, you came along." I imagine being displaced as the youngest in the family was hard on Lucy.

My full name, Victoria Grace Unruh, leant itself to variations. My mother never called me anything but a prim *Victoria.* To my father, I was *Vickie,* and when he was being playful, he'd call me *Vickie, Vickie, Vickie.*

I actually preferred Lucy's elegant little nickname for me, *Tori Grace.* On the rare occasion when she seemed to welcome my presence, she'd croon the name in the sweetest of tones, and I'd feel like the most beloved little sister on the planet. But most of the time when she called out *Tori Grace*, the three syllables were punctuated by a harsh exclamation point.

My father was a rural mail carrier, with a route on the west side of Goshen where we lived. My mother stayed home with me the first five years of my life, feeding me nutritious meals, keeping me in clean dresses, and deftly fixing my hair in two tidy braids every morning. At bedtime, she'd dutifully read me a story from the set of Bible Story books kept on a shelf in our living room, well-worn volumes that had also served as tools for the spiritual edification of my older siblings. She provided all this care without showing me much affection.

When I entered kindergarten at Model Elementary School, she took a part-time job as a secretary in the Bible and Religion department at Goshen College. She worked mornings while I was in school, and picked me up on her way home.

Those rides home were the closest she ever came to spending quality time with me. When she'd pull up to the school in her old, black Studebaker, I'd jump into the car, waving the picture I'd colored that morning.

"What did you learn today, Victoria?" she'd ask, almost smiling at me. I'd spout off the letters and numbers I'd so easily mastered, the simple sentences I'd learned to read. Then I'd chatter away about the social life in the classroom: who I'd played with that morning, who'd acted up and gotten punished by the teacher, who'd been mean to me and made me feel like hitting them.

My mother would invariably respond with a chiding,

"Victoria, you know I expect you to behave in school."

We often ran errands before going home, stopping by Salem Bank to deposit her paycheck or picking up a few groceries at Kroger's. I knew better than to beg for special treats when we shopped. Childish fussing never made an impact on my mother, as it simply bounced off the wall of sternness she'd built around herself.

My mother was a dedicated member of the Women's Fellowship at our church, Westside Mennonite. The ladies met in the church basement every Wednesday evening, where they devoted themselves to one charitable project or another. Their most notable activity was making quilts and comforters for the Mennonite Central Committee, a Christian organization that provided relief to impoverished people around the world.

After picking me up from kindergarten one afternoon, my mother drove to the G. L. Perry store to purchase quilting supplies. While she selected yards of fabric and spools of thread, I stood in front of the display of paper-dolls, admiring Patty Duke, Betsy McCall, and Cinderella. Their fabulous paper wardrobes, with outfits for every occasion, boggled my little Mennonite mind, as my closet held only a few plain dresses.

When my mother came to fetch me, she surprised me by saying, "Go ahead, Victoria, you can pick one." I happily chose Cinderella, and the checkout clerk tucked my acquisition into a separate bag that I proudly carried out of the store.

Later that afternoon, I sat on the living room floor, cutting out Cinderella's ball gown with my blunt-tipped scissors. Suddenly, I heard my father, home from his mail route, trudging heavily up the front steps and across the creaking porch. Momentarily distracted, I inadvertently cut off one of the tabs that folded over Cinderella's shoulder to hold the gown in place.

"Daddy!" I chortled, jumping up to greet him.

"Vickie!" he responded, playfully tugging one of my long, dark braids. He ambled over to his shabby armchair and wearily lowered his hefty body into it.

I picked up the paper ball gown and the severed tab. "Look what happened, Daddy," I whined, presenting the results of my mishap for his inspection.

"Oh, we can fix that just fine," he said. "Bring me the tape from the desk drawer."

After fetching the tape, I clambered onto his lap. "You've gotta sit still now, Vickie," he said. "When you wiggle around, your bony little bottom digs into my leg."

"Herr-mann!" my mother's fretful voice called from the kitchen. "I need your help out here."

"Give me a minute, Ada," he called back. "I need to catch my breath."

"Herr-mann, Herr-mann," I sang, imitating the cadence of my mother's voice. "Why are you named Herman, Daddy? That's a silly name."

"Well, Vickie," he said as he carefully reattached the tab to the gown with a strip of tape. "It's a family tradition. My grandfather was named Herman, my father was named Herman, and I was named Herman. The oldest son in every family was named Herman." His voice sounded wistful. "Three generations of Herman Unruhs lived on our wheat farm in Kansas."

"Why wasn't Michael named Herman?" I asked. "He's the oldest boy in our family."

"Well, your mother thought the name Herman was too old-fashioned. She wanted to name Michael something that sounded more modern. I suppose she was right. I don't think a boy would like to be called Herman in this day and age."

He sighed as he pulled me into the crook of his arm. "No more Herman Unruhs, Vickie. I'm the last one. No more farm in Kansas."

{Herman Unruh II and his wife Mary sit with their nineteen-year-old son at the kitchen table of their small farmhouse in western Kansas. Young Herman has known this day would come. He glances at his father, but can't bear to witness the expression of utter defeat etched into the lines of the older man's face. So he lowers his eyes, staring at the faded print on the frayed cotton tablecloth.

His father lays a work-worn hand on young Herman's arm. "This isn't going to come as any surprise to you, son. You've worked alongside me all these years, and you know what's happened as well as I do. With the depression, we've lost money on our wheat crop four years in a row. This year, the dust storms took out our entire crop. We had to let all the farmhands go. We have no money for seed next year, no money to buy feed for the animals. I'll have to sell them quickly. Otherwise, they'll die. We won't be able to feed ourselves if we stay here. We're losing the farm, son. I'll have to sell the land off cheap just to pay the debt we owe."

Young Herman's heart sinks like a rock and lies heavily in his stomach. All his life, he's imagined nothing other than working the wheat farm with his father, gradually taking over the operations as his father's strength declined. He pushes away from the table and stumbles over to the kitchen window, watching the unrelenting Kansas wind whipping through the sparse, scrubby trees in the distance and kicking up clouds of dust on the endless stretches of flat, barren land.

"What will we do now?" he mutters.

His father sighs heavily. "We've considered that, son. For the time being, your mother and I and the little ones will move to Hesston to stay with my brother and his family."

"And me? What's to become of me?"

The elder Herman stands up, walks over to his son, and places his arm around the young man's shoulders. "We've written to your mother's brother in Goshen, Indiana, your uncle Joseph Miller. He could use an extra hand on his dairy farm. His own boys are too young to be of much help. We've arranged for you to stay with him and his wife. You'll be able to earn your keep for a few years."}

"Herr-mann!" my mother called again. "Would you put that child down and come here for a minute? I need your help!"

My father gave me a gentle push. "Get up, now, Vickie. I need to see what your mother wants."

CHAPTER 2

"A soft answer turneth away wrath: but grievous words stir up anger." Proverbs 15:1

One evening when I was hardly more than a toddler, I scrambled onto the living room sofa next to my sister Lucy. Snuggling up against the warmth of her plump body, I absentmindedly began tracing the pattern of freckles on her arm with my index finger.

"Stop that, Tori Grace!" she snapped. She elbowed me away, toppling me over onto my side.

"Why don't you like me, Lucy?" I whimpered as I righted myself. "Everybody else does."

"Not everyone likes you as much as you think they do," she retorted. "You conceited little brat."

"Lucy," my father reproached from his armchair. As always, his scolding tone held little threat. "Why do you talk like that to your baby sister?" He held out his arms to me. "Come here, Vickie."

I was never daunted for long by the things Lucy said to me. If her harsh words did succeed in eliciting a few tears, my father's reassurance quickly restored my confidence in the fact that I was unconditionally lovable. "Don't pay her any mind, Vickie," he'd say as I'd climb onto his lap and huddle against his chest. "Your sister's just having a bad day."

But he showed ample affection to Lucy, also, as much as she'd allow. While she and my mother tangled incessantly, my father tried his best to remind his oldest daughter that she was loved. When she'd storm off to her upstairs bedroom after arguing with my mother in the kitchen, he'd stop her and try to enfold her in his arms.

"Lucy! Lucy!" he'd plead. "Take it easy now. It isn't good to get this worked up." I'd watch her surrender to his embrace for a second or two. Then she'd wrap her fury around herself again and stomp up the stairs.

One day when I was six and Lucy was fifteen, she stormed into the living room after her daily fight with my mother, tears pouring down her beet-red face. My father gently pushed me off his lap, saying, "It's Lucy's turn now."

He reached out his big hand and grabbed Lucy by the wrist, pulling her onto his lap. She was a hefty girl by then, heavy-set like her father. But he held her like she was a small child and allowed her to sob on his shoulder for a minute, until she pushed away from him.

As I watched the dramatic scene unfold, I felt miffed, thinking Lucy didn't belong on a lap that should have been exclusively mine. But at that moment, I knew she needed it more than I did.

My mother appeared in the doorway between the kitchen and the living room, hands on her hips, her dark eyes blazing with anger. She glared at my father, shook her head in disgust, then turned and disappeared back into the kitchen.

Years later, when I studied psychology in college, I realized that my parents' childrearing practices could have been labeled as dysfunctional. They constantly opposed and undermined each other's parenting efforts. But pulling together would have required my softhearted father to completely give over to my mother's harsh disciplinary standards. She never would have compromised with him. So the best he could do was to temper her stern sense of justice with a little bit of mercy.

My mother yelled a lot. Sometimes, the anger shooting from her eyes was loud enough that she didn't need to use her voice.

She yelled at Lucy on a daily basis, about her deplorable grades or her sloppy execution of some household chore. If she couldn't find anything else to accuse Lucy of, she'd blame her for having a bad attitude. I never quite knew what that meant, and I don't think Lucy did, either.

My absentminded father also served as a frequent target for my mother's wrath. Like when he trudged across her recently mopped kitchen floor with dirty shoes, or when he neglected to fix a clogged sink or a torn window screen in a timely manner. Or when she'd send him to Kroger's to get something she needed for a recipe, and he'd come home with the wrong product.

However, my behavioral infractions seemed to elicit a milder response from my mother. She never flew at me in an out-of-control way like she did with my father and Lucy. I'd see anger flare in her eyes, and then I'd watch her check herself before she administered her discipline. Unfortunately, this, coupled with my father's indulgence, resulted in me developing a belief in my own specialness. While I was a reasonably well-behaved child and not inclined toward rebellion, I also harbored the conviction that no one really had the right to stop me from doing whatever I wanted to do.

One thing Lucy said about me was undoubtedly true, that I was a little showoff. Usually, this annoyed her, but on occasion, it amused her. Whenever one of her friends came to the house and met her little sister for the first time, Lucy felt compelled to entertain them with a certain story.

My father used the term *cutting a wooly* to describe the event of someone passing gas. My mother thought this expression was vulgar, and seemed to think *breaking wind* was a more discreet way of referring to such an indelicate bodily function.

According to Lucy, one Sunday evening when I was two, our mother was presenting a flannel-graph lesson to the children in the church basement, the story about Jesus healing the ten lepers. She had put Lucy in charge of keeping an eye on me. I was sitting on Lucy's lap, perfectly behaved, when I suddenly passed some horrible-smelling gas.

Lucy abruptly put me off her lap, fanning her hand in front of her nose to ward off the evil odor. In telling the story, Lucy would say that she always thought lepers were stinky, and that it was like I'd provided the special effects for our mother's story.

Freed from Lucy's clutches, I walked up to the front of the room, prancing around in front of the other children. "I cut a wooly," I announced in my baby voice. "Phew! It stinks!"

My mother tried to ignore what I was doing, but when I repeated my announcement, she was forced to stop her story. "Lucy!" she hissed, gesturing toward me. Laughing, Lucy got up and tried to catch me, but I evaded her grasp. The other children began to giggle. Fueled by their attention, I danced back and forth in front of the group, chanting, "I cut a wooly, I cut a wooly. Phew! It stinks!"

My mother finally grabbed me and deposited me in Lucy's arms, instructing her to take me upstairs to where my father was sitting with the rest of the adults. Lucy always wrapped up her story by saying she was laughing so hard that she could barely make it up the basement steps with me.

Truly, I loved being in the spotlight, and I disliked sharing it with anyone else. My first experience on the stage was when I was a tiny tot. I had just completed the nursery class in summer Bible-School. Our church always held a program at the end of the two weeks, to demonstrate to the parents something of what their children had learned.

That first year, the task of reciting our simple Bible verses struck terror in the hearts of my little classmates. After we filed onto the stage, they all hung their heads and mumbled incoherently. But I had a strong voice and a great deal of nerve, and I held my head high and chanted the verses with confidence: "God is love." "Be ye kind one to another." "I will trust and not be afraid."

A titter of laughter ran throughout the audience. As soon as my class filed off the stage, I ran to the safety of my father's lap. "They laughed at me," I whimpered as I buried my face against his chest. "They think I'm stupid."

My father lifted my face and looked into my eyes. "They don't think you're stupid, Vickie. They laughed because you're so bloomin' cute."

His words were all it took to renew my confidence as a performer. The knowledge that I was *bloomin' cute* spurred me on. Time and again, I saved the day for my Sunday-School and Bible-School teachers, as I was the only pupil they could consistently count on to step up and pull off the show. They learned to place me front and center, where I belted out the words to *Jesus Loves the Little Children,* or dramatically executed the hand movements to *Building Up the Temple.* I began to take these star roles for granted, believing it was my God-given right to shine.

So I wasn't at all prepared for what happened when I was seven, when my Sunday-School class began rehearsing for our Christmas program. I'd been counting on singing the solo, *Away in a Manger,* but the part was given to one of my little friends, Rebecca Kauffman.

I couldn't believe I'd been slighted like that. I cried in the car all the way home from church. When we got home, I ran upstairs and flung myself across my bed, wailing loudly, wanting the whole world to know that I was mortally offended.

My mother finally had enough of my hysterics and stormed up the stairs. "It's time you stopped crying," she barked. "Now get up and come downstairs for dinner."

"But I'm upset," I sobbed. "I should get to sing *Away in a Manger.* I sing better than Becky Kauffman."

"Well, you can't always get everything you want," she retorted.

"But I wanted this really bad. I wanted this more than anything in the world."

My mother grabbed my arm and yanked me off the bed. "Victoria, we all want things really bad, and we don't always get them. Most of the time, we don't get what we want. You might as well get that through your stubborn little head."

{Seventeen-year-old Ada Hochstedler and a dozen other members of her church youth group have gathered in the backyard of their Sunday-School teacher, Joseph Miller. The raging bonfire Mr. Miller built earlier that day has diminished to embers, and the youth sit on a circle of logs around the dying fire.

Earlier in the evening, they'd roasted wieners on long sticks cut from the maple tree in Mr. Miller's yard. Then his wife had brought out a tray loaded with ingredients for making a special treat: graham crackers, marshmallows, and chocolate bars. After filling their stomachs with the hot dogs and s'mores, the youth had sung gospel songs in the Mennonite tradition of sublime four-part harmony.

In spite of the heat from the fire, the autumn night is starting to feel chilly. Ada tucks her long skirt around her slender legs and rubs her arms to warm herself. Her fingers are blackened from the charred hot dogs, and sticky from the marshmallows. The evening breeze has blown her hair into a state of disarray. A strand escapes her bun and catches on a sticky smudge on her cheek. Ada reaches up to pull it loose. She is normally a fastidious young woman, mindful of keeping herself clean and tidy. But tonight, she doesn't care much about her disheveled appearance. She can't remember when she's had such a good time. As she gazes into the dying fire, she feels relaxed, blissful, enveloped in a peace that her nervous disposition rarely allows her to experience.

Joseph Miller has invited a special guest to the youth

gathering, Reverend Samuel Graber, a missionary on furlough from central Africa. When Reverend Graber stands up to speak, his deep, spirit-filled voice sends a shiver of excitement through Ada's slight body. He recounts moving stories about his work at the mission station, how the African natives have been taught to read and write in the mission school, how their lives have been profoundly changed since they've come to know the Lord.

"So many people in this world are languishing in ignorance and misery," he intones. "Their souls long to hear the word of God. The Lord needs workers to spread the good news of His Gospel. Perhaps you are hearing the Lord's call in your own heart this evening. Many people hear that call, but they harden their hearts and turn away. If the Lord is speaking to you tonight, don't grieve Him by hardening your heart. God needs workers! God needs you!"

Ada's heart feels so full, she thinks it's going to burst. She knows the Lord is speaking to her. How she longs to serve God in some desperate foreign country, to take the Gospel to the poor and ignorant!

Reverend Graber brings his impassioned speech to a close. Then Joseph Miller leads the group in a final song. Tears stream down Ada's face as she sings.

Speed away! Speed away! Take the Gospel of light
To the lands that are wrapped in the darkness of night.
"Go ye into the world," is the Savior's command,
That the light of the Gospel shine o'er every land,
Go ye forth in his name and the Gospel proclaim,
Speed away! Speed away! Speed away!

After the closing prayer, the group disperses. The youth chat lightheartedly with each other as they leave for their homes, as if nothing of any importance had happened during that last hour around the bonfire. But Ada knows something happened to her. She needs to speak with Reverend Graber. The missionary is standing with his back to her, conversing with Joseph Miller. Timidly, she reaches out to touch his arm, and he turns to face her.

"May I . . . may I speak with you?" she stammers. Her body is trembling, both from the evening chill and from her overwhelming emotion.

"Certainly," Reverend Graber says.

"It's getting cold out here," Joseph Miller observes. "Why don't we go inside?" He leads Ada and Reverend Graber through the yard to the back door of his farmhouse, and then ushers them into the kitchen.

As soon as Ada sits down at the table with the visiting missionary, she begins to pour out her heart. "I know the Lord was calling me tonight," she says, her tears flowing again. "I don't want to be one of those people who harden their hearts. I want to serve God in the mission field. That's what I want, more than anything else in the world."

Reverend Martin stares at her, bewildered, as if he doesn't understand what she's saying.

"I want that more than anything in the world," she repeats.

Clearly, Reverend Martin hasn't anticipated such an outpouring of devotion from a young person that evening. He clears his throat, and when he begins to speak, his voice sounds matter-of-fact, no longer filled with spiritual conviction.

"Well, if that's what you want to do, you'll need to get practical about it. It's very difficult for a young woman to be on her own in the mission field. Perhaps you need to marry a young man who's interested in going into the ministry. Have you thought about things like that?"

Ada hesitates, and then nods. Truthfully, she hasn't thought about it in the past, but she's thinking now. Her mind flashes to the Mennonite Biblical Seminary on the Goshen College campus. There, she'd surely find lots of young men who shared her dreams.

A stocky, red-haired fellow walks into the kitchen. He's just come in from the barn, and his clothing reeks of cow manure. Ada puts her hand to her face, pretending to scratch her cheek, and then discretely covers her nose for as long as she can without appearing rude. She knows who the young man is: Joseph Miller's nephew Herman. He smiles at her. She wishes he wouldn't.

She gets up from the table, ready to leave. "It's really dark out there," Herman says. "Can I walk you to your car?"

She shakes her head. "I'll be okay." She doesn't want to give Herman the impression that she's interested in him. He's in his early twenties, way too old for her. She's more interested in his cousin, Joseph's son Eli, even though she knows Eli is going steady with another girl in their Sunday-School class. Still, that's the kind of guy she's drawn to: someone tall and slim with flashing dark eyes and a serious disposition. Someone capable of pursuing a college education. Someone cut out for a professional career.}

CHAPTER 3

"A righteous man regardeth the life of his beast . . . ."
Proverbs 12:10

"Be thou diligent to know the state of thy flocks, and look well to thy herds." Proverbs 27:23

Although my parents didn't own a farm, we lived in an old farmhouse, a two-story residence with a large front porch. Lucy and I occupied the two upstairs bedrooms. The downstairs consisted of my parents' bedroom, a single bathroom, a living room, and a large eat-in kitchen. A mudroom between the kitchen and the back door held my mother's washing machine and a seldom-used dryer, as she preferred to hang the laundry on the clothesline in our backyard. Our musty old cellar had an outdoor entry, and was used for storing the jars of fruits and vegetables my mother canned.

The acreage associated with our home had long been sold off by previous owners. While we were surrounded by cornfields, they didn't belong to us. However, our diminished piece of property did retain a ramshackle barn, and when I was a small child, it housed goats, rabbits, and a few stray cats. An old chicken coop sheltered half a dozen hens, one rooster, and two pairs of ducks.

Raising the animals was my father's project, something he'd shared with my brothers when they still lived at home. Neither my mother nor Lucy wanted anything to do with barnyard life. It seemed as if the only thing my mother and sister ever agreed upon was that the animals were malodorous and disgusting. My mother constantly complained about my father's smelly barn boots sitting in the mudroom by the back door.

From the time I was five, I joined my father in the evening feeding of the animals. During the summer months, I'd sometimes help with the morning feeding as well. This was never assigned to me as a chore, and I was always free to decline participating in animal-care duties. When it was time to go out to the barn, my father would say, "You comin', Vickie?" More often than not, I'd scramble up from whatever I was doing and grab onto his outstretched hand.

We'd stroll the distance from our back door to the barn, passing the clothesline, the vegetable garden, and the glorious arrangements of begonias, impatiens, geraniums and marigolds my mother planted in large wooden tubs. My father always carried a bag of birdseed out with us, and his first critter-feeding duty was replenishing the stock of seeds in the birdfeeder he'd installed for the cardinals, blue jays, robins and sparrows.

Our goats, Frederick, Bertha, Agnes and Annabelle, would be outside in their pen adjacent to the barn, waiting for us, bleating sorrowfully as we approached. "We're starving, we're suffering, feed us, feed us!" I imagined them to say. Sometimes, Frederick's pathetic cries became angry and demanding: "Get over here and give me something to eat! Right now!"

As we'd walk past their pen to enter the barn, the goats would bite at our clothing and nudge us with their silly heads. Chuckling at their ornery behavior, my father would take a flake of hay from the stack of bales along the back wall of the barn and toss it into their feeder. He'd scold Agnes, who, overcome by excitement at the prospect of food, would try to climb into the feeder. "Stop that, Aggie, you silly thing!" he'd say. "You don't belong in there!"

He'd grab the goats' drinking bucket hanging on a nail on the wall of the barn. Dumping out the dirty water, he'd head toward the pump to refill it. I'd grab the barn cats' water dish and go along with him. Then I'd carry the fresh water back to the thirsty felines. While they purred and rubbed up against my legs, I'd fill their food dish from the big bag of kibble we kept in the barn.

Our barn cat population tended to ebb and flow. A stray would show up out of nowhere, stick around for awhile, and then disappear. Occasionally, a litter of kittens would be born in the barn. I'd claim all the kittens with dark coats, but would designate the odd orange tabby as Lucy's, as its fur matched the color of her hair.

Disregarding my mother's injunction against cats in the house, I'd carry the adorable kitten up to Lucy's room, hoping she'd fall in love with it. "What do you want to call it?" I'd ask.

She'd hold up a protesting palm, keeping both the kitten and me at bay. "Call that stupid animal anything you want, Tori Grace. Now get out of here and stop bothering me."

I named one gray tabby *Milo*, because his face reminded me of a man who attended our church. The feline Milo could almost always be found lounging in the goats' pen during the day. At night, he'd curl up to sleep against the warmth of Annabelle's side.

"Milo's a crazy cat," I told my father. "He thinks he's a goat. He thinks Annabelle is his mother."

"Animals do things like that," my father mused. "I've seen barnyard animals pair up in a lot of strange ways. When I was a kid, our dog was best friends with one of our plow horses. You couldn't separate the two of them, and the dog always slept in the stall with the horse. Another one of our dogs hung around a goose, like he thought she was his girlfriend. So it doesn't surprise me to see a cat getting attached to a goat."

After feeding the demanding goats and cats, my father and I turned our attention to the rabbits. We'd make another trip to the pump to refill their water bottles. "Here you go," he'd say as he replenished the hay that lined their cages. "Just making your home a little more comfortable."

He'd offer them a little bit of the special timothy hay he kept for them, and they'd draw it into their mouths with their eager little teeth. "Yum," he'd say. "That's good stuff."

I'd dip an old cup into the tub of dry rabbit food and fill the feeders that hung on the walls of their cages. My father always reminded me to snap the lid of the tub firmly in place, in order to keep the bugs out of the food.

The rabbit cages were affixed to the wall of the barn, and when I was six or seven years old, they were at my eye level. I liked to peer into the cages, face to face with the twitchy-nosed creatures, but the nervous animals would shy away and scurry to hide in the little wooden boxes my father had constructed in the corners of their dwellings. Under my father's supervision, I was allowed to take out one rabbit each day to pet it. I'd pick a different color each time, alternating between the black, the brown, and the gray. The rabbits' luxurious fur astonished me, as it was so much softer than the fur of the barn cats. I loved holding the velvety animals up against my cheek.

Finally, we'd turn our care to the ducks and chickens. As we'd approach the henhouse in the morning, we'd hear an awful racket of clucking and quacking. "They're screamin' bloody murder today," my father would say.

He'd open the door to the coop, and the chickens and ducks would flap and flutter their way out into their fenced-in pen. I'd pour dry birdfeed into pans, while my father made another trip to the pump to refill their water bucket. I never lost my fascination with watching the birds drink. They'd dip their beaks into the water, and then tilt their heads up to swallow it. Sometimes, I'd imitate their technique when drinking a glass of milk at the dinner table, only to elicit a sharp, "Stop that, Victoria!" from my mother.

My father kept a plastic wading pool for the ducks, which he dumped out and refilled every day. They'd jump right in as soon as they had clean water, as if desperate for a swim.

Our rooster, whom my father named Orville, loved to strut around the barnyard, his haughty head held high, reminding everyone of who was in charge. "Now don't you think you're something!" my father would say to him.

Orville would watch my father and me with his wary, beady eyes, but he never bothered us. However, whenever my mother or Lucy came near him, he'd fly at them in a flurry of indignation. They hated him.

Our last chore of the morning was to gather the eggs

and carry them back to the house. My father would fill each of his big hands with four or five eggs from the hens' nests, and I'd carry the large duck eggs, one in each hand.

In the evening, we'd chase the birds back into their coop for the night. My rotund father looked comical, running in circles and flapping his arms. With a great deal of offended squawking, the ducks and chickens would flutter back into their shelter.

The feeding of the animals took a full thirty minutes, sometimes longer. My father savored each moment, conducting the routine like a sacred ritual, his movements slow and deliberate. The only time he'd quicken his pace was when my mother would yell out the back door, telling him she needed something.

I'm absolutely certain that my father would have taken first place in any contest involving the imitation of animal sounds. He could emit the cluck of a chicken, the quack of a duck, or the bleat of a goat. Without even thinking about it, he'd carry on a conversation with a critter in its own dialect. If I wasn't looking, I sometimes couldn't tell who was speaking, him or the animal.

Although we didn't keep cows, my father's cow imitation was my favorite. Whenever I'd request a bovine performance, his eyes would grow large and round, and he'd stretch out his fat neck and slowly raise his chin to the sky as he belted out a mournful, "Moo-oo-oo." I'd double over with laughter, begging him to do it again and again.

One day as I watched him shovel excrement out of the goat pen, I marveled at his cheerfulness in doing the dirty work. "You really love animals, don't you, Daddy?" I said.

He stopped for a moment, leaning on his shovel. "Yes,

Vickie, I do love them. I never wanted much more out of life than to raise animals. These critters might be filthy, and they can do some terrible things, like last week when the duck killed one of the hens. The animals might give me problems, but they can never hurt me on a deep level. They never judge a fellow, or make him feel like he's not worth anything. I would've been happy to stay on the farm forever."

He sighed, and then scooped another shovelful of goat droppings into the bucket. "That didn't work out, but I do count myself lucky to have this barnyard full of critters."

{Herman and his uncle Joseph have completed the morning milking, and the cows have been let out to pasture. Herman is hosing down the floor of the milk-house. He works carefully, knowing how important it is to keep sanitary conditions in the environment where the cows are milked.

The April morning is chilly, but the day promises to be beautiful, with temperatures in the seventies. Herman gazes out the back door of the milk-house, taking in the bright green spring grass in the expanse of the pasture. The apple trees along the fence row are in bloom. Several of the cows are heavy with their unborn calves, and their bulging sides make them look comical.

He reaches down to turn off the spigot, and when he looks up, he sees his uncle standing in the doorway. "We need to keep an eye on Buttercup," Joseph says. "She could deliver any day now."

Herman coils up the hose, and then steps out the door to join his uncle behind the milk-house, where the two men stand in a contented silence. "Herman, have you given any thought to your future?" Joseph suddenly asks. "What do you think you'll do when you move on from here?"

Herman winces at the sound of his uncle's words. The thought of leaving the security of the dairy farm is something he habitually pushes out of his mind.

Joseph senses his nephew's distress. "I'm not aiming to boot you out of here," he says. "You've been a big help to me. You can stay here awhile longer, if you want to. But my own sons are getting to the age where they can give me all the help I need. You're twenty-two. You don't want to settle for being a farmhand all your life."

Herman stands with his head bowed, listening.

Joseph knows his words are hard for his nephew to hear. His voice softens. "You're a hard worker, Herman. You're good with the animals. Handling the cows is like second nature to you. There's a lot you could do with your abilities."

Herman lifts his head, smiling. He thinks about the time he assisted the veterinarian when one of the cows was having a difficult delivery. It had taken the strength of both of them to pull the calf out of her birth canal. He thinks about the times he soothed the sick cows after the vet had given them injections. Then he dares to speak about a dream he's been harboring.

"I was thinking maybe someday I'd like to go to veterinary school."

Joseph smiles and claps his nephew on the shoulder. "I hear they have a good program at Purdue," he says.}

CHAPTER 4

"[Let] women adorn themselves in modest apparel,
with shamefacedness and sobriety . . . ." I Timothy 2:9

During my early childhood, my mother kept me in clothing that conformed to her idea of what a young Mennonite girl should look like. My daily attire consisted of plain dresses that modestly covered my little-girl body, preparing me for the day when I would need to hide the charms of a womanly figure. Sensible shades of brown, blue, and green prevailed in my wardrobe. Never would my mother have dreamed of putting me in something so pretentious or attention-grabbing as red, orange, or pink.

I couldn't help but experience surges of envy when I saw other little girls in the community decked out in cute, frilly outfits. However, I wasn't terribly discontented, as I was surrounded by Mennonite families whose daughters wore the same style of clothing I wore.

Then, in the mid-1960s, a new trend began to infiltrate Westside Mennonite Church, as a few of the teenage girls started wearing slacks.

Up to that point, wearing trousers of any kind had been off limits to females in our church. I'd grown accustomed to the sight of heavy-set church women in drab, full-skirted dresses that hung to the middle of their plump calves, dresses that camouflaged every unseemly part of their figures. In fact, I imagined that under the voluminous folds of fabric, these Mennonite matrons had skirt-shaped bodies. It seemed indecent to think of them as having legs that extended all the way up to their hips.

But change was bound to come, and with it came the fierce struggle between those who dared to step into a new era and those who defended the old traditions with every ounce of their moral strength. Some of the strongest resistance to the trend of wearing slacks came from the older women in the congregation, who'd spent their own youth clad in modest dresses, and who'd submitted to the restrictions imposed by those garments. And, of course, this conflict was played out in the tumultuous relationship between my mother and Lucy.

When Lucy was fifteen, a school friend gave her a pair of bright blue pedal-pushers, which she sneaked into the house and stashed in the back of her closet. Unsurprisingly, they were discovered by my mother when she was putting away Lucy's clean laundry.

That evening at the supper table, my mother seemed especially tense. As we passed the mashed potatoes and green beans, her movements were sharper and angrier than usual, and she plunked the dishes down on the table with unnecessary force. When we were finished eating and Lucy started to push away from the table, my mother pointed an accusing finger at her and said, "You stay right where you are!"

She got up and stalked off to her bedroom, emerging a moment later with the despicable pedal-pushers and a pair of sewing scissors. With a sweep of her arm, she brushed aside the dishes to clear a space on the table. Then, with my father, Lucy, and me as horrified onlookers, she hacked the blue trousers to death with her pinking shears.

"You have no right to destroy my personal property!" Lucy screamed. She made a grab for the scissors, but my mother held them behind her back, shooting her daughter a look that would have withered the giant maple tree in our front yard. Lucy finally gave up and flew up the stairs to her room, yelping like a wounded animal.

Shaken by the violent scene I'd witnessed, I slipped away from the table and went to huddle in the corner of the living room sofa, keeping an eye and an ear out for the parental exchange that was sure to follow.

"Young people want to keep up with the changing times," my father said to my mother in a tone of mild reproach. "It's more important to them than it is to you and me. Other girls in the church are starting to wear pants. When I was on my mail route the other day, I saw Reverend Schrock's granddaughter playing in the yard. She was wearing pants."

My mother shot him a scornful look and got up to clear the dishes from the table.

Those pedal-pushers were truly a lovely shade of blue, and I suppose my frugal mother thought it would be a shame to waste perfectly good fabric. One day, Lucy caught her in her bedroom, cutting blocks for a Mennonite Central Committee quilt out of the remnants of the ruined trousers.

"If those pants are so sinful, how can you put them in one of your church quilts?" Lucy bellowed in indignation.

My mother said nothing, but got up and slammed her bedroom door in Lucy's face.

Lucy didn't give up on the idea of wearing trousers, and she turned her pleas to my father. Time and again, I heard him say, "If your mother approves, then it's fine with me." One day, he said to my mother, "If you don't take your daughter shopping for some slacks, then I will. And I'm not going to let you to ruin them this time."

My mother finally relented and bought Lucy some slacks, and on the same shopping trip, she came home with two pairs of blue jeans for me. She told me they were for playing outdoors. I was surprised, as I hadn't even thought to ask for them.

Even at that young age, I was aware of the fact that I'd won the right to wear those controversial trousers without having to fight for them. I knew that I'd benefited from Lucy's painful struggle, and I felt a little sorry that my own privilege had come at such a cost to her.

But I loved wearing those blue jeans. They gave me the freedom to play like I wanted to play. I could turn cartwheels, hang upside down from a tree limb, or roll around on the ground with the barn cats, all without fear of being scolded by my mother for showing my underwear.

The summer after I turned six, I spent the months joyfully romping in the yard in my blue jeans, and my olive skin turned brown as a nut. When my father would come home from his mail route, I'd follow him into the house and climb onto his lap, both of us resting from the exertion of our day.

"Look, Daddy," I said one day as I put my brown arm next to his pale, freckled one. "I'm darker than you are. How's come?"

He looked strangely uncomfortable. "I guess with your dark hair and your dark complexion, you take after your mother and the boys."

"But I'm darker than Mom."

"She doesn't play outdoors in the sun and get tanned like you do, you silly thing."

I persisted with my pesky questions. "Why do you have all these freckles on your arms, Daddy? You have white hairs and a whole bunch of freckles."

"Well, I suppose it's because I have a little bit of Irish blood in me. My mother was part Irish. I get my red hair and freckles from her."

"Then Lucy must have Irish blood, too," I reasoned. "I wish I had Irish blood. I wish I had red hair and freckles like you and Lucy."

My father shifted in his chair, easing me off his lap. "Vickie, Vickie, Vickie. You're all mixed up about this Irish blood business, and I can't explain it to you. Just forget about it. Genetics is a hard thing to understand. That's one thing I learned before I flunked out of veterinarian school."

{The biology students file noisily out of the Purdue University classroom, but Herman Unruh has been asked to stay behind. He remains in his front row seat, facing the massive wooden desk of his biology professor, Dr. Horner.

The professor holds out a sheet of paper. Reluctantly, Herman slides out of his seat, walks up to the big desk, and takes the paper. He glances at it and sees the big red "F" emblazoned on his latest biology exam. He returns to his seat, turning the paper face down on his desk so that his most recent failure isn't staring him in the face.

Professor Horner clears his throat. "Mr. Unruh, I think you already know why I've asked to speak with you.

I'm sure you know that you won't be passing this course."

Herman hangs his head, nodding.

"I'm aware of the fact that this isn't the only course you're failing. Mr. Unruh, I'd advise you not to waste any more of your time here. I think it's best that you give up the idea of moving on in our veterinary program."

"I figured I'd have to drop out," Herman mumbles.

Professor Horner's voice softens. "It's really too bad. You have a friendly disposition and a gentle nature, and I'm sure you did well with the animals on the farm."

"Yes," Herman says. "I thought being good with animals would make me a good animal doctor. I guess I was wrong. I guess I don't have what it takes."

"Unfortunately, Mr. Unruh, the scientific side of veterinary medicine is something that a student must master. You don't seem to have a mind that easily grasps scientific facts. I know you've given it your best, but it isn't enough."

Herman sighs heavily. "I realize that. I know I don't belong here. I'll pack up my stuff and move on."

"You're such a likable fellow." There's a hint of sadness in Professor Horner's voice. "You get along well with the other students. I'm aware of the fact that when someone else is in need, you're the first to lend a helping hand. That's why this is so difficult. Mr. Unruh, I don't want you to lose heart. I'm sure you have a lot to offer in some other field. Maybe something that involves working with people, some field that doesn't require subjects like math and science. Maybe you could do some kind of social work or church work. Maybe you could be the pastor of a church."}

CHAPTER 5

"Lay not up for yourselves treasures upon earth,
where moth and rust doth corrupt, and where thieves break
through and steal: But lay up for yourselves treasures in
heaven, where neither moth nor rust doth corrupt, and
where thieves do not break through nor steal: For where
your treasure is, there will your heart be also."
Matthew 6:19-21

My parents practiced thriftiness and frugality, not only because those virtues were valued in our Mennonite community, but out of necessity. My father's wages as a mailman barely stretched to cover the family's basic needs. Even with the added income of my mother's part-time secretarial work, each dollar that came into the household was spent carefully.

My mother faithfully clipped grocery coupons from the insert in *The Goshen News*. Every summer, she canned green beans and froze peas from her vegetable garden. She bought bushels of apples from Kercher's Orchard, making enough applesauce to last us a year. She sewed her own dark, plain dresses, and my father wore the same flannel shirts and *Dickies* work pants for years on end.

I felt fortunate to get one new dress at the beginning of each school year. My mother made each purchase last two years by letting down the hem the second year. However, most of my dresses were hand-me-downs from Lucy. Because Lucy was plump and I was thin, my mother had to take in the bodices of the dresses. Even though she was a good seamstress, the alteration would leave the garment looking a bit lumpy and misshapen.

I was accustomed to our everyday frugality. Granted, I occasionally begged for things that were outside the bounds of our budget, telling my mother how desperately I needed a Chatty Cathy, an Easy-Bake Oven, or a hula hoop. But I never expected to get them.

However, as I grew older, I caught on to the fact that once or twice a year, a lump sum of money would mysteriously enter the household. The amount seemed significant to my parents, and it would generally be used for something practical. One year, they bought a sculpted beige carpet to replace the cracked linoleum in the living room. Another year, they purchased a freezer and installed it in the mudroom, then filled it with a side of beef.

For the first seven years of my life, my family didn't own a television set. The TV had long been a controversial topic in the Mennonite Church. While some Mennonite families had already broken down and bought one, my mother refused to have one in our household, as she viewed it as an instrument for bringing worldly influences into the home.

The only TV program I was allowed to watch during my early years was one I didn't enjoy in the least: Reverend Billy Graham's televised evangelistic services. Edna Schmucker, an elderly widow in our church, had purchased a television set to provide a pastime for her long, lonely days. My mother felt sorry for the old woman, and didn't seem to hold this worldly acquisition against her.

Every time Reverend Graham was to make a TV appearance, Edna would invite our family over to watch it.

My mother would sit with rapt attention, her eyes fixed on the screen, hungrily taking in every word imparted by the man of God. My father would fall asleep, snoring softly, his head resting on the back of the sofa. I'd fidget impatiently, fingering Edna's crocheted doilies on the armrests of the sofa, relieving my utter boredom by gazing at all the interesting knickknacks on her shelves and table tops. Lucy, of course, would refuse to come with us.

During my first and second grade years, I listened with envy as my classmates chattered about their favorite TV programs: *Captain Kangaroo, Batman, The Flintstones,* and *Flipper.* In first grade, I heard of the show about the weird *Munster* family. The father of the family was named Herman, which tickled me to no end.

"Daddy," I giggled as I climbed onto his lap one evening. "You're a Munster. You're name's Herman Munster."

"No," he protested playfully, "I'm not a Munster. I'm just an old bumble-head."

Suddenly, I felt sad. I stopped teasing and laid my head against his shoulder. "No, you're not," I whispered.

I probably heard my father utter the phrase, "I'm just an old bumble-head," a hundred times during my childhood. The words never failed to cause me pain.

Toward the end of my second grade year, the mystery money finally bought us a television set, which was ensconced in the corner of our living room. My mother quickly outlined the parameters of what we were allowed to watch, telling us that anything involving violence, bad language, or the use of alcohol was off limits.

"And anything else that's indecent," she added, although I didn't fully know what she meant.

Her monitoring efforts weren't entirely successful, as it turned out that my father got hooked on *Gunsmoke* and *Bonanza*. My mother would try to shoo Lucy and me out of the living room when he was watching his programs, but we'd drift back in when she wasn't looking.

She didn't mind too much if Lucy and I watched *The Partridge Family, The Flying Nun,* or *That Girl.* She refused to let us watch *Bewitched.* "That glorifies witchcraft," she told us, "and witchcraft is of the devil."

Knowing my mother's capacity for righteous anger, I rarely wandered outside the bounds of the list of shows she approved for watching. I knew that if provoked, my mother was fully capable of taking a hammer to the TV screen. And after such an event, there would never be another television set in our household.

Lucy, however, was always one to push the limits without regard to consequences. During the summer months, whenever my mother would leave the house to run an errand or work in her vegetable garden, Lucy would come downstairs and watch *Dark Shadows, As the World Turns,* or *Peyton Place.* When my mother would come back into the house, she'd march straight to the living room. Shooting Lucy a look of outrage, she'd switch off the TV. Lucy would howl in protest and storm up the stairs.

I watched this little drama play out more times than I could count. My mother and Lucy each had their roles down pat. Their performance made me terribly nervous, as each time, I wondered whether television doomsday had finally arrived.

When Lucy and I watched *Marcus Welby,* my mother would slip into the living room and watch with us. She never uttered a word about the show, but I always suspected she was a little sweet on the young doctor, Steven Kiley.

The summer after I turned eight, I overheard my mother and father discussing the mystery money at the table after supper. "You need tires for your car," my mother pointed out. "You shouldn't be driving your mail route on those bald tires."

My father bristled. "I'm not touching that money! I'll put tires on my car with my own damn money!"

"Herman!" my mother scolded. "Watch your language!" Then she lowered her voice. "Be reasonable. We should apply the money to what we need the most. That's what it's meant for. What would happen to us if you had an accident on those bald tires next winter?"

My father pushed away from the table and stood up, glowering down at my mother. "Use it for something the girls need!" he growled. "And I don't mean just Vickie. Get something for Lucy, too. For God's sake, Ada, treat the girl like she means something to you!" Then he stalked out of the house, slamming the back door behind him.

My mother sat motionless at the table, her head in her hands. I stared at her for a moment, and then ran out the door after my father, who was walking briskly toward the barn. Catching up with him, I grabbed his hand. "What's wrong, Daddy?"

For the first time in my memory, my father pulled his hand from mine. "I need a little time alone, Vickie," he said gruffly. Unable to comprehend his rejection, I trailed after him into the barn. He sat down on a bale of the goats' hay, breathing heavily, his face flushed, his eyes downcast, as if trying to quell an overwhelming emotion.

I stood transfixed, having never seen my father in such a state. After a few minutes, he raised his eyes and saw me watching him. His face softened. "Come here, Vickie."

I walked over to him, and he pulled me into the crook of his arm. "I don't want you to get into an accident, Daddy," I whimpered.

"Don't worry about it, Vickie," he said. "I'll get those tires one way or the other." Then he stood up and brushed the hay off the seat of his pants. "I guess it's time to feed the critters."

Two weeks later, when my mother took me shopping for school clothing, she astonished me by buying me three dresses instead of one. They seemed to be a bit more expensive than what I was used to, a notch above the usual plain garments she purchased for me.

When we got home, I carried my new dresses to my room and spread them out on my bed to admire them. In my eyes, these ordinary school dresses were exquisite. One was green and blue plaid, another was turquoise and yellow plaid, and the third was a purple print. All three had full skirts, bodices trimmed with buttons and lace, dainty little puffed sleeves, and Peter Pan collars.

An hour later, when my mother came upstairs to see what I was doing, she caught me dancing around my room holding one of the dresses up to my body. "I told you to hang those up in your closet," she barked.

Evidently, she thought I was taking far too much delight in my worldly acquisitions, possibly heading toward full-blown avarice. "You might think you've got it made now, Victoria," she said as she turned to leave my room. "But you need to know it's not going to be this way every year. Anyway, pretty dresses have no power to make you happy. Only the things of God can bring us true happiness. The Bible tells us to lay up our treasures in Heaven. Sometimes in this earthly life, we think we've struck gold, but after awhile, we realize we have no treasure at all."

"Not at all," I heard her mutter as she trudged down the stairs. "Not at all."

{Twenty-year-old Ada Hochstedler sits at the large wooden secretarial desk outside the office of the director of admissions. Although it's only mid-afternoon, she's bored and tired, feeling hot and sticky in her brown woolen work suit. She can't wait to go home and change into a cotton housedress.

She rests her chin in her hand, staring out the window, watching the students walk purposefully to their classes. Bitterness wells inside her. "They're getting what they want out of life," she whispers to herself. "Why can't I?"

Sighing, she turns back to her typewriter to finish up the letter her boss dictated to her that morning. But a minute later, her work is interrupted when a stocky young man in a well-worn suit walks through the door. He removes his battered gray fedora, exposing a mop of curly red hair. Holding his hat in his big, awkward hands, he glances around the room, as if trying to get his bearings.

Then his gaze falls on Ada. "I'm here to meet with the director of admissions," he says. A smile creeps across his broad face. "Say, don't I know you from somewhere?"

Ada has worked as the director's secretary for more than a year, and not a single seminary student has shown an interest in her. Although she does her best to be gracious and helpful, the serious, preoccupied would-be pastors seem to look right through her. Suddenly, this friendly, familiar face seems appealing, and something stirs inside her. She leans forward, returning the young man's smile.

"Yes," she says. "We've met before. How are you, Mr. Unruh?"}

CHAPTER 6

"I was glad when they said unto me, Let us go into the house of the Lord." Psalm 122:1

My sister Lucy hated being Mennonite. She resented every restriction our religion put upon her, seeing them as affronts to her personal freedom. Just as she'd been unwilling to accept the ban on wearing trousers, she refused to abide by any other rule designed to render her a modest and well-behaved young woman.

Before any of the other girls in the church dared to put a pair of scissors to their hair, Lucy stood in front of her dresser mirror and cut herself bangs. She hid her stash of jewelry and makeup from my mother, clipping on earrings and applying eye-shadow while riding the school bus in the morning.

In her later teen years, she grew so brazen as to smoke cigarettes in her bedroom. Once, my mother smelled the smoke and went charging up the stairs. When she burst into Lucy's room, she found Lucy, looking innocent and bewildered, sitting on her bed with her window wide open.

"I know you've been smoking in here," my mother barked, looking around for the telltale cigarette butts.

"How dare you accuse me of something so terrible?" Lucy wailed. "You never trust me! You always think I'm up to something!"

I never fully understood Lucy's rebellion. It seemed to me she was bent on making things difficult for herself, as virtually every time she broke a rule, she had to face the consequences. She'd end up being grounded or losing her meager allowance. It got to the point where she never had spending money or the privilege of going anywhere. She spent most of her teen years holed up in her bedroom, brooding on the unfairness of her punishment.

Granted, the fact that I was nearly a decade younger than Lucy made a big difference in our experience of growing up Mennonite. Although it always seemed to me that our church was behind the times, change did happen, and by the time I entered my teen years, the restrictions had softened considerably. I could wear stylish clothing, as long as it wasn't too short, too tight, or too revealing, and lip-gloss and a little bit of mascara weren't likely to create an uproar in our congregation. My friends and I trimmed each other's hair without any fear of the consequences.

Except for smoking, which never appealed to me, I ended up doing the same things Lucy did during her teen years, but without the struggle with my mother. When Lucy once pointed out that fact to me, I had to agree that it was, indeed, unfair.

From the time I was a tiny child, I loved the same church my sister hated. Every time we'd pull our family car into the gravel parking lot in front of the church, whether for Sunday services, Wednesday evening prayer meeting, or Vacation Bible-School, I knew I'd come to a place where I was loved and accepted, where I could count on being treated with kindness.

In keeping with the Mennonite value of eschewing worldly extravagance, the church building was a simple, white-painted wooden structure, with a tall steeple and an unembellished sign bearing the name of *Westside Mennonite Church.*

The interior of the church was as unpretentious as the exterior. Just inside the entry way, a small flight of concrete steps led to the level of the sanctuary. Narrower steps led to anterooms on each side, one for men and one for women. Presumably, this segregation was established to prevent any unseemly mingling of the sexes. Each anteroom contained a single bench, a rack for hanging coats, and a shelf for depositing hats and other personal items. The women's anteroom, larger than the men's, also doubled as a nursery, containing several baby cribs.

While little boys accompanied their mothers into the women's anteroom, the men's anteroom was decidedly off limits for a young girl. I was never allowed to set foot in there. For that reason, the space seemed mysterious and a little creepy to me, and I wondered what horrible things men did in there that would shock feminine sensibilities. Actually, the men seemed to pass through their anteroom quite quickly, divesting themselves of their hats and coats before moving on into the sanctuary.

However, the women's anteroom was an arena for socialization, a place where significant female bonds were forged. The ladies would take turns peering into the small mirror, making sure their long hair was properly secured into their buns. Then, with great precision, they'd perch their white head coverings over their mounds of hair, fastening them in place with straight-pins. No Mennonite woman wanted to be caught with her covering askew. The older women wore large coverings, while the younger women preferred something small and perky.

If a woman had young children to tend, or if she was experiencing menstrual cramps, she was likely to spend more time in the anteroom than in the sanctuary on a Sunday morning. If she'd had her feelings hurt by the thoughtless word of one of her friends, she might opt to sulk in the anteroom rather than to sit in the sanctuary with the one who'd offended her.

My mother complained about women who came to church Sunday after Sunday, but rarely set foot in the sanctuary. "They just come to church for the fellowship," she'd say. "They're not serious about their spiritual lives."

At the end of the sanctuary opposite the entry doors, a simple pulpit stood on a riser bounded by a wooden railing. Two dozen ancient, unpadded pews, arranged in three rows of eight, faced the pulpit. The old, arthritic wooden floors creaked in pain every time they were trod upon, embarrassing anyone who tried to slip out of the service undetected.

The sanctuary contained no stained glass windows, no display of religious icons. Nothing hung on the stark white walls, except for a single picture behind the pulpit depicting the radiant figure of Jesus gently rapping on a closed door. We Mennonite children were taught that this familiar picture symbolized the Savior's knocking on the door of the unbeliever's heart, patiently waiting for permission to enter.

The lighting in the sanctuary consisted of plain fixtures suspended on long chains. At times when the church service offered nothing to hold my attention, I entertained myself by imagining adorable cherubs cavorting on those fixtures, swinging from one to another in joyful abandon.

On Sunday mornings, after a hymn and a few opening words, the children were dismissed to go to their Sunday-School classes in the church basement. I must have walked down the concrete basement stairs a thousand times during my childhood. A relief map of the holy land was affixed to the left-hand side of the staircase wall, highlighting Nazareth, Bethlehem, Jerusalem, and other places where Jesus spent his life on earth.

The basement was dark and dank, with rough, cold concrete floors. Cement block walls divided the space into classrooms for children of various ages, ranging from preschoolers to teenagers. All the children were taught with standard curriculum from the *Mennonite Publishing House*. While the little ones colored pictures of Bible characters and sang simple songs, the older children contemplated the higher meanings of scriptural stories.

When the children departed for the basement, the adults met for their own Sunday-School classes. The men gathered in the pews on one side of the church, and the women formed their group on the other side. For many years, my mother served as the Sunday-School teacher for the women.

At the end of the Sunday-School hour, a buzzer rang, signifying that it was time for the children to join the adults for the second hour of the service. We'd traipse up the stairs, pausing in the entry way to scan the crowd of men in their dark suits and women in their white head coverings. When we'd spot our parents, we'd join them in the pews. Up until my teen years, I sat between my parents, sparing them the discomfort of sitting next to each other.

There was only one thing about the Mennonite church service that was lavish and sublime, and that was the singing, the traditional four-part a cappella harmony. The preponderance of talented singers in our Mennonite community suggested something about the genetic endowment of that ethnic group.

Some of the hymns were too slow for my childish taste. When the song leader, Alvin Troyer, announced the number of the hymn we were about to sing, my heart would sink a little when I realized it was something droning, like *Abide With Me, Often Weary and Worn, Precious Lord Take My Hand,* or *Must Jesus Bear the Cross Alone.*

I much preferred the up-tempo hymns, songs during which Alvin would beat the time with gusto as he belted out the melody in his magnificent tenor voice: *To God Be the Glory, Standing on the Promises, We're Marching to Zion, When the Roll is Called up Yonder, Revive Us Again.* But whether the hymn was fast or slow, it was impossible not to enjoy the singing.

I'd listen to my mother's rich, throaty alto voice hitting each of the lower notes in the treble clef with absolute precision. However, my father was an aberration among Mennonite singers. He was supposedly a tenor, but what he sang had nothing to do with the upper notes in the bass clef. The sounds that came out of his mouth could only be described as joyful howling. Whenever he'd get carried away while raising his voice in praise, my mother would shoot him a scornful look.

The free-spirited way in which my father sang sounded like fun, and I went through a stage in which I tried to imitate him. Whenever I'd howl along with him, my mother would squeeze my knee so tightly that I'd almost yelp in pain.

After the singing, we'd settle in for one of Reverend Delbert Schrock's interminably long, painfully boring sermons. I was required to sit still, an experience that, no doubt, taught me self-control. Thankfully, I was allowed to play quietly with a little plastic puzzle, a black frame containing movable red squares, each with a word on it. I'd move the squares around until the words formed a Bible verse. Then I'd scramble up the squares and start all over again.

My mother kept a small notebook in her purse. When the sermon grew especially long, she'd take pity on me and pull out the notebook, allowing me to draw pictures.

My father invariably fell asleep during the sermon. Whenever he'd let out a snort, my mother would nudge me, the signal that I was to nudge him. He'd startle and wake up, only to drift off again a few minutes later.

Evidently, one long service didn't provide enough edification for the week, as Westside Mennonite also held services on Sunday evening. My father routinely protested attending the evening service, saying he needed to stay home and rest up for the coming week's work. His line of reasoning never fell on sympathetic ears, because my mother always insisted that he come with us.

"If I let you stay home," she'd say, "then Lucy and Victoria will think they can be excused from church, too. And who knows where things would go from there?"

Thankfully, the children weren't required to sit through another sermon on Sunday evenings. After the opening hymn, we'd trudge downstairs to the basement, where we met in one large group to enjoy a Bible game or a flannel-graph story presented by one of our mothers.

Perhaps the Sunday evening children's hour in the basement was not as well-supervised as it should have been. When I was seven, something happened downstairs that became a legendary tale in our congregation.

A young couple in our church, Tim and Carolyn Shank, had a three-year-old son with a mop of blonde curls. Carolyn was loathe to cut little Timmy's gorgeous hair, which grew longer and longer, forming a bushy halo around his head.

Other congregational members teased Carolyn good-naturedly about her son's girlish appearance. "I know," she'd sigh. "But his curls are so beautiful. I just can't bring myself to cut them off."

Annette Nussbaum, the thirteen-year-old daughter of John and Irene Nussbaum, was an outspoken and impulsive teenager. She began calling the long-locked toddler "Timmy-etta." The name riled Carolyn, but not enough to make her cut her son's hair.

One Sunday evening when the children trooped up from the basement, the older children leading the little ones by the hand, Annette dutifully delivered young Timmy-etta to his mother.

Carolyn gasped and covered her mouth in horror when she saw the condition of her son's hair. Annette had fixed it in two tiny braids.

The following Sunday, it took the church members a few minutes to recognize the little buzz-haired tyke Carolyn Shank had in tow.

Sometimes, there was another delightful payoff for attending Sunday evening services. Mr. Campbell, an elderly man who lived on my father's mail route, never attended morning services, but on the occasional Sunday evening, he'd slip into one of the back pews. And the pockets of his old-fashioned baggy trousers were always filled with treats for the children, packs of *Double Mint* and *Juicy Fruit* chewing gum.

When the buzzer would summon us children upstairs, our eyes would light up at the sight of Mr. Campbell in the back pew. Shameless little beggars that we were, we'd descend upon him after the closing hymn. The smiling, twinkly-eyed septuagenarian would deposit sticks of gum into each our greedy, outstretched hands. It didn't take us long to come up with a new moniker for the kindly old gentleman: *Mr. Gumbell.*

Sunday after Sunday on our drive home from church, my mother complained bitterly about Reverend Schrock's inept preaching. "Give him a break," my father said one day. "Delbert Schrock is a good man."

"Well," my mother huffed, "that's easy for you to say. You don't have to put up with his preaching, because you sleep right through it."

She turned away from my father, staring out the car window in a sulk. Then she added, "He might be a good man, but if you ask me, someone who can't preach has no business going into the ministry."

{Ada Hochstedler Unruh sits in the cramped kitchen of the tiny apartment she shares with her husband. Pleased

that Herman has heeded the call to enter the ministry, their pastor and his wife are allowing the young couple to live in the upstairs of their home while Herman attends seminary.

Ada stares at the stack of papers on the table in front of her. When Herman announced that he was going to preach his next student sermon on the grace of God, she knew she'd have to take matters into her own hands. His last sermon, a disorganized, rambling discourse on God's love, had embarrassed her so profoundly that she'd wanted to crawl under the pew. She hadn't been able to tell what points he was trying to make, and he hadn't used any supportive scriptural references. Several times, he'd frozen, unable to utter a word for a full minute, his blue eyes wide with anxiety.

She can't bear the thought of sitting through another such disaster. She's decided to make a coherent outline for him to follow. She stares dejectedly at the meager notes Herman has scrawled, trying to make sense out of something she knows will never make sense.

Taking a deep breath, she straightens her shoulders and carefully prints, "God's Grace" in bold block letters at the top of the page. Then she prints a Roman Numeral I on the side of the page, ready to outline the first point of the sermon.

She peruses the scrawled notes again. Suddenly, anger wells inside her. She crumples the paper containing her husband's nonsensical ideas into a tight little ball and hurls it against the wall. Then she folds her arms on the table and buries her face, allowing the tears she's been holding back for weeks to leak out of the corners of her eyes.

"It's no use," she whispers to herself.

She knows Herman is right. "I'm not cut out for this," he told her yesterday. She knows he's ready to let go of his dream of pursuing a career in the ministry. She needs to let go, too.

Slowly, she raises her head and wipes her eyes. She swallows hard, pushing down the well of bitterness brewing in her soul.}

Thankfully, Westside Mennonite Church frequently hosted visiting ministers, which brought the congregation some much-needed relief from the insufferable routine of Reverend Schrock's preaching.

While the visitors weren't necessarily better preachers than Reverend Schrock, at least they were different. Reverend Daniel Amstutz, who hailed from Lancaster, Pennsylvania, came to Westside Mennonite at least once a year. With his slicked-flat hair and untamed beard, he reminded me of one of the men on the Smith Brothers cough drop box. His deep, growling voice and the peculiar cadence of his speech struck me as comical, and the week following his sermon, I'd walk around the house doing imitations of him. My mother would whack me on the bottom, telling me I shouldn't make fun of a man of God. But the fact that my imitations elicited hysterical laughter from Lucy made the occasional swat easy to bear.

Reverend Marvin Stoltzfus from Archbold, Ohio, was one of the homeliest men I'd ever laid eyes on, with his long, bony nose and receding chin. One Sunday when he was preaching, I was doodling in the notebook from my mother's purse, and I couldn't resist drawing a picture of him in profile. When my mother caught on to what I was doing, she snatched the notebook and put it away, snapping her purse shut with finality.

If the visiting ministers came from a distance, they stayed overnight at the home of Reverend Schrock and his wife Lydia. But one year when old Edgar Eash came to preach, Lydia Schrock was recovering from surgery and unable to provide her usual hospitality. My mother, always eager to demonstrate her spiritual devotion, offered to house Reverend Eash and his wife.

"Where will be put them?" my father asked when he heard about the commitment she'd made.

"In our bedroom, of course," my mother responded. "You and I can sleep on the living room floor."

"It's hard for a man to get a good night's sleep on the floor when he has to go to work the next day," my father grumbled.

Edgar Eash and his wife were some of the most ancient people I'd ever met. The short, rotund preacher wore a straight-cut coat with a high collar and no lapels, the style worn by old-time conservative Mennonite ministers. His plump little wife wore a bonnet-like head covering with strings that hung down over her ample bosom. I always wondered about the point of the strings if she wasn't going to tie them under her chin.

The night they stayed at our house, I headed downstairs to get a drink, but stopped on the stairs when I saw Reverend Eash and his wife in the kitchen. She was clad in a long flannel nightgown. He was wearing one, too.

I stood transfixed, staring at the two tubby little phantoms milling around the darkened kitchen in their white shrouds. Then I ran back upstairs and knocked on my sister's door. "Lucy! Lucy!" I whispered. "You've got to come see this."

She threw open her door, irritated. "What do you want, Tori Grace?"

"Come look," I said. "Reverend Eash is wearing a nightgown."

Her face lit up. "You're kidding me!"

"No," I said. "Come see."

We tiptoed partway downstairs, intending to spy on our guests without being detected. But at that very moment, Reverend Eash and his wife were leaving the kitchen, walking toward my parents' bedroom.

The nightgown-wearing preacher lifted a friendly hand in greeting. "Goodnight, girls," he called.

Lucy and I turned and flew up the stairs, stifling our laughter. When we were safely in her room, we subsided into uncontrolled giggles.

"He's wearing a nightshirt," Lucy explained to me. "That's what men used to wear in the old days." She allowed me to stay in her room for a full thirty minutes, while we giggled and made fun of Edgar Eash and all the other weird people we could think of.

There was, however, one truly exciting preacher that visited our church, and that was Reverend Harry Hahn. According to what I'd heard, Reverend Hahn had spent most of his pastoral career in Bakersfield, California. In the late 1950s, he'd toured the country from coast to coast, preaching in scores of Mennonite churches along the way. One of his stops had been at Westside Mennonite.

Several years later, he'd taken a pastoral assignment at First Mennonite Church in Warsaw, Indiana, a city twenty-five miles south of Goshen. Everyone in our congregation had been surprised by Reverend Hahn's move, wondering what on earth had prompted him to leave his enchanted home state of blue skies and ocean waves for the cornfields and blustery weather of northern Indiana. They were, however, quite flattered every time Reverend Hahn professed his love for the Midwest. Everyone agreed that California's loss was Indiana's gain, and they enjoyed the exotic west coast flair that Reverend Hahn brought with him when he preached at our church.

Because he lived so close to Goshen, our congregation was graced with Reverend Hahn's presence five or six times a year. Several years older than my father, he was not a young man, but his advancing years did not detract from the fact that he was extraordinarily handsome. He was tall, at least 6'4", with a slender build. His perfectly balanced features and his magnificent aquiline nose gave him a stunning profile. Irene Nussbaum, who'd grown up in a non-Mennonite, movie-watching family, insisted that Reverend Hahn's profile was even more striking than that of John Barrymore. None of the other church ladies had a frame of reference for Irene's comment, but they knew she'd paid the dashing minister a supreme compliment.

Reverend Hahn's black hair, streaked with gray, was swept back on the sides and held in place by Brylcreem. Like most other Mennonite ministers, he dressed conservatively, but his suits were well-made, perfectly tailored to fit his lanky frame. His sparkling white shirts were, no doubt, professionally laundered and starched.

Reverend Hahn's sermons were beautifully choreographed, perfectly executed performances. He held everyone, even the children, spellbound as he paced back and forth on the riser, gesturing with theatrical sweeps of his long arms, his expensive cufflinks glittering in the light. Occasionally, he stopped to thump the pulpit with his fist. He'd expound on truths from the scripture, holding a Bible in one hand and jabbing the air with the forefinger of his other hand, his dark eyes flashing with passion. He was undeniably charming, even when he thundered about the wrath of God and the fate of unrepentant sinners. Sometimes, he'd pause to pull a large white handkerchief out of his pocket and mop the sweat that trickled down the sides of his handsome face. By the end of the sermon, a strand of his Brylcreemed hair would have broken loose, hanging across his forehead and giving him a rakish look.

Reverend Hahn sometimes brought his wife Myrna with him. Like a male peacock, he was far more flamboyant than his female partner of the species. Myrna was a plain little woman with a thin, washed-out face and limp gray hair coiled into a bun at the nape of her skinny neck. While all eyes were riveted on her dashing husband, she'd sit inconspicuously in a back pew. The Hahns had no children, and rumor had it that Myrna was barren.

I'm quite sure that all the women in our congregation harbored a secret crush on Reverend Hahn. None of them could utter his name without blushing and batting her eyelashes. At the end of the service, they'd line up to greet him, clutching his hand and gushing, "Oh, Reverend Hahn, that was a wonderful sermon. You've given me so much to think about."

Thankfully, my grim mother refused to embarrass herself in such a way. She never offered the visiting minister more than a dour smile and a, "Thank you, Reverend Hahn."

Once a month after the Sunday morning service, our congregation held a potluck dinner. The capable Mennonite cooks always offered up a delectable spread, but when Reverend Hahn's presence was expected, their efforts were truly heroic.

Of course, the visiting minister was always directed to go first in the food line. Reverend Hahn would lavish praise on the platters piled high with ham and fried chicken, the crock-pots of baked beans, the savory casseroles, the luscious berry pies, and the decadent chocolate layer cakes with swirls of thick frosting.

As he ate, the church ladies would hover over him, asking, "Can I get you anything else, Reverend Hahn?"

"I couldn't eat another bite," he'd say, patting his stomach, as if the rich food had just put an extra twenty pounds on his lean physique.

It seemed the men of the church were not as charmed by Reverend Harry Hahn as were their wives. My father adamantly refused to attend any service where the debonair minister was scheduled to preach. When I'd ask him why he wasn't coming with us, he'd say, "I don't go for all that hellfire and brimstone stuff."

CHAPTER 7

*"And he took bread, and gave thanks, and brake it,
and gave unto them, saying, This is my body which is given
for you: this do in remembrance of me."*
Luke 22:19

*" He . . . laid aside his garments; and took a towel, and
girded himself. After that he poureth water into a bason,
and began to wash the disciples' feet, and to wipe them with
the towel wherewith he was girded." John 13:4-5*

"Salute one another with an holy kiss . . . ."
Romans 16:16

*"Then shall they deliver you up to be afflicted, and
shall kill you: and ye shall be hated of all nations for my
name's sake." Matthew 24:9*

There were other things about our church that my
father didn't fully agree with, although he never made
much of a fuss about them. While he was accepted and
well-liked by other church members, I knew he didn't quite
fit the mold of the typical Mennonite man, the type of man
my mother wanted him to be.

Unlike the other men in the church, my father rarely
wore a suit. Whenever my mother managed to convince
him that the occasion called for one, he'd reluctantly pull
out the old gray worsted wool suit he'd purchased a decade
before I was born. I'd feel sorry for him when he'd put it
on, as the jacket stretched tightly over his big stomach,

making him appear uncomfortable. To me, my father looked more like himself in plaid flannel.

When I was eight years old, my mother began schooling me in Mennonite history and theology. Over the years, she provided me with as much indoctrination as she thought I could take in. I learned that the Mennonite denomination had grown out of the Anabaptist movement during the sixteenth century Protestant Reformation in Europe. The Anabaptists were so named because they viewed baptism as a symbol of the believer's profession of faith. They rejected the idea of baptizing infants, who had no ability to understand the significance of the religious rite imposed upon them.

"Mennonites don't believe in baptizing babies," my mother told me, her tone reflecting her scorn for the denominations that held to that ridiculous practice. "Babies can't understand what baptism is about. Mennonites don't baptize their children until they're old enough to make a decision about dedicating their lives to God."

In our congregation, a child was typically baptized around the age of twelve. However, shortly after I turned ten, my mother steered me toward Reverend Schrock's baptism preparation classes, even though I hadn't yet given baptism any serious thought.

This was one time when my father spoke up. "Why are you doing this, Ada?" I heard him ask my mother. "Vickie's just a child. She's not old enough to know what she's doing."

"It's never too early to usher a child into the kingdom of God," my mother retorted.

"That doesn't make sense, Ada," my father said. "According to your line of thinking, we might as well do like the Catholics and baptize our children as babies."

"You know what I mean, Herman." My mother sounded flustered. "Anyway, I asked Victoria if she thought she was ready, and she said yes."

That was true. I had said yes. When my mother had asked me if I felt ready for baptism, her stern, questioning eyes told me she would accept only one answer. I sensed that, for whatever reason, my making a precocious statement of faith was important to her.

So, in spite of my father's protest, my mother had her way. Every Sunday evening for a month, I sat in Reverend Schrock's baptism classes along with five other young people, four boys and one girl. The girl happened to be my best friend, Judy Prentiss.

The Prentiss family lived on the west side of Goshen, and were on my father's mail route. Harold Prentiss was an alcoholic, known for going on benders that turned notoriously ugly. Barbara Prentiss, a haggard and discouraged woman who wanted to provide her children with some sort of positive influence, was most grateful when my father offered to transport Judy and her three older brothers to church on Sunday mornings.

The Prentiss children had attended our church for five years, and were regular fixtures in Sunday-School and Vacation Bible-School classes. Judy and I were also in the same grade at Model Elementary School, our birthdays being only ten days apart. Like me, Judy was a tall, thin, dark-haired girl with tomboy inclinations. At church, where one of us was found, the other was likely to be, and church members fondly referred to us as two peas in a pod.

My mother reluctantly allowed Judy to play at our house, but because of the sordid conditions in the Prentiss household, I was never allowed to go to there.

When Judy, who truly aspired to live a better life than her wicked father and her defeated mother, learned that I was going into the baptism class, she quickly decided to do the same. The two of us sat side by side through four Sunday evenings of Reverend Schrock's somber instruction.

On the Sunday morning of our baptism, the six of us young people sat in a row in the center front pew. The four boys sat to my right, and Judy sat on my left. As was the custom in our church, our regional bishop, Rupert Miller, had come to preside over the ceremonies.

Bishop Miller was another ancient relic of the Mennonite Church, an octogenarian with old-fashioned rimless eyeglasses and a few strands of gray hair combed over the top of his bald head. Like other conservative men of his era, he eschewed the worldliness of neckties and wore a straight-cut suit coat, shiny from decades of wear.

That morning, Bishop Miller preached a long, pious sermon which I didn't think I could endure without some sort of distracting activity, such as the little notebook from my mother's purse. But my mother had already warned me that after my baptism, I would be looked upon as a full-fledged member of the church, and that I would be required to behave accordingly. I would be expected to sit up straight, eyes toward the front, and pay attention to what the preacher was saying. In the eyes of God, I had reached the age of accountability, and I would no longer be allowed to entertain myself like a small child during the church service.

After the sermon, Bishop Miller came down from the pulpit to proceed with the baptism ceremony. Reverend Schrock came forward to assist him. As I'd witnessed baptisms before, I was aware of what was to come.

Starting with the boy on the far end of the row, Bishop Miller instructed him to kneel on the floor. Then Reverend Schrock handed him a pitcher of water. The bishop poured a small amount of water over the boy's bowed head, then laid his hands on his head and said a short prayer over him. Finally, he took the young man's hand, helped him to his feet, and did something quite disturbing in the eyes of a child: he planted a holy kiss on the boy's cheek.

I glanced over at Judy. Her eyes were wide with alarm.

One by one, the bishop worked his way down the line of boys, pouring the water, praying, and then imparting the holy kiss.

Judy's eyes now registered absolute terror, and I wondered whether she was going to bolt. I knew what she was thinking: that Bishop Miller, with his whiskery old face and his sour-smelling breath, was going to kiss her, too. I wanted to tell her that she didn't need to worry, as when it came time to baptize the girls, Bishop Miller's wife Dorcas would get up and do the kissing for him. But the eyes of the entire congregation were on us, and I couldn't very well nudge Judy and whisper in her ear.

Then it was my turn. I bit the inside of my cheek to keep from giggling as the cool water soaked my hair and dripped off my head, forming a puddle on the floor in front of me. I heard Judy's sigh of profound relief when the less-objectionable Dorcas Miller came up to plant the holy kiss on my cheek.

After our baptism, we newly-inducted members of the Mennonite church were expected to participate in the annual Holy Communion service that took place on Maundy Thursday, a ritual conducted in memory of Jesus' last supper with his apostles. Instead of remaining in the pews like the other children during this ceremony, Judy and I and the recently baptized boys filed up to the front of the sanctuary along with the adults. In a hushed voice, Reverend Schrock murmured the sacred words "Do this in remembrance of me," as he served each of us cubes of soft white bread and sips of grape juice from a communal cup.

I had no problem with the bread and the grape juice. For years, I'd watched in envy as the adults partook of these bits of sustenance that were off limits to un-baptized children. I did wonder about the health implications of so many people drinking from a common cup, but I figured the holiness of the act overpowered all the germs.

But there was one part of the communion service that I desperately wished to avoid, and that was the foot-washing ceremony. As a ten-year-old, having my feet washed by someone else was embarrassing, and washing their feet was positively disgusting.

True to the Mennonite practice of segregating the sexes during certain sensitive activities, the men and women never washed each other's feet. Tubs of water were set up in one corner of the sanctuary for the men, while the ladies were sequestered with their tubs in the women's anteroom.

The first time Judy Prentiss and I participated in foot-washing, we paired up. We didn't want to embarrass ourselves in front of the older women who knew what they were doing, and we watched them intently in order to learn the ropes.

One woman would sit on the bench, a tub of water at her feet. Another woman would kneel in front of the tub with a towel draped over her lap. The sitting woman would lower one foot into the tub. The kneeling woman would scoop up handfuls of water, adeptly splashing them over the foot. After drying the foot with the towel, she'd repeat the ritual with the other foot.

When we finally mustered the nerve, Judy and I rushed through our own ceremony, trying to keep our giggles to a minimum. Our inexperienced hands splashed awkwardly in the water, creating little puddles around the tub we were using.

Then, after all four of our collective feet were washed and dried, we faced another challenge. According to scriptural injunction, we were required to greet each other with the holy kiss. This was absolutely too much for two pre-adolescent girls, and we lost all ability to maintain our decorum. I'd pucker up my lips and move them toward Judy's cheek, but the giggling would take over. It took multiple attempts to finally get the holy kiss planted.

When we got home, my mother scolded me for the scene I'd made during a sacred ritual. But that was nothing compared to what happened a year later, when she caught me spying on the men.

I knew the men were also required to engage in holy kissing. At age eleven, I still delighted in being grossed out, and the image of the stodgy church men kissing each other's whiskery cheeks was just about the most revolting thing my imagination could come up with.

The older women took forever with their foot-washing, while Judy and I rushed through the ritual. After we hurriedly put back on our little-girl ankle socks and shoes, we ended up standing around, waiting while the women slowly pulled on their nylon stockings, discretely lifting their skirts to fasten their hosiery to their garter belts.

I was standing by the anteroom door that led into the sanctuary. Suddenly, I felt the urge to crack it open and peek at what the men were doing. And I saw the horror show I was hoping for, John Nussbaum kissing the grisly cheek of old Cletus Yoder. Then old Cletus returned the gesture.

I tried to stifle my giggles, but a few unladylike snorts escaped my tightly clenched lips. When Judy asked me what was funny, I whispered in her ear, telling her what I'd seen. We both clapped our hands over our mouths, trying to keep from howling with laughter.

My mother shot me an outraged look, her fierce eyes promising dire consequences for my wicked behavior. When we got home, she informed me of my punishment. Every evening after supper, I had to go to my room and stay there until bedtime, and while thus incarcerated, I had to write an essay on how to behave respectfully during a church service.

Upon the event of my baptism, I was required to start

wearing a head covering, something I considered to be a misfortune. On the morning of my baptism, my mother presented me with my personal little white cap.

I turned up my nose. "Do I have to wear that?"

"Yes," my mother replied.

"Why?"

"Because wearing a covering is the custom for women in the Mennonite Church. The Bible says it's dishonorable for a woman to pray with her head uncovered."

"But I'm not a woman," I retorted. "I'm just a girl."

"You're considered to be a young woman."

"Well, what if I don't pray in church? Do I still have to wear it?"

"That's enough of your nonsense, Victoria," my mother said sternly. She stood me in front of the bathroom mirror, and I scowled while she showed me how to secure the covering to my hair with straight pins.

She took an extra covering to church for Judy Prentiss, whose own mother had no way to provide her with such a necessity, and pinned it to her hair in the women's anteroom. Thereafter, Judy and I had to go through the covering-donning ritual before each church service.

The Sunday of our baptism, unmindful of the fact that we were wearing the unaccustomed coverings, Judy and I ran outside after the church service. Sitting on a low branch of our favorite tree behind the church, we giggled about all the weird stuff that had happened during the service. Judy inadvertently snagged her covering on a twig and ripped a sizable hole in it when she tried to pull it free.

When we shamefacedly presented the torn covering to my mother, we got the scolding we expected. From then on, my mother wisely collected our head coverings the moment the church service was over, keeping them in her care until the following Sunday's service.

When I became a teenager, I started wearing a type of covering that had come into vogue with the young women in our church. The new-style covering was essentially a lacy doily, which I thought was much more elegant than the old-fashioned coverings. As these new coverings came in both white and black, I could color-coordinate my covering with the outfit I was wearing.

Our church library, consisting of several shelves of books intended to strengthen the faith of both adults and children, was located in the back corner of the sanctuary. Most of the dry, serious volumes held no interest for me. However, I did enjoy the series of *Danny Orlis* books written by Bernard Palmer, stories about a young man who embarked upon one exciting adventure after another, and who never failed to witness to nonbelievers when the opportunity arose.

But I also had a strange attraction to a musty old tome called *The Martyrs Mirror*, published three hundred years before my birth. The book was made up of countless tales of courageous individuals who'd died for their Christian faith, beginning with Christ's apostles and including the Anabaptist martyrs executed in the sixteenth and seventeenth centuries. The book was large and very heavy, over a thousand pages of terrifying stories, detailed accounts of torture, beheading, and burning at the stake.

While my mother forbade me to watch horror and violence on television, she did not object to my reading stories about martyrdom. I was drawn to the particularly gruesome ones, reading my favorites over and over again. I also enjoyed the grisly illustrations, etchings by the Dutch artist Jan Luiken.

Sometimes, I'd lug the book over to my sister's room. "Listen to this, Lucy," I'd say.

Most of the time, she'd respond with, "Get out of here, Tori Grace. I don't want to hear that crap." But once in a while, I'd get her attention. Her blue eyes would grow round with horror, and she'd say, "Oh, gross!"

One day, my father came home from work and caught me sitting on the porch swing, pouring over the ghastly stories in *The Martyrs Mirror*.

"Put that book away, Vickie," he said. "You shouldn't be dwelling on that gruesome stuff. You should be filling your mind with more cheerful things."

At that moment, I was reminded once again that my father wasn't a very good Mennonite, as every other adult in my church would have been happy to see me schooling myself in the stories of the sacrifices made by our Anabaptist forebears. I also knew he was trying to protect me from something, and appreciation for him welled up inside me. The next Sunday, I lugged *The Martyrs Mirror* back to the church library, and I never checked it out again.

My father may not have been a stellar Mennonite, but being a mailman was where he shone. He drove the same route for over forty years, and he knew every family on the route. If someone was outside washing their car or mowing their lawn when he drove up to their mailbox, he'd linger to chat for a few minutes. If children were playing in the yard, they'd run over to his car. He'd hand them the mail and tell them to take it inside to their mother.

He watched these children grow up and become young adults with children of their own. He always knew who was graduating from high school, who was getting married, who was expecting a baby, whose elderly relative had just died. He never failed to offer words of congratulations or condolence.

Stopping to socialize meant that driving his route took longer than it needed to, which was a source of constant aggravation for my mother. "I need you to get home and help with things around here," she'd grouse.

The people on his route loved seeing my father's familiar face day after day, year after year. Every now and then, he'd open a mailbox to find a package with his name on it, containing a dozen cookies or a coffee cake.

At Christmastime, he reaped the benefits of all the goodwill he'd extended during the year. Every day for the three weeks prior to the holiday, he'd come home loaded down with Christmas cards, along with packages of cookies, fudge, peanut brittle, fruitcake, and every other kind of sweet treat imaginable.

I'd eagerly await his arrival home, and would prance around in excitement while he dumped his loot on the kitchen table. Together, we'd sort through it. As we'd read a card, he'd tell me something about the family who'd given it to him. I thought of him as popular, almost famous, in our small community, and I felt enormously proud of him.

"Daddy," I said to him one evening. "When I grow up, I'm going to marry a mailman like you."

"Oh, no, Vickie," he said hurriedly. "You want someone better than that. You don't want an old bumble-head like me."

{Herman Unruh trudges up the stairs to the tiny apartment he shares with his new bride. He has good news. At least, he hopes Ada will take it that way. He doesn't expect her to be overly impressed. After the way he's let her down, it will take a lot to get back into her good graces.

When he walks into the small kitchen, he finds Ada emptying the cupboards, packing their dishes into cardboard boxes. Now that he's no longer in seminary, they can't continue to rely upon the charity of their pastor and his wife. They need to find other housing.

Yesterday, when Ada told him she was carrying their first child, he knew he had no time to waste. He had to come up with a plan.

"I did what I told you I'd do," he announces. "I got a job."

She looks up from her work, and he sees the weariness on her pretty young face, the anger in her dark eyes. "Doing what?" she asks as she wraps a sheet of newspaper around the fruit bowl they received as a wedding gift.

"I signed up to be a mailman. I start my route next week."

"A mailman?" she sneers.

"At least it will pay the bills," he says, the coldness in his voice matching the ice in hers. "It'll put a roof over our heads. This is the best I can do for now, and we're going to have to live with it."}

CHAPTER 8

" . . . Inasmuch as ye have done it unto one of the least of
these my brethren, ye have done it unto me."
Matthew 25:40

My father never taught a Sunday-School class, never led a Bible study. He never stood up and gave his personal testimony during Sunday evening services. He never even prayed aloud during the Wednesday evening prayer meetings.

But he was the one who made sure the volleyball net was set up for the Mennonite Youth Fellowship on Friday evenings. During Vacation Bible-School, he helped supervise the children at recess, playing *Drop the Handkerchief* with the little ones, and *Duck, Duck, Goose* or *Dare Base* with the older ones. The kids loved fat old Herman Unruh and his goofy, boisterous laugh.

Whatever the church service, my father provided transportation for anyone who wanted to attend but couldn't find the means to get there. After driving all day on his job, he'd drive one more hour to pick up children for Vacation Bible-School. On Wednesday evenings, he'd fill his car with elderly widows and drive them to prayer meeting.

One lady in our congregation, Minnie Schumm, was crippled and unable to drive a car. On Sunday mornings, my father drove the ten miles to her home in Nappanee to pick her up for the church service. He'd help her into the front seat of his car, then would stash her walker in the trunk. After delivering her to the church and escorting her safely inside, he'd drive home to pick up my mother, Lucy, and me.

It may have seemed to others that my father did nothing to contribute to the spiritual life of the congregation. They may have been unaware of the fact that his kindly attention to the people on his mail route increased the attendance of our church by at least ten percent.

One afternoon when I was eight, my father came home from his route half an hour later than he normally did. As he trudged up the porch steps, his gait was slower and heavier than usual, and when he walked through the front door, his craggy face was twisted with pain.

"What's wrong, Daddy?" I exclaimed.

He said nothing, but walked into the kitchen where my mother was fixing dinner and slumped down at the table.

My mother looked up from the pot of chili she was stirring on the stove. "What's going on, Herman?"

"Little Scotty Thompson took his own life," my father choked out. "His parents found him hanging by his belt from the rod in his closet."

My mother's face went white. She turned off the burner under the chili and sat down at the table with my father. "How did you find that out?" she asked.

"The Thompson's neighbor, Roger Trumbull, told me. He and I talked about it for a while. He said Scotty had been getting into trouble in school, and that he'd been fighting with his parents."

My father stared down at the table, slowly shaking his big head. "I remember Scotty as a little tow-headed fellow.

From the time he was four or five, I'd see him out playing in the yard. As soon as he'd see me drive up, he'd run to the car. 'Got any packages for me, Mr. Unruh?' he'd say. His grandmother used to send him things in packages, and he always looked forward to that."

He reached up to wipe a tear that was sliding down his cheek. "When Scotty got to be a teenager, I didn't see much of him. I didn't think anything of that. I had no idea he was having problems. No idea at all. It makes a guy feel like he should've done something."

My father was quiet during supper. He had little appetite for the chili he usually consumed with gusto, and he declined a piece of my mother's banana cream pie. Suddenly, he pushed back from the table and stumbled into the living room, where he collapsed in his armchair.

I followed him and sat down on the sofa, watching him. He sat with his head bowed, his eyes squeezed shut, his shoulders heaving with silent sobs. At times, the sobbing erupted in big, noisy gulps.

My mother stepped into the living room. She watched my father for a moment, then moved toward him and laid her hand on his shoulder. I'd never before witnessed my mother expressing tenderness to my father. In spite of the grief permeating the room, the moment seemed perfect.

Then she stepped away and resumed her usual stern posture. Placing her hands on her hips, she said, "Herman, you can't take everything like this to heart."

On a Friday evening a year later, our telephone rang while we were eating supper. My mother scowled. "I'm just going to let it ring. People should know better than to call at mealtime."

"I think it's for me," my father said, a worried look on his face. He pushed back from the table and headed toward the phone, which hung on the kitchen wall by the door to the mudroom.

As he listened intently to the caller, he responded with an occasional, "Oh. Okay. I see." My mother, Lucy, and I could hear the frantic female voice on the other end of the line, but we couldn't make out what she was saying.

"I'll come right over," my father finally said. He hung up the phone and turned to us to explain. "That was Mrs. Prentiss. Harold's on another weekend bender. When I delivered their mail this afternoon, things were already getting out of hand. I told her to call me if she needed help."

Grabbing his car keys from the countertop, he headed out the back door. My mother scowled and bit her lip as she watched him go.

An hour later, I was holed up in my bedroom reading a *Danny Orlis* book when I heard a knock on my door. I jumped up to open it and found my father standing there with Judy Prentiss at his side. Her face was white, her eyes large and scared.

"Judy's going to spend the night with you," my father announced.

I didn't ask why, and Judy didn't offer any explanation as to why she was there. We played a game of Monopoly and watched a little TV. After she'd fallen asleep in my bed, I went downstairs to ask my mother for blankets so that I could sleep on the floor.

"Why didn't you consult me about this?" I heard her ask my father.

"I didn't have time," my father replied, his voice sounding apologetic. "It was an emergency. Mrs. Prentiss wanted her daughter to be somewhere safe."

My mother snorted. "Barbara Prentiss will pawn her children off on anyone who'll take them. You're way too easy, Herman. You'll let anyone talk you into anything."

{On a Sunday evening in March 1959, Herman and Ada Unruh sit in a pew at Westside Mennonite Church. Eight-year-old Lucy sits between them.

Ada listens with rapt attention to the visiting minister from California. Reverend Harry Hahn is delivering an impassioned speech about a mission project he's taken an interest in, a fledgling Mennonite church in the Mexican state of Sonora.

"These people are impoverished," he cries out in an anguished voice, "but so devoted to the Lord. Their devotion touches my heart. They deserve my help. They deserve your help. Their church building is little more than a hut. They want to build an addition so they can hold Sunday-School classes for their children."

Reverend Hahn's dark, burning eyes sweep across the congregation. Then it seems to Ada that they stop and stare at her. It feels as if his gaze penetrates her soul all the way to the core of her being, to the unspoken longing she's harbored for years.

"Perhaps the Lord is laying it on your heart to make a financial contribution to this project," he intones. "Or

perhaps He's moving you to come to Mexico and help with the labor."

Ada's mind flashes back twenty years, back to the bonfire in Joseph Miller's backyard, where she listened tearfully to a missionary's fervent speech about God's need for workers. Sorrow engulfs her heart. At thirty-eight, she feels old, her life spent, her dreams unfulfilled.

She glances over at her husband, expecting to see him dozing like he usually does during church services. But he's wide awake, listening intently to Reverend Hahn's words. He turns to meet her gaze, and his eyes register understanding.

That night in bed, Herman reaches over and takes her hand. "Ada." His voice is tentative. "Why don't you go to Mexico this summer? Call Reverend Hahn and tell him you want to volunteer."

Ada pulls her hand away. "You're talking nonsense, Herman. Don't tease me like that."

"I'm not teasing," he says. "Ever since the day I met you, I've known you had your heart set on doing something like this. Being married to me has held you back."

Ada shakes her head. "Don't say that, Herman."

"I know you feel that way," he says, "and I don't blame you. This might be your last chance. Take it, Ada. I don't want to hold you back any longer."

She can't believe what she heard him say. "But the children . . . ."

He interrupts her. "The kids and I can manage on our own this summer. Reverend Hahn is staying at Delbert Schrock's house tonight. Call there tomorrow and tell Reverend Hahn that you want to go to Mexico."

Ada is silent for a long moment. "Okay," she finally says. "I'll call first thing in the morning."

She knows she owes Herman a mountain of gratitude. No other husband would be so generous. She knows she should reach over and take his hand and tell him how much she appreciates his understanding of her needs, his respect for her hopes and aspirations.

But she doesn't. Contempt for her husband sours the pit of her stomach. Herman should have some self-respect and put his foot down. He should stop this silly fantasy of hers and remind her that she needs to take care of her responsibilities. She has two teenage sons and a young daughter. She knows that her being gone for three months will leave the household in a state of upheaval. Her husband and children will struggle to get by without her.

But excitement bubbles up inside her. Never in her entire life has she traveled any farther than Ohio or Michigan. She wants to leap out of bed and dance around the room, singing, "I'm going to Mexico, I'm going to Mexico." But she doesn't want to embarrass herself in front of Herman. She'll allow herself to get excited tomorrow, when he's gone.

She rolls over in bed, facing away from her husband, and says nothing more.}

CHAPTER 9

*"Thou hast turned for me my mourning into dancing: thou
hast put off my sackcloth, and girded me with gladness."*
Psalm 30:11

Lucy grew up believing she wasn't pretty. During
elementary school, her classmates teased her and called her
carrot-top, a nickname that never failed to ignite her fiery
temper. In high school, her red hair and freckled
complexion weren't considered to be the standard of
beauty, and her chubby figure didn't attract boys.

Our mother's lack of reassurance only served to
reinforce Lucy's negative opinion about her looks. Mom
was never one to shore up her daughter's sagging self-
esteem. She was determined to nip any tendency toward
vanity in the bud, as she considered self-admiration to be a
sin that could lead to all sorts of dangerous consequences.

But from my little-girl point of view, my big sister was
pretty. I envied her red hair and freckled complexion,
judging my own dark hair and olive skin to be inferior
traits. When Lucy's blue eyes weren't blazing with anger,
they were undeniably gorgeous. They were large and
round like my mother's eyes, but cornflower-blue like my
father's. While she flaunted church rules and cut a few
inches off her mane of curly red hair, she left it long, in
keeping with the fashion of the late 1960s. However,
instead of confining her locks to a proper Mennonite up-do,
she allowed her luxurious curls to cascade down her back.

During her senior year of high school, Lucy decided to
exercise some control over her weight. She started
skipping lunch at school, no doubt using her lunch money

to buy cigarettes. She picked at her dinners, pushing away the noodles and mashed potatoes and declining our mother's rich desserts.

One morning during the summer following her high school graduation, Lucy came tiptoeing down the stairs, apparently wanting to slip out of the house undetected by our mother. I was standing in the living room, and I gasped with delight when I saw her.

She was wearing hip-hugger bell-bottom blue jeans with red and yellow flowers embroidered on the length of the legs. A red tube top stretched over her ample bosom. The expanse between the skimpy top and her low-slung jeans left her slender waist and belly exposed. The lines of her body were quite striking, from her full breasts to her narrow waist to the curve of her hips.

She wore heavy eye-shadow and thick eyeliner that made her big blue eyes appear dramatic. Her curly red hair rippled down over her shoulders, framing her no-longer-chubby face. Oversized hoop earrings added an exotic touch to her appearance. Her flowing hair and half-naked body reminded me of the picture of a mermaid I'd seen in the book of fairy tales I'd once borrowed from my school library.

"Oh, Lucy!" I exclaimed. "You look beautiful!"

She put a finger to her lips. "Shhh."

But my exclamation had alerted our mother, who stepped out of the kitchen to see what was going on. When she laid eyes on Lucy, her face darkened with anger. I knew she recognized that her once plain, heavy-set daughter now presented a stunning appearance, and that she believed this transformation boded nothing but trouble.

Pointing a judgmental finger at Lucy, she said, "Young lady, you are not leaving the house looking like that."

"Why not?" Lucy snipped, tossing her magnificent mane of hair.

"You look like a . . . . " My mother searched for an acceptable word to express her contempt. "You look like an immoral . . . . "

"Don't you dare say it!" Lucy bellowed. "Don't you dare! You, of all people!" She glanced toward me. "Tori Grace, go up to your room before I say something I'm not supposed to say."

I stood there refusing to budge, not wanting to miss what was coming. "Go on, get out of here," Lucy barked, flipping the back of her hand at me.

When I didn't move, she turned back to my mother. "You!" she hissed. "Where do you get the nerve to talk to me like this? You haven't exactly played by the rules, you know."

My mother's face went white. The righteous anger seemed to drain from her body, and she suddenly appeared small and fragile. Lucy brushed past her and slammed out of the house.

{It's a scorching day in July 1959. Ada Unruh has been in Mexico for a month, along with the other Mennonite volunteers who've come to build the addition to the church in Sonora. While the men are occupied with making and laying the adobe bricks, Ada works alongside a few of the local women, preparing meals for the building crew, doing laundry, and cleaning up the living quarters and construction site.

The crew is housed in an old school building. The men camp out in the classrooms, while Ada sleeps in the former school teacher's quarters. As it turned out, she's the only female member of the Mennonite volunteer crew. But she doesn't mind. Under the wing of Reverend Harry Hahn, she feels secure and protected. When a local man made improper advances toward her, Reverend Hahn had intervened. "Leave Senora Unruh alone," he'd commanded. "She's a married woman."

Today is laundry day. Ada picks up the last of the freshly washed shirts from her basket and pins it to the clothesline. The shirt belongs to Reverend Hahn, and she handles it with special care. He's praised her for the excellent work she does with the laundry in these makeshift arrangements. She has to scrub the clothing by hand in tubs of hot water. But she doesn't mind the hard work. She's willing to do anything Reverend Hahn asks of her.

She stops to gaze at her surroundings, the acres of sun-baked soil dotted with cactus and scrubby brush. Several local men are napping in the shade of a mesquite tree, straw hats pulled over their faces. The scene is so different from the lush green landscape of her native Indiana. But she loves it here. She still can't believe how suddenly her mundane existence changed, how unforeseen circumstances led her to this strange land.

She wipes the sweat from her forehead with the back of her hand. Untying the red ribbon that holds back her long, dark hair, she combs through the locks with her fingers and then reties the ribbon. She's no longer wearing her Mennonite bun. It seems out of place in this enchanted country, this land of starry nights, softly strumming guitars, and the sultry rhythm of the rumba.

With all the bending and reaching involved in doing laundry, her blouse has pulled out of her skirt. She takes a moment to tuck it back in. She's wearing a bright yellow cotton ensemble that she purchased from the merchant at the nearby adobe dry-goods store. A pattern of colorful embroidered flowers encircles the neck and sleeves of the blouse. The full skirt, also embellished with embroidery, swirls with her movements.

Her hands linger on her slender waist, and she smiles. With the hard physical labor and her limited tolerance for the beans and tamales she and the Mexican women prepare for the building crew, she's shed a few pounds. She's enjoying a slimness she hasn't known for years, not since Lucy was born. She's exhausted, but in spite of working day after day in the dry, scorching heat, she feels more alive than she has in decades. She's doing something with a purpose.

When she looks into the eager eyes of the dark-skinned Sunday-School children who call her "Senora Unruh," her life seems fulfilled. She's taught them how to sing "Heavenly Sunshine" and "This Little Light of Mine" in English, and they've taught her the Spanish words for "Jesus Loves Me."

One little orphan boy begs her to take him back to the states with her. "I want you and Senor Hahn to be my mother and father," he tells her. In the minds of the children, she and Reverend Hahn are linked together.

The little boy's request pleases her. Ada wishes she could tell him such a thing was possible.

She wishes this summer would never end. The Indiana farmhouse she shares with her husband and three children seems a million miles away. She's worked closely with Reverend Hahn, trying to be as helpful to him as possible. In spite of the seriousness of their work, there are many light-hearted moments between the two of them. She enjoys engaging in witty banter with the jovial but highly intelligent minister. She loves it when one of her humorous quips sets off his hearty laugh.

She often watches him when he's not aware of her presence. She memorizes little details about him: the rhythmic movement of his long arms as he slaps down a line of mortar, then reaches for the adobe bricks and lays them in place; the way strands of his sleek, black hair fall in his face while he works; his deep sigh as he pauses to pull his handkerchief from his pocket and mop the sweat from his forehead; the way he stands back to inspect a row of bricks he's just laid, one hand on his hip, the other caressing his chin.

"Whoever said doing the Lord's work is easy?" he invariably tells the spent and exhausted volunteer crew at the end of the day.

Ada picks up her laundry basket and carries it back into the school building. It's time to take drinking water to the men. As she approaches the crew carrying the big clay jug of cool water, she sees Reverend Hahn working shirtless in the scorching heat.

She stops, taking a few moments to admire his long, lean, deeply tanned torso. Mennonite men in her community never expose their naked torsos in the presence of women. She knows she is indulging in a guilty pleasure, but she can't bring herself to turn her eyes away.

Reverend Hahn lifts his head, and their eyes meet. Smiling sheepishly, he reaches for his shirt.

That night is hotter than ever. Ada tosses and turns on her narrow cot. The residents of a nearby home are hosting some kind of party, and the strains of their sweet music fill the night.

She gives up on sleep. Pulling on the yellow skirt and blouse, she tiptoes toward the door. Then she pauses, turns back, and runs her hairbrush through her tousled hair. She doesn't want anyone to catch her looking disheveled. But she doesn't bother to tie her hair back with the ribbon, allowing her long locks to fall over her shoulders.

Silently, she slips out of her quarters, and from her vantage point outside the school building, she watches her neighbors' celebration. She doesn't know their customs well, but she's learning.

A pig is turning on a spit, and the savory smell of roasting pork fills her nostrils. The lively rhythm of the guitars and concertina makes her body want to move in blissful abandon. Festive strings of colored lights illuminate the figures of the dancers, the lavish skirts of the women swirling with their joyful movements. Ada feels a twinge of envy. How she longs to be that free!

Suddenly, she hears footsteps behind her, and she turns to see Reverend Hahn approaching.

"You couldn't sleep, either?" he says, chuckling. "I don't know how anybody could with all this going on. But I don't mind. I love it."

He stands beside her, gazing up at the night sky, hands

clasped behind his back. *"Just look at these stars, Ada.
Everywhere I travel, I experience the beauty of God's
creation in a new way. Just think, if you hadn't mustered
the courage to leave your sheltered home life in Indiana,
you never would've known some place like this existed."*

She nods. She couldn't agree with him more. It seems
that Reverend Hahn knows the unspoken passions of her
heart better than she knows them herself.

Reverend Hahn begins humming to the music, his long,
lean body swaying to the beat. Suddenly, he says, *"Dance
with me, Ada."*

She stares at him, horrified. Never in her life has she
been allowed to dance, and she can't imagine a Mennonite
minister making such an unthinkable suggestion.
"Reverend Hahn!" she protests.

He laughs. *"In the second book of Samuel, the Bible
tells us that King David danced before the Lord with all his
might. The Psalmist says, 'Thou hast turned my mourning
into dancing.' Dancing is a beautiful way of expressing
joy, our gratitude for God's gift of life."*

He takes her in his arms, and she trembles at his touch.
"The rumba is easy," he says. *"It's slow, quick, quick.
When you get the hang of the footwork, then you can add
the hip movement."}*

CHAPTER 10

*"With [his] much fair speech [he] caused [her] to
yield, with the flattering of [his] lips [he] forced [her]."*
Proverbs 7:21

While I never struggled with my mother to the extent
that Lucy did, there was one issue on which we constantly
bumped heads: my relationship with the opposite sex.

Our church issued plenty of injunctions against
improper conduct between the sexes. But my mother took
an even more extreme position than did the average church
member. If she'd had her way, I wouldn't have gone
within a hundred feet of a man or a boy.

It seemed to me that, in my mother's eyes, the male of
the species was a loathsome and dangerous creature. She
didn't often smile, and on the rare occasion when her face
did light up with pleasure, it was never in response to, or
even in the presence of, a man. If a man stepped too close
to her, she'd look uncomfortable, and I could almost see
her drawing an invisible veil of protection around herself.

The struggle between my mother and me wasn't just
about dating, although that battle certainly took place
during my teen years. Her desire to shield me from any
unfortunate experience with the opposite sex probably
began the day I was born. As a tiny child, she'd allow
women to fawn over me, to pat my cheek or stroke my hair
or cuddle me on their laps. But the minute a man would
bend down to engage me, she'd pull me back, holding me
firmly at her side.

When I entered the nursery Sunday-School class at age

four, my mother periodically checked with my teacher, Thelma Kauffman, to see how I was doing. The peace-loving Mennonites in our congregation abhorred conflict on every level, from the international to the interpersonal, and were thus hesitant to do something so provocative as to confront another church member about the conduct of her child. So it was with considerable reluctance that Thelma admitted to my mother that I'd been misbehaving in class. I'd bothered several little boys while they were coloring their Bible story pictures, and had made one of them cry when I stole his crayons.

My mother's quick response to this small crisis was to instruct Thelma to make sure that I was always seated between two girls.

One Sunday when I was six, I was playing in the church parking lot after our monthly potluck dinner. When my mother came out to check on me, she caught me teasing a little boy by tickling him in the ribs. Grabbing me by the arm, she marched me back to where she was sitting with a group of church women. "You'll stay right here with me, Victoria," she announced, "until you learn to keep your hands off the boys."

She'd tell me that when playing *Drop the Handkerchief* with the other Vacation Bible-School children, I should never drop the handkerchief behind a boy. When it came to *Red Rover*, she'd instruct me to call to the other team to send a girl over, not a boy. She'd caution me to chase only girls when I was *it* during a game of tag.

"Why?" I'd ask her, pouting.

Her answer was invariably along the same line: "It

isn't becoming for a girl to give off the impression that she's boy crazy."

The evening before Valentine's Day during my second grade year, I sat at our kitchen table with the box of valentine cards my mother had bought for me. Laboriously, I addressed each card in my newly learned cursive handwriting. My mother occasionally interrupted her supper preparations to peer at what I was doing.

"You don't need to give valentines to the boys," she said when she saw me writing the name *Kenny Miller* on one of the envelopes.

"Yes, I do," I retorted. "My teacher said we should give valentines to everyone so nobody gets hurt feelings."

A minute later, she caught me writing, *Love, Victoria,* on the back of a card. "What are you doing?" she barked. "You can't be telling the boys that you love them."

"You write, *Love, Ada* when you send Aunt Myrtle a letter," I said.

"That's different. She's my sister."

"Well, aren't you supposed to tell people you love them on Valentine's Day?" I persisted.

"Oh, Victoria!" my mother said, exasperation in her voice. She turned off the burners on the stove and sat down beside me, making sure that I didn't include any inappropriate sentiment on the cards I was addressing to my male classmates.

My mother also bombarded me with rules about my day-to-day conduct at school: "Don't bump up against the boys when you line up for recess." "Don't sit beside the

boys in the cafeteria. You should always sit with girls."
"Don't let your skirt fly up when you're on the playground.
You shouldn't let the boys see your underwear."

Her assumption that I was overly drawn to the boys
was correct. But it wasn't because I thought of them in
romantic terms. They were just fun to play with. While I
occasionally enjoyed dolls and other girly pastimes, I
usually preferred the rough and tumble games of the boys.

Admittedly, there was one boy in my class at Model
Elementary that I liked in a different way, and that was
Michael Nelson. He was tall and good-looking, smart and
athletic, and I wasn't the only girl in our class to harbor a
secret crush on him.

I tried my best to impress him by beating him in
competitions. But when it came to contests of doing long-
division or multiplication problems on the chalkboard, he
always beat me by a second or two. Once, I raced him
from the playground to the softball diamond, my long legs
pumping furiously, but he easily stayed several strides
ahead of me.

Michael, whose father was an attorney, was one of the
rich kids in the class. His family lived in a newly
constructed brick home on Greene Road. It seemed huge to
me, a veritable mansion with a flawless lawn and perfectly
groomed shrubbery. In comparison, my family's shabby
farmhouse seemed pitiful. Michael seemed to be above me
in every way. I could do nothing but hold him in the
highest regard, hoping that someday I would earn his
admiration.

In fifth grade, when we drew names for our gift
exchange at Christmastime, I was ecstatic when I drew

Michael's name. A moment later, anxiety replaced my excitement. I couldn't imagine what I could buy with a few dollars that would impress someone so special.

When my mother took me shopping at G. L. Perry's to purchase the gift, I was in an ornery mood. Nothing she suggested struck my fancy.

"How about a car?" she asked, pointing to a display of *Hot Wheels*. "Boys always like cars."

I wrinkled my nose and shook my head.

"How about *Lincoln Logs? Tinker Toys?*"

I snorted. "Those are for little kids. Michael wouldn't want anything like that."

My mother continued to peruse the merchandise in the toy section. Knowing full well I was doing something I'd never get away with, I sidled over to the display of *Marvel* comic books.

Because Michael Nelson's family wasn't Mennonite, his parents allowed him the pleasure of reading comic books, something off-limits to me. I'd often hear him talking about his favorite characters, and I always wished I had enough knowledge of the subject matter to discuss them with him.

Michael was a well-behaved kid, and he hardly ever got into trouble at school. But once, he got caught reading an *Iron Man* comic book that he'd tucked inside his geography book. In my eyes, this infraction only demonstrated his devotion to the characters he loved. As I began picking out copies of *Spiderman, Thor, X-Men,* and *Captain America,* I knew for certain I'd found a gift that would please the boy I admired so much.

Seconds later, my mother was at my side. Deftly

plucking the comic books from my hands and putting them back in the display, she said, "You know better than this, Victoria. I don't allow you to read comic books, and I won't let you buy them for someone else."

Shooting her a look I knew would get me in trouble, I stomped my foot. "That's not fair! This is something Michael would like."

My mother grabbed my shoulders and brought her face close to mine. "I know what you're up to, Victoria," she hissed. "You're trying to get this boy to like you. Well, I'm not having it. If you want to get him something to read, we'll go to Provident Bookstore and buy his gift there." With that, she turned and headed out of the store.

In my mind, a Mennonite bookstore was the worst place in the world to buy a gift for the boy I wanted to impress, and I knew my mother was doing her best to squelch my romantic fantasy. "They just have stupid church books at Provident," I muttered as I followed her.

In the end, my mother and I came to a compromise, and we bought Michael Nelson one of the *Hardy Boys* books. I wanted to at least impress him by wrapping his gift in colorful, glossy paper and topping it with a lavish bow, but my mother provided only plain white tissue paper and cheap, skinny ribbon.

If a neighbor man stopped by to chat while my father and I were feeding the animals, my mother would invariably find a reason to call me inside.

If she saw me standing by the side of our county road watching the road construction crew fill the potholes, she'd march out of the house, grab me by the arm, and escort me back to the porch.

"You can sit on the swing and watch," she'd say, "but you may not go any closer than that." If she'd catch me wandering off the porch and heading toward the road again, she'd haul me into the house and forbid me to go outdoors for the rest of the day.

Her watchfulness both aggravated and mystified me, as I never felt threatened by men. My strong bond with my father provided the model for absolute safety in a relationship with a male, and it never entered my mind that he would betray my trust.

And I never felt intimidated by boys my own age. I was as quick and strong as most of them, and I knew full well that, with the exception of Michael Nelson, I was smarter than the whole lot of them. No doubt, I posed a greater threat to them than they did to me, as I was bossy and manipulative, and would invariably outwit them and get them to do things my way.

By the time I was eleven, I'd had my fill of hearing my mother's cautionary rules about interacting with the boys on the school playground. After her umpteenth warning, I planted myself in front of her, scowling, my arms crossed huffily over my chest.

"I don't know what's wrong with you," I said. "The boys at school haven't done anything bad to me. You act like they're monsters."

She looked startled. Then the grim lines of her face softened. She sat down on the sofa and pulled me toward her, taking my hands in hers. "I guess I've been too hard on you, Victoria," she said. "I don't mean to give you the impression that the boys at school are bad. But in a few years, you're going to be a young lady. You'll need to be really careful then. I don't want you to get hurt."

"Those boys won't hurt me," I scoffed. "I won't let them."

She dropped my hands, and the strange look in her eyes made it seem like she'd gone a million miles away. I thought she was done with our little talk, and turned to leave.

But then she spoke again, in a low tone that sounded almost ominous. "You never know, Victoria. Men can be silver-tongued devils."

Her last sentence made me spin around and stare at her. My mother's style of speech was generally blunt and to the point, and she rarely expressed anything in a poetic or metaphorical way. I had no idea what she was trying to tell me. I'd heard the devil's attributes discussed plenty of times at church, but no one had ever mentioned the color of his tongue.

"What are you talking about?" I asked.

She shook her head, as if sloughing off the daze that had come over her. Looking intently into my eyes, she said, "Men can be smooth talkers, Victoria. If they want something from you, they have a really sweet way of talking you into it. You start thinking you mean something special to them. Then you find out it was all a big lie. You realize they never cared about you at all."

I continued to stare at her, horrified. "Dad's not a silver-tongued devil, is he?"

My mother's laugh was contemptuous. "Herman? No. Not him."

{It's the last day of August 1959, and Ada Unruh's summer volunteer work has come to an end. Her Mexico experience will soon be behind her. She and the other volunteers from the states are loading their luggage into the battered old bus that will transport them to the airport. All of the volunteers are leaving today, except for Reverend Harry Hahn, who is staying on an extra week.

Ada wants a moment to speak with Reverend Hahn in private. She needs to clarify where she stands with him. But it seems he's been avoiding her all morning. Every time she sees an opportunity to corner him, he's gone before she can reach him.

She doesn't want to make a fool out of herself, but she can't go back home to Indiana in this state of mental turmoil. She walks up behind him as he heaves a piece of luggage onto the bus.

"Harry?" she says, laying a hand on his arm. She's long past the point of calling him Reverend Hahn.

He turns to look at her, and her eyes search his face for evidence of what she hopes is true. He winces and glances away.

When he meets her gaze again, his eyes are those of Reverend Hahn, authoritative, self-possessed, and aloof. "Ada," he says, his voice so cool that it makes her shiver in the blistering heat. "We need to be realistic."}

CHAPTER 11

"Wash you, make you clean . . . ." Isaiah 1:16

"Let all things be done decently and in order."
I Corinthians 14:40

My mother was an immaculate housekeeper. Although our home was old and rundown, our furnishings shabby, she didn't complain much about that. I never knew her to hanker after fancy things. She didn't need a lot, but what she did have needed to be clean. For her, cleanliness was part of righteous living.

Germs never had a chance to multiply in my mother's kitchen. Dishes were washed at least twice a day, and were never allowed to pile up in the sink. Every inch of the cracked and warped laminate countertop had to be scrubbed down on a daily basis. On the rare occasion when my mother succeeded in getting Lucy to wash dishes, she'd grumble about her lack of thoroughness, cleaning up after her in a flurry of anger. She cleaned up after me as well, even though I applied myself to the dishwashing task more diligently than Lucy did.

Once a week, my mother did a thorough cleaning of our downstairs rooms. She often listened to music while she worked. Sometimes, she'd tune our old radio to WGCS, the Goshen College station. Other times, she'd put an album of spiritual music on our *RCA* record player. If she was particularly tired, the upbeat tempo of The Chuck Wagon Gang gave her the pep she needed to get through her task. Whenever she needed a good cry, she'd listen to Elvis Presley's soulful gospel songs. While Elvis crooned

Peace in the Valley or *How Great Though Art,* tears would stream down my mother's face as she dusted and scrubbed.

She'd sweep and mop the cracked linoleum in the kitchen and bathroom. She'd give our ancient bathroom fixtures a scrub-down with a *Clorox* bleach solution. She'd run the dust-mop over the scuffed hardwood flooring in her bedroom. Hauling out our old Hoover vacuum cleaner, she'd sweep the sagging living room sofa and my father's ragged armchair.

The only carpet in our house was in the living room. My mother took special care of it, vacuuming it at least every other day. She tried, albeit unsuccessfully, to get the rest of us to remove our shoes before walking into the living room. Twice a year, she'd get down on her hands and knees with a bucket of water, a rag, and a can of aerosol carpet shampoo.

My mother complained bitterly and incessantly about her lack of help with the housework. She had a valid point, as she worked much harder at chores than did the rest of us household members. But helping her often seemed like an exercise in futility, as none of us could ever complete chores up to her standards.

When I was a tiny child, my mother taught me the step-by-step process of cleaning my bedroom, a task she required me to complete every Saturday morning. When I'd announce to her that I was finished, she'd come upstairs to inspect my work. She never failed to point out something I'd missed: a smudge on my dresser mirror, dust bunnies under my bed, or the nightgown that I'd forgotten to fold up and tuck under my pillow.

The fact that the other upstairs bedroom was completely overrun by filth and clutter aggravated my mother to no end. The harder she tried to instill in Lucy the virtues of cleanliness and tidiness, the harder Lucy dug in her heels. My mother issued dire warnings about the future consequences of such slovenly habits, while Lucy insisted on her right to take care of her personal belongings in her own way.

As I grew older, Lucy's housekeeping style repulsed me nearly as much as it did my mother. But when I was little, I rather liked going into her bedroom, as it was an adventure. I'd poke around in the piles of rubbish, never knowing what treasures I might unearth.

At the end of Lucy's senior year, she and a few of her closest friends began scheming about what they were going to do on their *senior skip day*. While the teachers expressed mild disgruntlement about this breaking of the rules, the annual event was expected, and none of the participants got into serious trouble. Lucy's friends had all decided to spend the day at Warren Dunes State Park in Michigan, and Lucy desperately wanted to go with them.

My mother objected, saying that condoning senior skip day was supporting irresponsible behavior. Furthermore, she pointed out that Lucy's sassy backtalk and her refusal to help with household chores didn't warrant such a privilege. However, my father held the opinion that she should be allowed to go.

"After all, Ada," he said, "this is a once-in-a-lifetime experience for the girl. She needs to have some good memories from her youth." My mother petulantly gave in.

Then Lucy pushed her luck by asking for spending money. When my father pulled out his wallet, my mother stood her ground, insisting that Lucy needed to earn the money.

Lucy angrily planted herself in front of my mother, hands on her hips. "How do you expect me to do that?" she demanded to know. "I don't have a job because you barely let me out of this house."

"You will earn your spending money by cleaning your room," my mother retorted. "Before you take that twenty dollars from your dad, you will clean your room from top to bottom. I mean everything: your drawers, your closet. That room has to be spotless."

Lucy glanced over at my father, as if expecting him to bail her out. But all he said was, "Do what you mother told you to do."

My mother smirked, knowing she'd finally gained the upper hand in the interminable power struggle over the condition of Lucy's bedroom. Lucy shot her a malevolent look, then thundered up the stairs and slammed the door of her room behind her.

After a minute, I followed my sister up the stairs and stood outside her closed door, wondering what she was going to do. All was quiet. I thought for sure Lucy's stubbornness was once again going to prevail, that she'd forgo another privilege in favor of thwarting my mother's will. Then I heard her moving around, muttering to herself.

I cracked open her door and peered inside. "Want me to help you, Lucy?" I called. When she didn't respond, I stepped inside the room.

She scowled at me, and then said, "Alright, Tori Grace,

you can help. Go downstairs and bring me up some trash bags."

I ran down the stairs and fetched a handful of paper grocery sacks that my mother had stashed under the kitchen sink. When I went back upstairs, I found Lucy burrowed deep inside her closet, angrily flinging out items of clothing she wanted to get rid of.

"Tori Grace, put this crap in the bags and take them out to the burn barrel," she ordered.

"Uh oh," I taunted her. "You said crap. That's a bad word."

"Shut up," she retorted, "or I'll use more bad words."

I filled one bag with the discarded items, clothing Lucy hadn't worn in years. "Shouldn't you give these to Goodwill?" I asked. "That's what Mom always does with my old clothes."

"No," she said. "I don't want to bother. I'm just going to burn these and be done with it."

I filled another bag, but then I got distracted and began poking through the clutter on Lucy's dresser top. I found half a pack of cigarettes hidden under a rumpled shirt.

"Lucy," I scolded, "you're not supposed to have these. I'm going to tell Mom."

She swung around, glaring at me. "No you won't, you little twerp, because if you do, I'm kicking you out of this room and I'll never let you back in again."

I pulled one of the cigarettes from the pack. Holding it between my first and second fingers, I put it to my mouth and pretended to inhale. Then I blew out the pretend smoke.

"Get that thing out of your mouth," Lucy snarled as

she grabbed the cigarette from me. She put it back in the pack, which she stuffed into the pocket of her jeans.

Continuing my exploration of the messy dresser top, I pulled a scrap of paper from under an empty tissue box. On it was written, "Dear Jimmy." The rest of the note that Lucy had composed was scribbled out by a seemingly frustrated hand.

"Dear Jimmy," I read aloud in a gushy voice. Lucy grabbed the paper from my hand, ripped it up, and tossed the scraps into one of the trash bags.

"If you want to be in here, Tori Grace," she warned, "you better do what I tell you to do." She pulled an old pair of shoes from the closet and threw them in my direction.

One of the shoes slid along the surface of the linoleum floor and ended up under the bed. When I got down on my belly to fish it out, I found an open bag of pretzels under the bed.

"Where did you get these?" I asked, holding up the bag. "You're not supposed to have food in here. Did you steal these from the kitchen?"

"No," she said, "I bought them myself."

I took a bite of a pretzel, but promptly spit it back into the bag, as it was dry and stale. "Yuck," I said. "These are awful!"

"That's what you deserve, you little brat." Lucy grabbed the pretzels from me and tossed them into one of the garbage bags.

Wondering what other illicit goodies Lucy might have stashed in her room, I began rummaging around in the rumpled covers of her bed. When I moved her pillow, I discovered a half-eaten chocolate bar. It looked as if she'd lain on the candy while she was sleeping, as the chocolate was partially melted and had stained her sheet.

I broke off a piece of the candy, ready to sample it.

"Tori Grace, if you put that in your mouth, I'm gonna smack you silly!" Lucy held out one of the garbage bags. "Throw it in here. It's nasty. I swear, if you do one more thing, I'm kicking you out of here."

"You're mean!" Pouting, I turned back to my task of filling the bags with the clothing she was yanking out of her closet.

Suddenly, she pulled out an item I'd never seen before, a little white cotton blouse with puffed sleeves and a gathered neckline embellished with colorful embroidery.

She looked at it for a long moment, a strange expression on her face. Instead of throwing it on the floor with the rest of her discarded items, she stuffed it down the side of one of the bags I'd already filled.

"Where did you get that?" I asked. I scrambled up to pull the blouse out of the bag. Holding it up to me, I said, "It's pretty. Can I have it?"

"No!" Lucy barked, snatching the blouse from my hand and shoving it back into the bag.

"Why not?" I asked. "It looks like my size."

"It's too big for you."

"Let me try it on," I pleaded. When I reached into the bag again, she caught my wrist and squeezed it so hard that I gave up my effort. But I made a mental note of which bag contained the blouse.

After all the bags had been filled, Lucy said, "Tori Grace, go get me some more bags."

"Okay." I picked up two of the bags, one of which contained the pretty white blouse. "Since I'm going downstairs, I'll take these out to the burn barrel."

"Whatever," Lucy said absentmindedly, clearly not suspecting my nefarious intentions. She opened her window wide, then pulled the half-pack of cigarettes out of her pocket and lit one. As I was caught up in my own deceptive scheme, I didn't bother to scold her.

I carried the bags down the stairs, out the front door, then around the side of the house to the burn barrel in our back yard. Before dumping the contents of the bags into the barrel, I retrieved the little blouse and slipped it on over the shirt I was wearing. Just as I thought, it fit me perfectly. I sauntered back to the house, ready to prove to Lucy that the blouse was wearable by me after all.

Instead of going around to the front of the house, I walked through the back door and the mudroom and into the kitchen, where my mother was peeling potatoes at the sink. She turned around when she heard me come in, and her face went white. Putting aside her knife, she sat down at the table, staring at me as if I were a ghost.

"Where did you get that blouse?" she whispered.

Bewildered by her reaction, I said, "It was in Lucy's closet. It's too small for her, but it fits me."

"Take it off," she commanded.

"Why?"

A dazed look crossed my mother's face, and she remained speechless for a few moments. Just when she opened her mouth to say something, Lucy came down the stairs. She stopped short when she saw what I was wearing.

My mother looked up at her, instantly finding a target she could blast with her upset feelings. "Why did you give that to her?" she snarled.

"I didn't give it to her." Unlike her usual arrogant retort, Lucy's protest sounded weirdly vulnerable. "She wanted it, but I told her she couldn't have it. I put it in one of the trash bags she was supposed to take to the burn barrel. She sneaked it out of there."

Mother turned back to me. "Take it off!"

As I struggled to pull the blouse over my head, she stood up, and with a few harsh jerks, removed it from my body. I gave a little yelp when I heard the fabric rip.

Wadding up the garment, my mother reached into the drawer by the sink for a box of matches. Then, without saying a word to Lucy or me, she walked out the back door. I followed her out of the house and stood on the back steps, watching as she strode purposefully to the burn barrel and threw the blouse in with the two bags of Lucy's discarded clothing. Then she struck a match on the side of the box and tossed it into the barrel. Within seconds, flames leaped into the air.

{On a Sunday night in October 1959, Lucy Unruh lies wide awake in her bed, too excited to sleep. Tomorrow is the day when school pictures will be taken, and she's thinking about what she wants to wear.

Two weeks ago, she celebrated her ninth birthday, and her mother gave her a special gift she'd brought with her from Mexico: a white blouse with puffed sleeves and embroidery around the neck. Her mother had said it was the kind of blouse little Mexican girls wear on holidays.

It's the most beautiful garment Lucy has ever owned. She'd wear it every day, if she could. But her mother said she needed to save it for special occasions.

Lucy wonders if picture day could be thought of as a special occasion. Even though she knows her mother will scold her for not being asleep, she decides to go downstairs and ask.

Silently, she creeps down the stairs and tiptoes to her parents' bedroom. Their light is on, the door is open a crack, and she can hear her mother and father talking. They sound upset. She peeks through the cracked door, watching and listening.

Her mother is sitting on the bed, her back to Lucy. Her father is pacing back and forth, looking angrier than Lucy has ever seen him look. Then he stops and takes a step toward her mother, who draws back as if in fear.

"I'm not going to hurt you, Ada," he says. "You know me better than that."

He resumes his pacing, and then stops again. "Are you sure it's not mine?" Then he laughs bitterly. "Of course it's not. You wouldn't let me touch you for weeks before you left."

Lucy opens the door a little wider, and when it creaks, both of her parents swing around to look. "Lucy!" her mother exclaims. "How long have you been standing there?"

Lucy doesn't answer. As she turns to run away, she hears her father say, "Go talk to her, Ada. You're the one who needs to take care of this."

Lucy rushes up the stairs and into her room. Throwing herself onto her bed, she buries her face in her pillow, sobbing. *A few moments later, she hears her mother's footsteps enter the room. Ada sits down on the bed and lays a tentative hand on Lucy's back.*

"Why is Daddy so mad at you?" Lucy asks, her voice muffled by the pillow.

Ada hesitates a long moment. "Because I made a mistake," she finally says in a tone of weary resignation. "He's angry because I made a mistake."

"What did you do?" Lucy wails. Her sobbing intensifies.

"Be quiet, Lucy!" Ada commands, her voice suddenly harsh. "You'll wake up your brothers." She rolls Lucy over to face her, then grabs her by the shoulders and shakes her.

"Listen to me, Lucy," she hisses. "You must never tell anyone about this. Never. Do you understand me?"

Lucy nods, terrified by the venom in her mother's voice.

"Just put this out of your mind. Don't think about it anymore."

When her mother leaves the room, Lucy realizes she didn't remember to ask about wearing her new blouse to school tomorrow. But she doesn't care. Suddenly, she hates that blouse. She feels like she hates everything.}

CHAPTER 12

"Love worketh no ill to his neighbor . . ."
Romans 13:10

". . . Take no heed unto all words that are spoken . . ."
Ecclesiastes 7:21

Our nearest neighbors, Wendell and Marilyn Hooley, lived on a tidy piece of property a quarter of a mile down the road from us. Like our family, they were Mennonites, and they attended the same church we did.

My father admired and respected Wendell, who farmed most of the land adjacent to our property. Wendell kindly supplied my father with hay for our goats, always refusing payment for it. The two heavy-set men could often be found standing together beside our barn, beefy arms crossed over their broad chests. Wendell, wearing his trademark overalls and a feed cap pulled low over his sunburned face, stood a head taller than my flannel-shirted father. They'd discuss the weather, the prediction for crops that year, and the latest farm implement Wendell had acquired.

If my mother ever would have claimed to have a best friend, it would have been her plump, pretty, sweet-natured neighbor. Marilyn Hooley was a frequent visitor in my mother's kitchen, where the two of them exchanged recipes, quilt patterns, and cuttings from their favorite houseplants. My mother considered Marilyn to be an expert gardener. She drew inspiration for her own gardens from the flawless beds of shrubs and flowers Marilyn cultivated around the perimeter of the Hooley home and along the edge of their long driveway.

Wendell was also my school bus driver, and the first stop on his route was at my house. His two shy, tow-headed, chubby-cheeked sons would already be on the bus, sitting quietly in the front seat behind their father. Daniel was a year older than me, and David a year younger. I thought the two of them were the cutest little boys I'd ever seen, and I tried to get their attention by teasing them. However, they were too well-disciplined to respond to my annoying behavior.

I tended to bother not only Wendell's sons, but also the other children on the school bus. Every now and then, Wendell had to remind me to lower my voice, stay in my seat, and keep my hands to myself. Unfortunately, his gentle reprimands had little impact on me. Finally, he resorted to having a few words with my father, who then had a talk with me. This was all handled quietly and with goodwill, and when I finally decided to behave myself on the bus, any tension between us and the Hooleys was over and done with.

So, up until I was eight years old, my parents considered the Hooleys to be ideal neighbors in every way. But that all changed when Marilyn's widowed father, Melvin Horst, moved in with them.

Unlike his polite daughter and son-in-law, old Melvin was an ornery, foul-mouthed busybody. He was a wiry, diminutive man with stubbly whiskers and a shock of unruly white hair. Wendell and Marilyn had long ago taken away his car keys, but Wendell did allow his father-in-law to cruise up and down the county roads near their farm on an old *John Deere* tractor.

At least three afternoons a week, when he knew my father would be home from work, old Melvin would come putt-putting up the road and pull his tractor into our driveway, hoping for an opportunity to shoot the breeze. If he'd catch my father outdoors, he'd corner him and start yakking the nonsense that got on everyone's nerves, even the nerves of kindly, longsuffering Herman Unruh.

When Melvin would sidle too close to the goat pen and get nibbled on by Agnes or Annabelle, a stream of vulgarity would spew out of his mouth. If Orville the rooster would fly at him, the old man would flail at the bird with his skinny arms, cussing a blue streak.

"Take it easy, there, Melvin," my father would say. He developed discreet techniques of getting Melvin to move on down the road. "Gotta get these critters fed. Talk to you later, Melvin." "Need to go inside now. Ada needs my help."

Time and again, old Melvin caught my mother outside working in her flowerbeds. She'd be down on her knees with her hands in the dirt, her apron soiled, her hair in disarray. At those moments when she was looking her absolute worst, he'd inevitably say, "Ada, you just keep getting prettier all the time." Her face would turn beet red, and I knew she knew he was mocking her.

Once, I heard him say, "Looks like you've put on a little weight there, Ada. That's good. I like to see a woman with a little meat on her bones." Then he made a lewd clicking sound with his mouth. "That Herman's a lucky man."

Utterly mortified, my mother got up and walked into the house without saying a word to the old man.

It seemed as if Marilyn was constantly apologizing for something her father did. Like when he ran his tractor off our driveway, gouging furrows in our front lawn and taking out several of my mother's hydrangea bushes. Or when he absentmindedly opened the gate to the goat pen, allowing the freed animals to cavort around the yard and chew on the new bath towels my mother had just hung out on the clothesline.

"We just don't know what to do with him," Marilyn would fret. "He wasn't like this when he was younger."

My mother would reply with, "It's okay, Marilyn," even though I knew it wasn't okay, and that she hated the old man. But no one hated Melvin Horst more than I did.

Every time he'd pull up on his tractor and spot me in the yard, he'd call out in his evil old voice, "There's that orphan!"

"Why did you call me that?" I asked him the first time he said it.

"Because you don't look like the rest of the family," he said with an ugly cackle. "You must be a foundling. Somebody must've left you on their doorstep."

"That's a lie," I shot back, but my retort only made him laugh harder.

After hearing, "Hey, orphan!" half a dozen times, I learned to run and hide when I heard the sound of a tractor.

I never gave much thought to my physical appearance during my early childhood. However, by the time I was ten, I started becoming conscious of my height. At 5'2", I was as tall as my mother, and only an inch shorter than my nineteen-year-old sister. When my music class at school put on our Christmas concert, my teacher put me in the back row with the other tall kids. I was forced to stand next to creepy Wallace Morgan, who was older than the rest of us because he'd been held back two years.

One day, I was outside shooting baskets at the hoop my father had, years earlier, attached to the front of our garage for my brothers Michael and Robert. Because his tractor was either broken down or out of gas, old Melvin came walking, instead of driving, up the road. I wasn't aware of his presence until I heard him shriek, "Hey, orphan!"

Startled, I stopped and stared at him. "Orphan, you're growing like a damn weed," he hooted. "Pretty soon, you're gonna be tall enough to dunk that ball like an NBA player."

I'd been raised to respect my elders, but this nasty old man had poked a very sore spot, and I lost control. "Shut up!" I screamed at him.

His grisly face contorted in anger. "You need to learn some manners," he snarled. "Haven't your parents taught you to mind your manners?"

"You're the one who needs to learn manners," I yelled back at him. "You're rude!"

At that point, my mother stepped out the back door, grabbed me by the arm, and pulled me into the house. "What did I hear you say to him?" she asked after plunking my bottom down on a kitchen chair.

"I told him to shut up," I said. "He's always making fun of me. I'm sick of it."

"Victoria," my mother said, "Melvin Horst is just a stupid old man who's losing his mind. You can't stand out there getting into arguments with him. Just ignore him. Walk away from him. That's what I do. People are always going to say things you don't like, and you can't let it get to you. You need to make up your mind that you're not going to stoop to their level."

{"I can't believe how big you're getting with this pregnancy, Ada," Irene Nussbaum says one Sunday morning at church. "You must've gotten pregnant the minute you got home from your trip."

Ada shoots Irene a haughty look, but says nothing. Irene Nussbaum has a reputation for blurting out things other Mennonite women wouldn't dream of saying. The other women in the church have talked about Irene behind her back. They've attributed her indiscretions to the fact that she didn't grow up Mennonite. She joined the church when she married Sam Nussbaum, and she doesn't know how to guard her tongue.

"You and Herman must've had quite a reunion when you got home," Irene says, smirking.

Ada wonders if the other women in the church are thinking along the same line, or whether they're imagining something else. She searches for words to rebuff Irene's lewd insinuation.

"Wouldn't you expect that?" she says. "Wouldn't you and Sam do the same thing if you'd been apart for awhile?"

Irene pats Ada's arm, a lascivious grin spreading across her face. "You bet we would!"}

CHAPTER 13

*". . . The [mothers] have eaten a sour grape, and the
children's teeth are set on edge." Jeremiah 31:29*

The differences between my conservative home life
and the seemingly lavish lifestyles of my non-Mennonite
friends often embarrassed me. But never was the pain of
this disparity so keenly felt as at Christmastime.

Over the years, my mother grudgingly gave in to some
of the lifestyle changes thrust upon her by her husband and
children. However, when it came to the worldly influences
of the Christmas season, she was unmovable. She viewed
the Christmas tree as a pagan symbol, and was not about to
contaminate the purity of the story of Christ's birth with
something so offensive. Likewise, Santa Claus was viewed
as an abomination, a secular distraction from the true
meaning of Christmas, and no images of him were allowed
in our home.

Every year, a certain activity at the beginning of
December marked the onset of our family's holiday season.
On the first Saturday of the month, my mother would carry
a bag of gifts to the post office, to be mailed to her sons,
daughters-in-law, and grandchildren in Virginia. Each time
I accompanied her on this mission, I sensed that it was one
of sorrow rather than joy.

"Why don't Michael and Robert come home for
Christmas?" I asked her one year as we drove home from
the post office.

She was quiet for a minute, staring straight ahead as
she negotiated her old blue Ford through the congested

traffic of holiday shoppers. "Because the weather is too bad this time of the year," she finally said. "It's too dangerous for them to make that long drive in the winter."

I looked out the window, noting that the winter roads were clear that day, but I didn't voice my observation.

After making her annual holiday trek to the post office, my mother would invariably come home and rummage around in her bedroom closet, pulling out the ancient nativity scene that had been part of her family's Christmas celebrations when she was a child. It was in a sorry condition. The shepherd's staffs were broken, and the donkey and sheep were missing ears and tails. The paint on the face of the Christ child was chipped, giving the poor infant a blotchy complexion.

I'd help my mother set up the figures on the coffee table, but the antique pieces held little charm for me. I longed for something newer, shinier, and more dazzling.

My mother also set a trio of electric candles in the living room window, the bulbs burning with a white glow that symbolized the light of Christ. Several years, Lucy and I were allowed to decorate the window with artificial snow from an aerosol can. Spiritually speaking, snow scenes were neutral. They weren't holy like the Baby Jesus, but neither were they sacrilegious like Christmas trees and Santa Claus.

The afternoon of Christmas Eve day, my mother would disappear into her bedroom to wrap gifts for Lucy and me. This mysterious activity always stirred my curiosity. I'd allow myself to hope for something spectacular, knowing full well my fantasy would never become a reality.

On Christmas morning, I'd awaken to find a few gifts wrapped in white tissue paper surrounding the nativity scene on the coffee table. Each year, I'd get one inexpensive toy: a baby doll, an *Uncle Wiggily* game, a kit for weaving potholders. Then there would be several practical items, such as socks or a flannel nightgown that my mother had sewn out of fabric left over from one of her Mennonite Central Committee comforters.

Several particularly bitter years stand out in my memory. When I was nine, my Christmas toy was replaced by my first Bible. I was so disappointed that I wanted to hurl the holy book across the room, but I didn't.

Another year, Lucy opened the one and only package with her name on it, only to find it contained nothing but a note informing her that her gift was "debt credit." Lucy looked up at my parents, bewildered. My mother, trying unsuccessfully to keep the smirk off her face, explained the meaning of the gift: regarding the debt Lucy had incurred by accepting the unearned allowance my father had slipped her behind my mother's back, the slate had been wiped clean. Lucy spent most of that Christmas crying in her room. My father wouldn't look at my mother for the rest of the day, let alone speak to her.

It seemed my mother realized that while her gift of debt credit could have been construed as just, it was undisputedly mean-spirited. Two days after Christmas, she left the house, then came home an hour later carrying a shopping bag from G. C. Murphy's. Ascending the stairs, she knocked on Lucy's door. I heard a muffled conversation between the two of them. My mother came downstairs a few moments later, without the bag.

Christmas celebrations at our church were also a modest affair, following the same tradition year after year. On Christmas Eve, the teenagers, along with some of the young adults, would form a troupe of carolers. They'd go to the homes of the poor, the elderly, and the infirm, standing outside in the cold and the dark to offer up a heavenly serenade in four-part harmony. When I grew old enough to join the outdoor caroling, I discovered that the warmth welling up in my heart more than made up for frozen fingers and toes.

On the Sunday morning before Christmas, the Sunday-School children would present their program. They would line up on the podium to sing a few carols. Then they would act out the story of the birth of Jesus, drawing on the account from the second chapter of the Gospel of Luke. When I was ten, I was chosen for the role I'd coveted for years, the angel who announced the birth of the Christ child to the shepherds.

My mother was almost as pleased about my good fortune as I was. She bought yards of inexpensive white cotton fabric at G. L. Perry's and sewed me a voluminous robe. Going farther than I thought she would with the project, she bought a length of gold ribbon to tie around my waist. Then she used gold trim to adorn the neckline and sleeves of the robe, and to fashion a halo for my head.

Even Lucy got in on the act, apparently enjoying the idea of transforming her annoying little sister into a star performer. One evening when my mother had me try on my robe so she could mark the length of the hem, Lucy said, "Angels don't wear braids. Tori Grace needs to let her hair down."

Surprisingly, my mother allowed her to have her way. Lucy unbraided my long hair and brushed it out. The braids had created a myriad of rippling waves, which troubled Lucy. "You need to wash your hair right before the program," she said, "so it won't be all lumpy and bumpy."

As it was bedtime, my mother didn't bother to braid my hair up again. When I went upstairs, Lucy opened her door and hissed, "Come in here, Tori Grace."

She stood me in front of her mirror, where she brushed out my hair again. Then, pulling a pair of scissors from her dresser drawer, she said, "Your hair is straggly on the ends. I'm going to trim it."

I cringed when I heard the scritch-scritch of the scissors on my hair, wondering if I was going to get in trouble. A minute later, Lucy held out three inches of severed hair for me to see. "It looks a lot better now," she said.

The next morning, I held my breath while my mother braided my hair, but she made no comment about what Lucy had done. That evening, I heard her say to my sister, "It's up to me to decide whether my child's hair needs trimming. You keep your hands off of it."

Thelma Kauffman was in charge of the Sunday-School Christmas program that year. I was glad, as she was more enthusiastic and imaginative than some of the adults who'd supervised the production in previous years. She served as the narrator of the drama, standing inconspicuously on the edge of the podium while reading the portions of the story that didn't involve speaking parts.

"And it came to pass in those days, that there went out a decree from Caesar Augustus, that all the world should be taxed."

Thelma eliminated a few verses that she deemed inconsequential to the story. *"And Joseph also went up from Galilee, out of the city of Nazareth, into Judea, unto the city of David, which is called Bethlehem . . . to be taxed with Mary, his espoused wife, being great with child."*

Then Joseph and Mary, played by my neighbor Daniel Hooley and Reverend Schrock's granddaughter Beth, plodded across the stage. Daniel pulled along a large cardboard donkey that his father Wendell had mounted on a wooden platform with wheels. Skinny little Beth's abdomen was conspicuously flat, as it would have been unthinkable to simulate a pregnancy in a Sunday-School production.

Thelma had written a few lines for Joseph and Mary. In monotone voices, Daniel and Beth each commented on how weary they were from their long journey.

"And so it was," Thelma continued, *"that, while they were there, the days were accomplished that she should be delivered. And she brought forth her firstborn son, and wrapped him in swaddling clothes, and laid him in a manger, because there was no room for him in the inn."*

Several more scenes ensued: Joseph knocking on the cardboard door of the inn, pleading with the innkeeper for shelter; Joseph and Mary hovering over the manger, gazing adoringly at their doll-child.

"And there were in the same country shepherds abiding in the field, keeping watch over their flock by night."

Three boys wearing their fathers' old bathrobes scrambled onto the stage and crouched on the ground, cardboard sheep in hand.

"And, lo, the angel of the Lord came upon them . . ."

That was my cue, and I stepped regally onto the stage.

"And the glory of the Lord shone round about them: and they were sore afraid."

The shepherds cowered in front of me, shielding their faces from my dazzling presence.

"And the angel said unto them . . ."

I stepped forward, spectacular in my gold-trimmed robe, my sleek, freshly washed hair cascading over my shoulders. Raising my arms in the air, I called out in a loud voice, "Fear not!"

The congregation went dead silent. Suddenly, I felt a surge of power, like I was holding all of them captive.

"For, behold, I bring you good tidings of great joy. . ." I said the words *great joy* slowly and dramatically.

"For unto you . . ." With a flourish of my hand, I indicated that I was addressing the entire congregation. ". . . is born this day in the city of David a Savior, which is Christ the Lord."

Raising my finger in the air, I intoned, "And this shall be a sign unto you. Ye shall find the babe wrapped in swaddling clothes, lying in a manger."

Then Thelma read, *"And suddenly there was with the angel a multitude of heavenly host, praising God and saying . . ."*

Several timid, white-robed six-year-olds were urged onto the stage by their mothers. They were too frightened to utter their lines, so I was the only angel who raised her eyes and her hands heavenward and proclaimed in an ecstatic voice, "Glory to God in the highest, and on earth peace, good will toward men."

A murmur of appreciation spread throughout the audience, and I realized the people had been moved by my angelic performance. I knew it was more than a matter of me doing a good job of remembering my lines. It was as if I had personally delivered the good news of Christ's birth to them, in a way that had touched their hearts.

I glided off the stage, and the program settled back into its previous level of mediocrity. But I felt giddy and elated, knowing something important had happened to me that morning.

After the service was over, I stood at my mother's side, still wearing the angel costume I was reluctant to take off, while one person after another came up to congratulate me on my performance.

"You did a wonderful job, Victoria."

"That was truly inspiring, Victoria."

"You make a beautiful angel, Victoria."

"You brought tears to my eyes, Victoria."

Then Irene Nussbaum said to my mother, "Victoria is so comfortable in front of an audience. If she were a boy, I'd say she'd make a great preacher."

Suddenly, a note of anger tinged my euphoric mood. *Why did being a girl mean that I couldn't be a preacher?* I knew I could preach better than any boy in my entire congregation, and I was dead set on proving everybody wrong.

After dinner that day, my parents lay down for their Sunday afternoon naps. I took the opportunity to sneak out to the garage, where I poked around until I found several orange crates. Hauling them back into the house, I stacked them one on top of the other, building myself a little pulpit in the corner of the living room.

Then, brandishing the New Testament I'd received when the Gideons handed them out at school, I waved the other hand in the air, imitating what I'd seen Reverend Hahn do the last time he held an evangelistic service at our church. "Repent, ye wicked sinners, lest ye be cast into the fires of hell," I thundered.

On and on I ranted, in short order waking up my parents. My bewildered father wandered sleepily into the room and sat down in his armchair. After hearing just a few moments of my righteous rage, he said, "Cut it out, Vickie."

My father virtually never spoke to me in such a sharp tone. I paused, staring at him in confusion. But I was on a roll I didn't feel like stopping, and I resumed my preaching with increased energy.

Then Lucy entered the room, followed by my mother. "What the heck are you doing, Tori Grace?" Lucy asked.

She stared at me, wide-eyed. All of a sudden, she inhaled sharply, covering her mouth with her hand. "Oh my God, oh my God!" she exclaimed.

Horrified, she turned to my mother. "It was HIM, wasn't it? Oh my God, it was him! I can't believe I didn't know that all along."

White-faced with shock, my mother opened her mouth to protest.

"Don't say anything!" Lucy screamed, pointing an accusing finger at her. "I don't want to hear you say a goddamn word!" Then she turned and rushed up the stairs.

My mother quickly retreated into her own bedroom.

By that time, I'd stopped my preaching, startled and baffled by the strange little drama playing out before my eyes.

"Vickie, take those crates back out to the garage," my father commanded. "And don't ever do this again."

"Why not?" I asked. "Why can't I preach?"

"I told you before," he said. "I don't go for that hellfire and damnation stuff. I won't have that nonsense going on in my house."

Then he picked up a newspaper and hid himself behind it. The dreadful silence in the house was broken only by the sounds of Lucy sobbing in her upstairs bedroom.

{Eleven-year-old Lucy Unruh sits in the classroom with the other sixth-grade girls. They are having a private meeting with the school nurse. The boys have been taken to the gymnasium for a meeting of their own.

The nurse has just shown the girls a filmstrip about the female anatomy and the changes that take place in a girl's body when she becomes a woman.

Lucy feels sick to her stomach. She wishes she didn't have to grow up. She doesn't want to become someone like her mother, an unhappy woman who hates the life she is consigned to lead. She hopes it will be a long time before these changes happen in her body.

The nurse explains how the woman's egg is fertilized by the male sperm, and how that results in an embryo that lodges in the uterus and grows into a baby.

When the class is dismissed, Lucy walks up to the nurse. "I have a question," she whispers.

The nurse searches Lucy's face, sensing the girl's distress. "Let's go to my office," she says.

When she and Lucy are safely behind her closed office door, Lucy blurts out, "How does the sperm get inside the woman to fertilize the egg?"

The nurse looks uncomfortable. "Hasn't your mother talked with you about these things?"

Lucy shakes her head. "No. She won't. And I don't want her to."

As the nurse discreetly describes the act of human copulation, horror creeps over Lucy. She suddenly grasps the nature of her mother's mistake, the one that had so enraged her father just months before her little sister was born.

She clutches her stomach. "I'm going to throw up."

The nurse quickly fetches a basin. "I know all of this can be upsetting to a young girl," she says as she hands Lucy a damp towel to wipe her face. "You'll understand better when you're older."

Lucy shakes her head. She'll never understand.}

CHAPTER 14

"When I was a child, I spake as a child, I understood as a child, I thought as a child: but when I became a [woman], I put away childish things." I Corinthians 13:11

Up until I was twelve, my mother conducted the daily ritual of braiding my long hair. The hair-braiding station was the kitchen chair at the end of the table closest to the living room. Each morning when I traipsed down the stairs after dressing myself for the day, my mother would have the chair pulled out and would be standing there with comb and hairbrush in hand.

I'd sit sideways on the chair so that she could have access to my long locks. Combing out and braiding my hair took no longer than three or four minutes, as she was very proficient with the task. I'd seen other girls come to church with crooked parts or lopsided braids. My mother would have been ashamed to let me out of the house in such a state.

She kept me in those tidy braids long after the other Mennonite girls my age started wearing more grown-up hairstyles. When I turned eleven, I started disliking my little-girl hairstyle, but every time I asked my mother if I could wear it differently, she found a way of deflecting my request.

The Saturday morning after my twelfth birthday, I decided to take matters into my own hands. As I stood at my dresser mirror brushing out the hair I'd washed the night before, I admired its sleekness, and I determined that it would never again be confined to braids.

"Hurry up, Victoria," my mother said when I came

down the stairs. "I have things to do." She pulled out the hair-braiding chair, impatiently waiting for me to take a seat.

"No," I said. "I'm not letting you braid my hair anymore."

She stared at me, bewildered. "Well, how do you want to wear it then?"

"I'll decide that," I said in a haughty tone. Then I turned and headed back up the stairs, where I knocked on Lucy's door.

"I want you to trim my hair again," I told my sister when she granted me entrance. "And this time, cut me bangs."

Fifteen minutes later, I stood in front of my dresser mirror admiring my new look. I blew my breath upwards, ruffling my newly cut bangs. I bounced up and down, watching my unconfined hair flying in the air, then settling on my shoulders. I swung my head from side to side, chortling, "Whee-ee, whee-ee," as my hair whipped back and forth. Flinging my arms in the air, I twirled and danced, feeling freer than I'd ever felt before.

Then I stopped to admire myself again. "My mom's not in charge of me anymore," I announced to my smug reflection.

Thereafter, I wore my long hair trailing down my back, looking like every other adolescent girl in the early 1970s. My mother registered her displeasure over my new look by making the occasional snide remark.

"I guess you don't mind being straggly-haired," she said when I walked into the house one blustery day, the wind having blown my hair into a state of disarray.

Another day when she watched me brushing my hair, she said, "You seem to think you can do whatever you want to do, no matter what the Bible says or what the church teaches."

I shot her a scornful look. "My hair is still long. And if you can show me anywhere in the Bible that says braids or buns are holy, then I'll start wearing my hair like that."

Entering seventh grade at Towncrest Junior High marked the beginning of other significant changes in my life. At the tender age of twelve, I took several more steps down the road of self-determination.

Unlike Lucy, I didn't accomplish these changes through a stormy rebellion against my mother. I simply asserted the imperious attitude that was rapidly becoming an integral part of my personality, an attitude that my mother had difficulty standing up to.

A month before I started seventh grade, I opened my closet to find half a dozen of Lucy's old dresses hanging there, recently altered by my mother. Snorting in disgust, I carried them downstairs to the kitchen, where my mother was rolling out crusts for rhubarb pies. "You might as well give these to Goodwill," I told her, "because I'm not wearing them."

"Why not?" she said. "They're perfectly good dresses."

"They're out of style," I replied.

She shrugged and turned back to her pie crusts. Before going back upstairs, I threw the dresses on her bed. My mother never said another word about them.

Two weeks later, she took me school shopping. Each time she picked out an outfit for me to try on, I wrinkled my nose and shook my head. I could tell she was becoming more frustrated by the minute, which both amused and empowered me. Finally, she sat down on a chair beside the dressing room and said, "I give up, Victoria. You go find what you want. But you have to try it on so I can see it."

Gleefully, I gathered up armloads of all the dresses, skirts, and tops that struck my fancy. While my mother vetoed a few of my choices, I still started out my seventh grade year with a stylish wardrobe.

During my years at Model Elementary School, I'd earned good grades, without trying very hard and without caring very much about my performance. However, in junior high, I became conscious of the fact that I was considered to be a top-notch student, even a gifted student, and I began investing a great deal of energy in maintaining that identity. My teachers' praise for my outstanding work fueled my burgeoning attitude of superiority and invincibility, spurring me on to even greater achievements.

In elementary school, I'd been competitive with the boys on the playground, but in junior high, I threw myself into competing academically with the two brainy boys in my class: Thomas Eads, the son of the eighth grade math teacher, and Maurice Landis, the son of a local heart surgeon. I did everything I could to edge them out by a few points on a math or science test, and wasn't hesitant to rub my victory in their faces.

One day when my English teacher handed me back an essay with an A+ on it, she said, "Excellent work, Victoria." Then she furrowed her brow and asked, "You're Lucy Unruh's sister, aren't you?"

"Yes," I replied.

"Hard to believe," she murmured as she walked away.

For a few minutes, I felt dejected. I didn't mind showing anyone else up, but somehow, it didn't feel good to put my sister in a bad light.

For a year and a half, I sailed along, fully convinced of my right to do anything I wanted to do, confident in my ability to accomplish anything I set out to achieve. However, during the second semester of my eighth grade year, I bumped up against a roadblock, as I inadvertently gave my mother the perfect opportunity to put her foot down.

When my music teacher, Mrs. Tilton, announced our school's plans to put on a production of the musical *Brigadoon*, it never occurred to me to ask my parents' permission to try out for a part. Being in a play was something I wanted to do, and no one was going to stop me. Of course, I had my heart set on the lead female role of Fiona.

During the *Brigadoon* auditions, I watched in disdain while the other girls stood motionless on stage, arms glued to their sides, singing *Waitin' For My Dearie* in breathless little voices. When my turn came, I belted out the sweet lyrics from the depths of my heart, floating dreamily around the stage, gesturing gracefully with my uplifted arms.

When Mrs. Tilton posted the outcome of the tryouts late on a Friday afternoon, I wasn't a bit surprised to see that I'd been cast in the role of Fiona. Neither was anyone else. Everyone agreed that the part was rightfully mine.

For a moment or two, I worried about the implications of my height. At 5'7", I was the tallest girl in my class, taller than the vast majority of the boys. I didn't relish the idea of playing opposite a leading man a head shorter than me. But as I continued to peruse the list of cast members, I breathed a sigh of relief when I saw that my neighbor Daniel Hooley had been cast in the lead male role of Tommy.

Daniel, a ninth grader, was destined to be a large man like his father Wendell, and was at least an inch taller than me. He wore his blonde hair as long as the school dress code would allow, a style which all the girls at Towncrest thought was incredibly sexy. Although Daniel was quiet, his sky-blue eyes twinkled with friendliness, and he was undoubtedly one of the best-looking guys in the school. The idea of playing opposite him in *Brigadoon* was quite a pleasant prospect for me. My female classmates gushed about how much they envied me, as I'd probably have the chance to kiss the boy of all their dreams.

I rode home on the school bus in a jubilant mood, feeling a new, special bond with the magnificent Daniel Hooley. Keenly aware of his presence three seats behind me, it was all I could do to keep from turning around to catch his eye and smile at him. But I was beginning to understand that I needed to be less assertive with boys, that if I wanted them to like me, I needed to stand back a bit and let them pursue me.

When Wendell stopped the bus at my house, I jumped off and ran all the way up the driveway and onto the porch. "Guess what!" I exclaimed to my father as I bounded into the living room and flopped down on the end of the sofa next to his armchair. "I got the lead part in our school musical!"

"Well, good for you, Vickie!" My father reached over and patted my arm. "You're such a smart girl."

By that point in my life, I'd come to realize that my father wasn't a very worldly-wise man. He had no understanding of plays and musicals, or anything else related to the arts. But I didn't care, because being happy for me was all that I needed from him.

I headed up the stairs, ready to sequester myself in my room and indulge in delightful fantasies about the future of my acting career. But I was stopped short when I heard my mother's voice barking from the kitchen, "Victoria, you come down here right now!"

Reluctantly, I turned around and walked back downstairs, the air leaking out of my euphoric mood. I could tell my mother wasn't going to be nearly as easy to deal with as my father.

"Sit down," she commanded, pointing to a kitchen chair.

I obliged, but not without shooting her a haughty look. "Why am I in trouble? I didn't do anything."

"What's this about you getting a part in the school musical?" she demanded to know, hands on her hips, her elbows jutting out aggressively. "You didn't ask my permission to do this." Her clenched jaw and narrowed eyes made her pretty face seem ugly and suspicious.

Trying to shore up my wavering confidence, I looked her dead in the eye. "I didn't think you'd mind. There's nothing wrong with it."

She sat down on the chair across the table from me, ready to begin her interrogation. "What's the name of this musical?"

"Brigadoon."

"What's it about?"

"What does it matter?"

She glowered at me. "Don't sass me, Victoria. It's my job to decide whether the subject matter of this play is appropriate for a Christian young lady."

I knew I was in for a very hard time, and I scrambled to pull my wits together. Taking a deep breath, I said, "Two guys from New York go to Scotland on a hunting trip. They discover a little town called Brigadoon. It exists for just one day every hundred years, and it never changes."

"Hmph!" my mother snorted. "So this musical is based on a lie. It's trying to get a person to believe in something that isn't true."

"It's like a fairy-tale, Mom," I protested. "No one believes it. It's just for fun."

"So what happens in the story?"

"One of the men falls in love with a girl from the village. They can't get married, because if she leaves Brigadoon and goes back to New York with him, Brigadoon won't exist anymore. So he goes back to New York alone. But he misses the girl so much that he decides to go back to Brigadoon to be with her and stay there forever."

"What role are you supposed to play?"

"Fiona."

"Who is she?"

I hung my head. "The girl the man falls in love with."

"That's what I figured!" My mother smacked the table with an angry hand. "I know you, Victoria. You'll do anything to get close to boys." She leaned toward me, eyeing me quizzically. "Are there going to be love scenes in the play?"

I knew I was plunging deeper and deeper into hot water. Feigning innocence, I asked, "What do you mean?"

"You know what I mean. Hugging and kissing and things like that."

"I don't know," I lied. "If there is kissing, it will just be pretend kissing. Mrs. Tilton wouldn't let us kiss for real." I desperately hoped my mother's penetrating eyes couldn't peer into my mind, because if they could, she'd know that I wasn't at all averse to the idea of kissing my co-star.

My mother leaned back in her chair. "No, Victoria," she said in a low, ominous tone. "You're not doing this. I'm not going to have you shaming yourself by making out with some boy in front of an entire audience. You tell Mrs. Tilton that she needs to find someone else to play the role of Fiona."

"Mom!" I wailed.

My father had gotten up from his chair, and was standing in the doorway between the living room and the kitchen. "Ada," he interjected.

My mother ignored him and plunged ahead. "And what about dancing? Is there going to be dancing in this musical?"

"Maybe," I admitted.

"Victoria Unruh!" she thundered. "You had no business even trying out for this! You know you aren't allowed to dance!"

"But it won't be the bad kind of dancing," I protested. "It's . . . it's just folk dancing."

"But you'll be kicking up your heels, looking indecent, showing everything you've got. The answer is still no. We're not going to discuss this anymore." She stood up and walked over to the kitchen counter, where she began angrily tearing up a head of iceberg lettuce, tossing the bits into a salad bowl.

I knew my ship was sinking rapidly, and I pulled out the only lifeboat I could think of. "But Daniel Hooley gets to be in the musical. He's a Mennonite, and Marilyn and Wendell are letting him do it."

My mother swung around to look at me, a strange expression on her face. "What role is Daniel playing?"

"Tommy."

"Who's Tommy?"

I realized my lifeboat had just pitched me overboard into churning waters. "One of the men from New York."

My mother's wary eyes peered at me suspiciously. "He's the man that falls in love with Fiona, isn't he?"

I nodded, my eyes flickering downward to avoid her accusing stare.

"Victoria," she said, her voice filled with disdain, "I know how you are with Daniel Hooley. You'll do anything you can to get his attention. I absolutely will not allow you to play love scenes on stage with that young man!"

"Ada," my father protested.

She turned to glare at him. "I said the answer is no! She's my daughter, and I have the right to say no!"

"I'm dad's daughter, too," I wailed in my last futile attempt to reason with her. "He thinks it's okay!"

Over the weekend, I lost my arrogant composure and resorted to Lucy-like behavior: screaming that my mother was ruining my life, flinging myself across my bed and crying hysterically, refusing to come downstairs for meals.

My mother was well-practiced in responding to such theatrics, having gone down that road with her older daughter, and she stubbornly refused to budge in the face of my histrionics. So on Monday morning, I had no choice but to tearfully inform my music teacher that my mother wouldn't allow me to participate in the production of *Brigadoon.*

Mrs. Tilton shook her head sadly. "That's such a shame, Victoria. You're perfect for the role of Fiona."

That evening, she called my mother, and they talked for half an hour. I sat at the foot of the stairs, straining to hear my mother's end of the conversation. Apparently, Mrs. Tilton gave her a full explanation of what would happen in the musical, reassuring her that the young cast would be carefully supervised at all times, and that nothing indiscreet would be allowed on the stage.

To my delight and amazement, my mother grudgingly gave Mrs. Tilton her consent for my participation. I figured she didn't want to appear unreasonable in the eyes of the school. But when she hung up the phone, she glared at me with fierce eyes. When I exclaimed, "Oh, thank you, Mom," she refused to speak to me.

She remained in a huff for a few days, giving me the cold shoulder. I knew she realized she'd completely lost control over the direction my life was taking, and that she didn't like it, not one bit.

For the next three months, my life revolved around preparing for the production of *Brigadoon*. The cast rehearsed twice a week after school. I leaped and twirled while practicing the *Wedding Dance*, kicking my long legs high, enjoying what my lithe young body was capable of doing. Daniel and I practiced Tommy and Fiona's duets, *The Heather on the Hill* and *Almost Like Being in Love*, and Mrs. Tilton gushed over the beauty of our harmony. We occasionally brushed lips during our pretend kissing, but my mother's protest was far from my mind. She no longer had the power to hold me back.

At home, I diligently rehearsed my lines in the privacy of my bedroom, doing my best to infuse them with a Scottish brogue. Whenever my mother left the house, I took the opportunity to practice my songs and my dance steps. I knew better than to flaunt in her face the fact that I'd won our power struggle.

I'd been well-liked during my first year at Towncrest, but my participation in the musical elevated my status, boosting me into the ranks of the popular kids. Other students began clamoring to keep company with me. Melissa Adkins, a short, chubby girl who followed me around like a lost puppy, said, "It's not fair, Victoria. You've got everything. You're pretty and smart, plus you can sing and act. I wish I was like you."

"I'm not perfect," I responded in an attempt at modesty.

"It seems like you are," Melissa sighed.

Every day, at least one of my classmates asked me whether Daniel Hooley was my boyfriend, as he and I were frequently seen walking down the halls together. I'd always say, "Oh, no, he's just my friend," even though I thought of him as a little bit more than that.

On the evening of our performance, I smugly assessed the acting skills of my fellow thespians to be amateurish, typical for middle-schoolers. But in my mind, Daniel and I were Broadway-bound, our talent soaring far above the rest. As he and I sang *From This Day On* in Tommy and Fiona's heart-wrenching parting scene, I experienced the exhilarating sense of holding the members of the audience in the palm of my hand. They were my emotional captives, and I loved it.

When Daniel and I came out for our curtain call, the audience applauded wildly, and a few of the people gave us a standing ovation. I bowed repeatedly, making sure to catch every corner of the auditorium in the beam of my smile.

Suddenly, my eyes fell upon a tall, gray-haired gentleman standing in the back row, clapping enthusiastically. I was momentarily bewildered, as I'd never seen Reverend Harry Hahn anywhere other than at church. It took me a moment to register the fact that he could indeed have a life outside of that setting. I wondered whether he had a relative in the play, perhaps a niece or a nephew.

My parents had attended the performance. After pulling myself away from the post-production fanfare, I had to face the sobering fact that I'd now have to contend with my mother's reaction. I was pretty sure she hadn't really wanted to watch the musical, and that she'd only come to spy on me, to find out what I'd been doing behind her back for the past three months.

As he drove us home, my father periodically glanced over his shoulder at me in the back seat, saying things like, "That was real nice, Vickie." "You did a real good job." "I really enjoyed your play."

But my mother sat beside him in a stony silence, eyes straight ahead, presumably wanting me to know how badly my worldly performance had offended her Christian sensibilities. I was afraid that, at any moment, she might turn around and start berating me for how immodest I'd been in my dancing, or for how passionately I'd kissed Daniel Hooley in our parting scene. As a way of distracting her, I said, "I saw Reverend Hahn sitting in the back row. What was he doing there?"

The silence engulfing my mother became heavier, more ominous. I wondered whether she was so angry with me that she was refusing to speak to me on any subject. Finally, she muttered, "Well, the man has a right to go anywhere he wants to go."

{On a sweltering summer evening in 1961, the phone rings while Ada is scrubbing a skillet in the kitchen sink. "Will you get that, Herman?" she calls to her husband who is sitting in the living room.

Carrying their one-year-old daughter in the crook of his arm, Herman walks into the kitchen and picks up the receiver. His jaw tightens when he hears the familiar voice on the other end of the line. He wishes the man would disappear and leave him and his wife in peace, but he knows that isn't likely to happen. Not for many years.

"May I speak to Ada?" the caller asks.

"Okay." Herman's voice is flat. He holds the receiver out to his wife. "It's Reverend Hahn."

Ada grimaces, but she obligingly dries her hands on a dish towel and takes the phone.

"Ada," Reverend Hahn says, "I need to inform you about the plans I've made."

"Yes?" she says, irritated.

"I've accepted the pastorate of the First Mennonite Church in Warsaw."

Ada thinks he's referring to Warsaw, Poland. She wonders why he feels the need to tell her that he's taking a position in another country. As far as she's concerned, Reverend Hahn can carry on his disreputable missionary work anywhere he pleases. At this point, she couldn't care less about church work in foreign lands.

"Okay," she says.

"Warsaw, Indiana," Reverend Hahn clarifies. "Myrna and I will be moving to Indiana in two months."

Ada inhales sharply, leaning against the kitchen counter for support. "Why?" she asks when she finds her voice again. "Why are you doing this, Harry?"

"I need to be near her." His voice is thick with emotion. "She's the only child I have. I can't raise her, but I can at least be close enough to watch her grow up."

An angry fire burns in the pit of Ada's stomach. It moves up through her chest and her throat. Her face turns hot and red, and the pressure in her head makes it feel as if it's going to explode into a million pieces. One hand squeezes the phone receiver like she wants to crush it, while her other fist is clenched at her side. Once again, she realizes that a foolish mistake, a moment of misguided passion, is going to follow her for the rest of her life.

"I don't think this is a good idea," she says, not bothering to hide the antagonism in her voice. "You know this will make things awkward for Herman and me. But I suppose you have the right to live anywhere you want to live."}

CHAPTER 15

*"Children, obey your parents in all things: for this is
well pleasing unto the Lord. [Parents], provoke not your
children to anger, lest they be discouraged."*
Colossians 3:20-21

My English teacher wasn't the only one who
questioned how Lucy and I could come from the same
family. Lucy struggled with her schoolwork, plodding
along in the bottom half of her class. When I came along
years later, I excelled academically, soaring to the top of
my class. And being a tall, overly-confident brunette, I
bore not the slightest resemblance to my short, red-headed
sister with the reputation for a fiery temper.

Lucy hated everything about school. She always
seemed to be at odds with one or more of her female peers.
When my mother wasn't around, she'd be on the telephone
with a friend, ranting about what some other girl had done
to make her mad. Although she refused to talk with me
about her upset feelings, I often sensed that the crying
spells behind her closed bedroom door had to do with boys
who didn't reciprocate her affection.

And she repeatedly butted heads with her teachers.
Halfway through her senior year, she got into a heated
argument with her home economics teacher, who'd
criticized the uneven hem on the skirt Lucy was sewing.
Lucy came home enraged, announcing to our parents that
she was dropping out of school.

My mother turned on her in a fury. "I absolutely will
not allow you to make such a foolish decision!"

"I might as well quit," Lucy protested. "I don't even have enough credits to graduate on time."

As usual, my mother stood as solid as a brick wall. "You're going to stay in school until you have that diploma in your hand! I don't care if it takes you until you're twenty-one!"

"You go against me on everything," Lucy wailed. "You've never loved me. You just enjoy making my life miserable."

While I, too, had often questioned my mother's affection for my sister, it occurred to me that her insistence on Lucy finishing high school was the most loving thing she'd ever done for her oldest daughter.

Lucy's shocking announcement brought fear to the eyes of my placid father, and he heaved himself out of his armchair and stood behind my mother while she railed at Lucy. No doubt, his show of support for my mother's stance at that critical moment helped keep Lucy in school.

So Lucy stumbled through the last few months of her senior year. She ended up participating in her graduation ceremonies, although she had to attend summer school to retake the government class she'd failed.

While Michael and Robert had gone on to college right after high school, there was never any talk in our household about Lucy doing the same. My parents knew she couldn't make it in college, and Lucy showed no interest in furthering her education.

After completing her term of summer school, Lucy lay around her room for the rest of the summer, passing the daytime hours by sleeping. Late at night, she'd rouse herself, going out to join the party life of her like-minded friends. In a futile attempt at reforming her indolent daughter, my mother badgered Lucy incessantly about the need to abide by household rules, telling her she was expected to clean her bedroom, do her own laundry, help with the dishes, and come home by her 11:00 PM curfew.

Lucy would laugh in my mother's face. "I'm eighteen now. I'm an adult, and you can't tell me what to do anymore."

"If you're an adult," my mother would retort, "then you need to take on adult responsibilities. If you want to continue living here, then you need to pay for your room and board."

Fortunately, Lucy had a friend who worked at the Dairy Queen on Pike Street in Goshen, and she managed to get Lucy some part-time hours there. Lucy ended up working that job for the next three or four years. However, my parents never saw a dime of rent money, as she spent her earnings on after-work partying and cheap, sleazy clothing.

My father would drive her to the Dairy Queen store for her evening shift. "You don't need to pick me up," Lucy would tell him. "I'll find another ride home." She'd come stumbling into the house at three or four in the morning, reeking of alcohol and cigarette smoke.

I didn't see much of Lucy during those years, as whenever she was home, she was usually asleep in her bedroom. Sometimes while getting ready for school in the morning, I'd crack open her door and peer into her room. I'd see her body, once again heavy from the cheeseburgers and banana splits she was eating on her breaks at work, forming a large mound under her bedcovers.

"Lucy?" I'd whisper.

She'd roll over, mumbling, "Leave me alone, Tori Grace."

Whenever I'd catch a glimpse of her face, I'd see the profound despair in her eyes. I knew my sister was a miserable young woman, living a pitiful life.

But every now and then, Lucy would snap out of her dark mood and join family life for a few hours. She'd share a pleasant Sunday dinner with the rest of us, or would play a board game with my father and me on one of her evenings off work. I could see that, in spite of her rebellious ways, my sister longed to be an upstanding member of our family.

I did everything I could to make her feel like she belonged with us. Knocking on the door of her bedroom, I'd call out, "Wanna play *Aggravation* with Dad and me? Mom said we could have popcorn." Or, "Mom made a chocolate pie for supper. Wanna come down and have some?" Even though Lucy responded to my invitations only a fraction of the time, I never gave up my efforts.

Whenever Lucy did emerge from the cave of her despair, she'd be fine as long as my mother managed to refrain from berating her about her many shortcomings. But it was extremely difficult for Mom to stay off her case, and Lucy's good mood would inevitably vanish in a blaze of anger.

Time and again, my mother confronted my father, demanding action from him. "I want her out of here!" she'd hiss, as if her own daughter was a fugitive from the law, hiding out in our attic and putting the rest of us at risk. "She's a bad influence on Victoria."

My father would turn his head to avoid her angry stare. "Vickie's not going to follow Lucy's example," he'd say. "She knows better than that."

Once when Lucy heard my mother speak of her bad example on me, she pointed an impertinent finger at her and said, "I should think you'd be worried about your own example on Tori Grace."

One day when Lucy was twenty-two, she didn't come stumbling home in the wee hours of the morning. Out of habit, I peeked into her room while getting ready for school, and a bolt of fear shot through me when I didn't see her body creating a mound under the bedcovers. She still wasn't there when I came home from school. I found my parents conversing in low tones in the kitchen, worried expressions on their faces.

An hour later, a car pulled up in our driveway, driven by a scruffy-looking young man. Lucy was beside him in the passenger seat. She jumped out of the car and strode into the house and up the stairs to her room, without saying a word to my mother, my father, or me. Ten minutes later, she came down again, carrying a bulging duffle bag and an armful of clothing.

"What are you doing?" my mother asked.

"I'm doing what you want me to do," Lucy snapped as she headed out the door. "I'm getting the hell out of here."

"Where are you going?"

"What do you care?" Lucy slammed the door behind her.

My father and I followed her out the door and stood on the porch, watching while she opened the car door and threw her belongings into the back seat. Then, with a laugh and an arrogant wave, she climbed in beside the young man.

As the car pulled out of our driveway, I was overcome by sadness and a sense of foreboding. I looked up at my father and saw the sorrow on his face. "What's going to happen to Lucy?" I asked him.

He put his arm around my shoulders. "I don't know what's going to happen to her, Vickie. All I know is that Lucy's got to find her own way in life. All I can do right now is pray and trust the Lord to watch out for her. Yup, I'll be praying for my girl, day and night."

"I'll pray for her, too," I promised.

That evening, my mother didn't utter a single word about Lucy's departure. The next day when I went upstairs after coming home from school, I found her in Lucy's room, pulling things out of the closet. She was sorting items Lucy had left behind into three boxes, each bearing a hand-printed label: *garbage, Goodwill,* and *quilt blocks.*

"What are you doing?" I asked.

Scowling, she gingerly picked up a pair of unwashed panties from the closet floor and tossed them into the *garbage* box. "I'm cleaning up your sister's mess," she muttered.

The next day when I came home, I again found my mother in Lucy's room. This time, she was pulling down the soiled curtains from Lucy's window, adding them to the pile of rancid sheets and blankets she'd removed from the bed. The following day, she was scrubbing the yellow cigarette smoke stains off the beige walls. The day after that, I found her on her hands and knees with a rag and a bucket of bleach water, scrubbing the sticky black grime off the old linoleum.

She looked up at me as I stood in the doorway, her face red from exertion, her messy hair standing out from her head like a deranged halo. "She's never going to do this to me again," she muttered. "Running out of the house and leaving all this filth for me to clean up. No one is ever going to do this to me again."

{On a warm, sunny morning in May 1962, Ada Unruh carries a basket of freshly laundered sheets out to the clothesline in her backyard. She brings two-year-old Victoria outside with her, as no one else is home to watch the child.

As she hangs the sheets on the clothesline, Ada glances around to make sure her daughter is playing within her line of vision. Little Victoria is a cheerful toddler who seldom clings or fusses, and she is prone to wandering off to explore her surroundings.

Suddenly, Ada realizes that today is Victoria's birthday. She knows she needs to do something to mark the occasion, although her heart isn't in it. Celebrating the day seems like celebrating the sin that brought the child into the world.

As she lifts another sheet from her laundry basket and drapes it over the clothesline, she mentally takes stock of the ingredients in her pantry. She thinks she has what she needs to make a chocolate cake, although she tells herself it doesn't really matter. Victoria is too young to know anything about birthdays.

Her sons don't care about Victoria's birthday. They barely even acknowledge their little sister's existence. Neither one of them shows any interest in family life anymore. Michael is at college in Virginia, and Ada rarely hears from him. Robert is finishing up his senior year at Goshen High School, and he finds every reason not to be at home in the evenings. But Herman and Lucy will be there for dinner, and they will scold her if she hasn't remembered to do something special for Victoria.

An anguished cry jolts Ada out of her thoughts. She glances around and sees that her child has wandered all the way over to the vegetable garden. Little Victoria is standing motionless, as if frozen. As Ada runs toward her, she sees that the toddler is surrounded by a swarm of honey bees. She is whimpering pitifully, gasping for breath. One side of her face has begun to swell, distorting her dainty features.

Ada's quick assessment tells her that Victoria's reaction to a bee sting is different than that of her other children. When Michael, Robert, and Lucy played in the backyard as youngsters, an occasional bee sting was nothing to be alarmed about.

Grabbing the toddler, Ada rushes into the house for her car keys. Then she lays her child in the back seat of the car and heads toward Goshen General Hospital.

On the drive to the hospital, a horrible thought flits through her mind. If her child dies, her life will be less complicated. Her secret burden of shame could be laid to rest. Deeply penitent, Ada counteracts her despicable thought with a desperate prayer, beseeching God to spare little Victoria's life.

In the emergency room, Victoria is promptly treated with an injection of epinephrine. The doctor informs Ada that the child had gone into anaphylactic shock due to an allergy to bee stings. "Have any other family members ever had reactions like this?" he asks.

"I don't think so," Ada mumbles. The truth is that she doesn't know. She has no information about the medical history on her daughter's paternal side of the family.

The doctor keeps Victoria in the emergency room for observation for a few hours. Late that afternoon, Ada takes her home and places her in Herman's comforting arms. While Ada dutifully mixes the ingredients for a chocolate birthday cake, Herman croons a Sunday-School song to the swollen-faced child.

"Yes, Jesus loves me. Yes, Jesus loves me," he sings in his errant tenor voice, tears of sympathy running down his craggy cheeks.

The next day, Ada does something she doesn't want to do, but knows she must. She picks up the phone and dials the number of the office at the First Mennonite Church in Warsaw. Reverend Hahn has instructed her to call there in case of an emergency. He's made it clear that she is never to call his home.

"Harry," she says when he answers the phone in his lofty pastor's voice. "We had a problem with Victoria yesterday. She went into anaphylactic shock after being stung by a bee."

"Oh no!" he gasps. "Is she okay?"

"She's fine now," Ada assures him. "But the doctor asked me about her family medical history, and I realized

that I don't have anything on your side of the family. Does anyone in your family have an allergy like that?"

"Not to my knowledge," he replies.

"Well, I need a medical history from you, in case something else comes up."

"Of course. I'll write up what I know and put it in the mail for you."

"Thank you," she says, ready to hang up the phone.

"Wait just a minute, Ada."

She cringes, knowing she isn't going to like what her child's father is about to say.

"How did this happen?"

"She was with me in the backyard while I was hanging out laundry."

"Weren't you watching her?"

"Of course I was watching her! Things like this happen. My other children got stung every now and then when they were little, but they never had a reaction like this."

"How could you let a two-year-old run around the yard without keeping your eye on her every minute?" Reverend Hahn's voice sounds contemptuous.

Ada's stomach churns with anger. "Harry, you have no right to criticize me. You don't know what it's like to raise a child."

"Ada," he says, drawing his voice out slowly like he does when making a righteous point. "I'm keeping my part of the agreement we made. If you think about it, I've done more than my part. I've gone above and beyond what you and Herman have asked of me. And I expect you to do your part."

Ada can barely contain her rage. "You have the easy part, Harry. You send a check a couple of times a year. I'm stuck with the daily job of taking care of your child. I never get a break."

Reverend Hahn gives an exasperated sigh. "We've been over all of this, Ada. You and I made a mistake. We've confessed our wrongdoing, and the Lord has heard our prayers. Our sin has been forgiven. Now we need to move forward in alignment with God's will, and do the best we can for the sake of our child. You and I both know we've made the best arrangements for Victoria's care."

In her mind's eye, Ada sees Reverend Hahn sitting in his desk chair, leaning back with one long leg crossed over the other, looking as dashing as ever in his expensive black suit, the man of God discussing the welfare of his illegitimate child.

She bites her tongue to keep from railing at him. "WE did wrong?" she wants say. "You laid a trap for me, and I was stupid enough to walk into it. How dare you make me an equal partner in your sin?"

She hangs up the phone without saying goodbye to Reverend Hahn. "No one is ever going to do something like this to me again," she hisses through clenched teeth. "No one!"}

CHAPTER 16

*"Take fast hold of instruction; let her not go: keep her,
for she is thy life." Proverbs 4:13*

One morning during the summer between my eighth
and ninth grade years, my mother sat down at the table with
me while I was eating breakfast. "Victoria," she said, "how
would you like to go to Conrad Grebel Christian High
School next year?"

I stared at her, dumbfounded by the question that had
seemingly come out of nowhere. A few of the youth from
our church attended Conrad Grebel Christian High, their
parents opting to send them to the private Mennonite
school rather than to Goshen High School. But I'd never
imagined going there. During our *Brigadoon* rehearsals,
Daniel Hooley had told me his parents were thinking about
sending him to Conrad Grebel High for his sophomore
year. I'd suppressed a surge of envy, knowing full well
that such an opportunity was out of the question for me.

Even though my brothers had been earnest young
Christians and excellent students, they hadn't been granted
the privilege of attending Conrad Grebel High. The issue
hadn't even been raised when Lucy was in high school. I'd
long ago accepted the fact that my parents couldn't afford
the tuition for private schooling. If they'd had the money,
my mother undoubtedly would have sent her misguided
oldest daughter to a school where she'd be surrounded by
godly influences.

So I'd envisioned nothing other than attending ninth
grade at Towncrest Junior High. I'd anticipated enjoying

the status of being one of the older kids in the school, looked up to by the seventh and eighth graders, more popular than ever.

I sat there at the table with my head spinning, as my mother pontificated on the merits of attending a Mennonite high school. "Academically, Conrad Grebel is a top-notch school," she informed me. "Ninety percent of the graduating seniors go on to college. That's way above the national average. Conrad Grebel High would challenge you more than the Goshen public schools. I think you need that, Victoria. And you could even sing in the choir. You'd love that."

I perked up my ears at her last few sentences. The Conrad Grebel Christian High School choir, the cream of the crop of young Mennonite singers, was well known throughout Goshen. The choir gave concerts at all the Mennonite churches in the area, and even traveled to venues in other communities. I'd heard them sing at Westside Mennonite a number of times. No doubt about it, they were impressive.

As my mother continued her efforts to sell me on the idea of attending our denominational high school, I realized she wasn't going to stop until I consented to what she wanted me to do. By the time I'd finished my cornflakes, my mind was already shifting gears, carrying me toward a new venture that was becoming increasingly attractive by the minute.

But I had to ask the obvious question. "How can you and Dad afford this? You didn't send Lucy or the boys to Conrad Grebel High."

My mother stood up abruptly, as if she was suddenly

finished with our conversation. "Things are different now, Victoria."

A month later, my mother and I made the fifteen-minute drive to Conrad Grebel High School on the east side of Goshen, for an appointment with Mrs. Hunsberger, my new guidance counselor. Mrs. Hunsberger had my transcript from Towncrest Junior High in hand, and immediately congratulated me on my academic record. "You'll fit right in here," she told me. "We have a number of strong students here at Conrad Grebel Christian High."

She cheerfully ran down the list of the school's extra-curricular activities, asking, "Are you interested in this? Are you interested in that?"

I responded to each of her queries with an enthusiastic, "Oh, yes!"

She smiled at me. "Well, we don't want to overload you the first year. I'd suggest you try out for one athletic team, and then limit yourself to just one other extra-curricular activity. See how that goes before adding anything else."

As there was no bus service to Conrad Grebel High, my mother and father formed a carpool with the parents of other students who lived on the west side of Goshen. When it was my parents' turn to drive, my mother transported Daniel Hooley, Beth Schrock, Rebecca Kauffman, and me to school in the morning before heading off to her job at Goshen College.

Then my father would pick up the four of us after he finished his mail route in the afternoon. He'd park his tired old mail-delivery Chevy at the far end of the parking lot, as if he wasn't good enough to mingle with the other parents waiting in their much nicer vehicles. I'd come out to the car to find him snoozing, his head resting on the back of the seat, his eyes closed, shutting out a world in which he didn't belong.

I was not a young person who clung to the security of the familiar. Rather, I was inexorably drawn toward the excitement of new experiences. Within several days of starting my freshman year at Conrad Grebel High, I'd put behind me any feelings of loss associated with leaving Towncrest Junior High, and was eager to explore what opportunities my new school held for me.

It took me only a few weeks to identify the strong students Mrs. Hunsberger had spoken of, and I figured out who was going to form my competition at the top of the class. Several new friends, Jill Schwartzentruber and Angela Hess, persuaded me to try out for the girls' volleyball team, where my height in the front row proved to be an advantage in spiking the ball. In spite of Mrs. Hunsberger's caution, I ended up joining both the theatre group and the speech and debate team my freshman year, adding choir membership my sophomore year.

Many of the students at Conrad Grebel Christian High were not residents of Goshen. Some of them drove in from nearby Dunlap, Elkhart, or Warsaw. Others came from distant parts of Indiana, even from other states, and lived with host families in Goshen. Meeting young people from outside the community made me feel like I was broadening my horizons.

But the most exciting thing was meeting the students from missionary families stationed in Africa, Bolivia, Nicaragua, and Puerto Rico. Their parents had arranged for them to pursue their high school education in the United States. These brave teenagers had come on their own to live with host families in a country that was strange to them. Getting to know these young people who'd grown up in foreign lands gave me a new perspective of the breadth of the Mennonite Church, carrying me far beyond the narrow confines of my home congregation.

Most of my fellow students came from families more affluent than mine, families with connections and influence in the Mennonite church. I liked to think that I was mingling with the Mennonite elite, and I pretended that I was one of them. This engendered in me a superficial sense of loyalty to the church. I took on a contrived piety, spouting words that I heard other students say, words that made the older generation believe that I was on the path to becoming an upstanding member of our spiritual community.

When my Old Testament teacher Mrs. Haarer told me what a pleasure it was to have me in her class, I said, "I believe God led me to Conrad Grebel High."

She beamed at me and said, "I'm so glad that He did." As I moved on to my math class, I felt guilty for half a minute, knowing full well that I'd manipulated her in order to gain her approval.

"Why don't we host a Conrad Grebel student at our house?" I asked my mother one morning as we headed out to pick up Daniel, Beth, and Rebecca. "Maybe we could take in a missionary kid. They could stay in Lucy's room."

"I've thought about doing something like that," my mother replied. "But your father doesn't like the idea."

As my father drove me home that afternoon, I broached the subject with him. "Vickie," he said, "our family's been through a lot of stress lately. Now is not the time to take on that kind of thing."

I turned away from him, pouting. I suspected he wanted to keep Lucy's room ready for the event of her return home. I wished he'd get over the fact of her unceremonious departure. I had.

After I began my freshman year at Conrad Grebel Christian High, my mother distanced herself from family life. She expanded her secretarial hours in Goshen College's Bible and Religion department from part-time to fulltime. I assumed she needed to do this to pay for my private school tuition, and I felt a little sorry for her. But as the months passed, I realized she didn't at all mind working forty hours a week, and that she was happier when she spent most of her time away from home.

Fulltime employees of the college were granted the privilege of taking one free course per semester. My mother immediately took advantage of this opportunity, and at the age of fifty-three, she embarked upon her college career.

Instead of coming home for dinner on Tuesdays and Thursdays, she stayed after work to attend her two-hour evening class. On Wednesdays, she went directly from work to her women's group at church. Sometimes, she'd leave the house on a Monday or Friday evening or on a Saturday afternoon. When I'd ask my father where she'd gone, he'd shrug and say, "I think she went to her study group, or something like that."

On her evenings at home, my mother busied herself with her class assignments. She bought a second-hand typewriter and set it up on a card table in her bedroom. One of the kitchen chairs was always missing from the table, as it had become a permanent fixture at her writing station. She'd hole herself up in the cave of her room, never speaking to my father and me unless it was to poke her head out the door and yell, "Would you turn that TV down? It's so loud that I can't hear myself think in here."

"What are you going to major in, Mom?" I asked her one morning as we headed out to pick up the other students in our carpool.

She sighed. "Victoria, I'll probably never get my degree. I'm past that point in my life. But at least I can learn about things I'm interested in."

"Like what?" I asked.

"Psychology, sociology, religion. Those kinds of things."

"That's cool," I said. I'd never considered the possibility that my mother had interests outside of homemaking tasks like cooking, sewing, and gardening. The idea was oddly reassuring.

{Ada Unruh sits on the back steps of the farmhouse, shelling a batch of peas for supper. Earlier in the day, she'd taken two loaves of freshly baked bread to Marilyn Hooley, and her neighbor had returned the favor by supplying Ada with a heaping basket of peas from her vegetable garden.

Three-year-old Victoria is keeping her mother company. She prances around the yard, prattling away in her sweet baby talk. The child can't seem to be quiet or still for a minute. Ada sometimes jokes with the other women in the church, saying that her precocious daughter came out of the womb talking.

Little Victoria reaches into the basket for a pea pod. Her tiny, determined fingers twist and rip at the pod until she gets it open. Then she fishes out a tender pea and pops it into her mouth. Her eyes widen with delight as she chews it. "It's good!" she exclaims.

Ada smiles. Truly, she and Harry have created a beautiful child, with her sparkling brown eyes, her sleek dark hair, and her silky olive skin. Victoria's delicate facial features are perfectly formed, a superb combination of Ada's and Harry's features. It appears the child is going to be tall and slender like her father. She possesses an irresistibly engaging personality, and is the brightest little child Ada has ever known.

"If she'd come into the world in any other way," Ada whispers to herself, "I'd be very proud of this little girl."

A wave of sadness washes over her, and she suddenly feels tired. Taking care of a three-year-old isn't what she'd envisioned for herself at age forty-two. When Lucy had entered elementary school, Ada had begun to consider the possibility of going back to school to earn a degree. She longed for a career that would make a difference in the world, something more rewarding than secretarial work.

But Victoria's arrival had dashed that dream to pieces. One error in judgment had sent her life down a completely different path.

Holding the bowl of shelled peas, Ada stands up and opens the battered screen door. "Time to go inside," she calls to her child.}

I could tell my father had no comprehension of what my mother was up to when she started attending her college classes. He had no idea what inner longings drove her in that direction. She was moving far away from the simple little world they had shared, and she apparently had no interest in taking him with her. In spite of their marital problems, my father had always found a measure of contentment in home life, loving my mother even if she didn't return his affections. But while my mother had dutifully carried out her domestic responsibilities, it had been, for her, a life of bleakness and drudgery.

At that time, I was of an age where I was allowed to sit with friends during church services. Sometimes, I'd look at my parents sitting far apart in their pew, never looking at each other, never touching. There was no child sitting between them to link them together. I'd feel sad, and a little guilty.

"What are you studying, Ada?" my father asked one evening when my mother emerged from her bedroom to get a glass of water. I knew he was searching for a way to connect with her.

"I'm taking a class in Women's Studies," she said stiffly as she marched past him toward the kitchen. Then she turned to face him. "You know, Herman, women have endured oppression at the hands of men for hundreds of years. Thousands of years. It's been horrendous, shameful. A blight on our society."

My father looked stricken, as if she was accusing him personally. "I've done the best I could for you, Ada," he mumbled. She waved a dismissive hand at him, got her drink of water, and disappeared into the bedroom again.

During my younger years, my mother had often brought her portable sewing machine out to the kitchen table whenever she was making a dress or piecing together quilt blocks. Now, when she wasn't studying, she set the sewing machine up on her bedroom card table, remaining out of sight and inaccessible to my father and me. If I needed something from her, I'd have to go through the formal process of knocking on her door and asking for permission to enter.

I began noticing a subtle change in the style of her clothing. Instead of sewing dark, drab garments, she now bought fabric for her dresses in brighter colors: yellow, purple, and royal blue.

One Saturday morning, I almost fell over from shock when she emerged from her bedroom, ready for the day's housework, wearing a long, colorful patchwork skirt. It reminded me of the quilt blocks she'd constructed over the years, and looked decidedly hippie-like.

"That's a cool skirt, Mom," I said. She glanced at me with a hint of a smile on her face, and then went on about her business.

I didn't mind my mother distancing herself from my father and me. It was a relief not to have her grim presence hanging over us like a dark cloud, and I was happy to see a spark of interest in her eyes.

Most evenings, my father and I were on our own for dinner. Having never cooked a day in his life, my dad was completely inept in the kitchen. But my mother didn't seem at all worried about this. She never bothered to tell us what to make when she was gone. I suspected she'd decided it was time for equal opportunity to reign in the kitchen.

Sometimes, I tried my hand at fixing dinner. I experiment with recipes I'd learned in my home economics class, something like Spanish rice or chicken chow mien, different than the routine meat and potato dishes my mother prepared. But I couldn't muster much enthusiasm for cooking, and all too often, my father and I settled for bologna sandwiches.

However, at least once a week, he'd say to me, "Why don't we go out tonight, Vickie?" We'd go to the A & W Root Beer Stand for hot dogs and root beer floats, to Burger Chef for cheeseburgers and fries, or to the South Side Soda Shop for a bowl of chili. If we were in the mood for tenderloin sandwiches, we'd drive all the way over to Penguin Point on the east side of town.

Occasionally, my father would splurge and take me to the Plain and Fancy restaurant in downtown Goshen, or to the newly opened Peddler's Village buffet. Wherever we'd go, he'd invariably run into someone he knew. He'd get caught up in shooting the breeze, sometimes for so long that I'd have to remind him I needed to get home to do my schoolwork.

Whenever he'd introduce me to someone I'd never met, he'd always say something to express his pride in me: "My daughter's quite the athlete. You should see her spike a volley ball." "Vickie's smart as a whip. She brings home all A's on her report card." "Vickie's on the debate team at school. You wouldn't want to go up against her. She can argue the fuzz off a peach."

Those first two years of high school were some of the best times I ever had with my father. We were at ease with each other, unencumbered by the prickly personalities of my mother and Lucy. While I thought I'd outgrown the childish pleasure of helping my father with the evening chores, I'd often push aside my homework to wander out to the barn, joining him in his never-changing routine of feeding the animals.

But in spite of his ready smile and cheerful demeanor, I could see the well of sorrow in my father's eyes. Although he never uttered a word about Lucy, I knew he worried about her. Sometimes in the evenings, when I'd have my schoolwork spread out on the kitchen table, he'd say, "I'm going out for a few minutes, Vickie. I'll be back in a bit."

I knew he was going out to see Lucy, to catch her at her shift at the Dairy Queen. As much as I loved all the soft-serve ice cream treats the Dairy Queen had to offer, I never once asked to go there for our evening meal. I didn't want to run the risk of seeing my sister. I had an abundance of good things going on in my life, and had no desire to take time out for sadness.

CHAPTER 17

"O come, let us sing unto the Lord: let us make a joyful noise to the rock of our salvation." Psalm 95:1

During my freshman year at Conrad Grebel Christian High, I had more than my share of boyfriends. My roving infatuation focused on any given target for about three weeks at a time. First, it was Greg Baumberger, then Robbie Zook, followed by Ben Birkey, Zach Gingerich, and Russell Kreider. I even went with each of the Liechty twins, going with Jeffrey in November and Jeremy the following January.

My mother made it clear to me that I was not allowed to go out on actual dates until my junior year of high school. Thus, my involvement with my so-called boyfriends was limited to walking down the halls of the school together, plus the occasional telephone conversation in the evening. While I was not at all averse to initiating the phone calls, my mother told me she wouldn't tolerate such audacious behavior on the part of her daughter. So I was forced to wait until the young men called me.

In spite of my fleeting interest in other boys, my feelings for them never came close to the deep affection I felt for Daniel Hooley. Daniel and I had been good friends ever since working together in the production of *Brigadoon.* Daniel never talked much, but he was easy to be around, and I felt safe and comfortable with him. Like my father, he always called me *Vickie.* Whenever another boy made me angry or hurt my feelings, I'd gravitate toward Daniel's soothing presence.

162

While I maintained my right to play the field, I hated the thought of Daniel doing the same. He was undeniably handsome and one of the most outstanding athletes at Conrad Grebel High. All the girls considered him to be "hot." I wanted to slap the face of every female who giggled and acted coy in his presence. And whenever I'd see him walking down the hall with another girl, I'd be overcome by powerful surges of jealousy.

Early in the first semester of my sophomore year, I saw Daniel talking with Deanna Yordy by her locker. She smiled up at him, batting her long lashes, and he responded with an awkward grin.

That was the last straw for me. Deanna was very pretty and very popular with the boys, but in my mind, she was a conceited bitch. She'd boss her boyfriend around until she grew tired of him, and a day or two after she'd broken up with him, his place would be filled by another glutton for punishment. Never did it occur to me that others might rightly categorize me as the same type of girl.

Fuming, I told myself there was no way I'd allow Deanna Yordy to hook her evil talons into my Daniel. It was time for me to stake my claim on Daniel Hooley once and forever. The next day, I approached him during our lunch hour.

"I need to talk to you," I said. He looked surprised, but followed me as I led him out the door and around to the side of the school where we could be alone.

"I like you, Daniel," I said. "I want us to be together."

He stared at me, startled and speechless. Then his face reddened, and he looked away. I thought he was about to refuse my overture, and my heart sank.

"I thought you had a boyfriend," he finally said. "It seems like you're always with somebody. Aren't you going with Brian Schertz?"

"Not anymore," I said, instantly breaking up with Brian in my own mind. "I was just messing around with him. I'm sick of him. I don't like anyone but you."

Daniel brought his gaze back to my face, and I saw confusion in his gorgeous blue eyes. "I've always liked you, Vickie," he mumbled. "But I didn't think you felt that way about me. I never thought I was good enough for you."

"That's bullshit!" I said, using a word I wasn't supposed to say in order to get my point across. "You're the best there is."

"Are you sure about this?" he asked.

I nodded.

"Really sure?"

"Totally sure."

"You're not going to dump me in a couple of weeks? Because I couldn't take that."

"No, I won't dump you, Daniel. Never. I promise."

He continued to stare at me, almost warily, as if he didn't fully trust my intentions. Then, in the sweetest of gestures, he reached over and took my hand. "Okay, Vickie," he said.

From that point on, Daniel and I were officially boyfriend and girlfriend. I made a point of talking about that in front of my classmates, until word of us going together spread around the school. We became one of the premier couples at Conrad Grebel High, the handsome, athletic Daniel Hooley and the pretty, talented Victoria

Unruh. No one could touch us. No one dared try to break us up.

When Daniel started his junior year, he stopped riding in our carpool. Wendell had supplied his trustworthy son with a used vehicle and allowed him to drive to school on his own. Daniel offered to pick me up and drive me to school as well, and I thought that was a splendid idea. So I proposed the new arrangement to my father, withholding the fact that Daniel and I were now more than friends.

"Just think," I told him. "You won't have to bother with the carpool anymore."

My mother overheard us talking and emerged from her bedroom study cave long enough to put her foot down. "Absolutely not, Victoria," she said. "I won't allow you to spend that much time alone with a boy."

"It's just Daniel," my father protested on my behalf.

"That's the whole point," my mother said. "It's Daniel. I know how she is around him."

Thereafter, she periodically reminded my lenient father that I wasn't allowed to spend any unsupervised time with a young man until I was at least sixteen. From time to time, she'd drop comments in my presence about the problems teenagers encounter when they allow their passions to run unchecked. "Exercising control over your lower nature is a sign of maturity," she'd tell me.

For nearly a year, Daniel and I had to satisfy our longing for each other through stolen moments at school. However, the fact that we both sang in the Conrad Grebel choir provided us more time together than we otherwise would have had. I was a member of the alto section, and Daniel was right behind me in the bass section.

The choir frequently traveled to venues outside the school for performances, visiting nearly every Mennonite church in Goshen, Elkhart, and the surrounding communities: College Mennonite, East Goshen, Benton, Yellow Creek, Pleasant View, Clinton Frame, Walnut Hill, Waterford, Belmont, Sunnyside, Hively Avenue, and more.

We were transported in a bus driven by crotchety old Henry Mast, who kept a wary eye on all of us kids in his rearview mirror. Our soft-spoken choir director, Dennis Rheinheimer, rode with us in the bus, helping Mr. Mast maintain control over the upstanding young people who couldn't always curb their impulses to behave like rambunctious teenagers.

Daniel and I would sit together in the back seat holding hands, occasionally allowing them to rest on each other's thighs. Sometimes, I'd snuggle close to him, resting my head against his shoulder while he wrapped a protective arm around me.

On our way to the concert, we students would generally behave ourselves, as we'd be anxious about the upcoming performance. But on our way home, when it was typically late in the evening, we'd be relaxed and giddy. Taking it for granted that Mr. Mast and Mr. Rheinheimer would be busy policing the unruly behavior of the other students, and feeling confident that we'd be undetected in the darkness, Daniel and I would indulge in some heavy make-out sessions.

I was generally the one who instigated the out-of-bounds activity, as Daniel was more cautious than I was about taking such risks. But I loved getting him all hot and bothered, and he'd reach a point where his hands began roaming to places where they shouldn't have gone.

One Sunday night on our way back from Prairie Street Mennonite Church in Elkhart, Mr. Mast suddenly bellowed, "Daniel! Victoria! If the two of you want to sit together, you need to keep your hands off each other."

A titter of laughter ran throughout the bus. Embarrassed, we untangled our intertwined bodies and sat up straight in the seat.

The next day, kindly Mr. Rheinheimer kept Daniel and me after school for a few minutes. Looking terribly disappointed in us, he proceeded to tell us that we were two of the best students in the choir, that the other students looked up to us, and that it was imperative that we conduct ourselves in a manner befitting of role models. Then, in his gentle voice, he informed us that any future episodes of such behavior on the bus would constitute grounds for expulsion from the choir.

I knew then that I had to take Mr. Rheinheimer seriously and curb my behavior. If any word about my unseemly conduct got back to my mother, she would erupt in a fury that would make Mount Vesuvius pale in comparison. Thereafter, Daniel and I didn't even touch shoulders as we sat together on the bus. If I sneaked a hand over to touch his thigh, he'd push it away, whispering, "Not now, Vickie. We'll get in trouble."

I had inherited my mother's pitch-perfect alto voice. But my voice was bolder than hers, unbridled, not meant to remain in the background. Thus, Mr. Rheinheimer often chose me for solos in the alto range. My favorite solo was *Jesus Walked this Lonesome Valley*. The lyrics were touching, and the sweet, haunting tune lent itself to an emotional performance, at which I was quite adept.

On a Sunday evening late in my sophomore year, our choir climbed into the bus and rode the twenty-five miles to the First Mennonite Church in Warsaw, where Reverend Harry Hahn was the pastor. Toward the end of our concert, I stepped forward to sing my solo, while the rest of the choir hummed softly behind me in four-part harmony.

> *Jesus walked this lonesome valley.*
> *He had to walk it by Himself;*
> *O, nobody else could walk it for Him,*
> *He had to walk it by Himself.*

As my eyes swept over the audience, I saw a number of women, touched by my performance, dabbing at their eyes with tissues. Then my gaze rested on mousy little Myrna Hahn sitting in the front row next to her peacock of a husband. Her blue eyes were large and round with sorrow. For reasons I didn't understand, the anguish on her pinched face amped up my emotion in the second stanza.

> *I must walk this lonesome valley.*
> *I have to walk it by myself;*

Tears spilled out of Myrna Hahn's eyes. She buried her face in her hands, her shoulders heaving with sobs. Reverend Hahn sat unmoving at her side, seemingly oblivious to his wife's pain, his attention riveted on me.

Self-centered teenager that I was, I was not inclined to agonize over the sorrows of other people. But I suddenly wondered why the drab little woman was so moved by my song, and her suffering struck me so deeply that my voice caught as I sang the last two lines of the stanza.

> *O, nobody else can walk it for me,*
> *I have to walk it by myself.*

A murmur spread throughout the audience, and I realized everyone thought I was singing from a well of emotion in my own soul. For a moment, I felt like a fraud. I was not walking through any lonesome valley. I was surrounded by friends. I had a wonderful, faithful boyfriend. And every moment of my young life had been sustained by my father's affection and unwavering support. I lacked for nothing. Yet, I continued my last stanza in a tearful voice.

> *I must go and stand my trial,*
> *I have to stand it by myself;*
> *O, nobody else can stand it for me,*
> *I have to stand it by myself.*

As I stepped back into my place in the alto section, the audience was dead silent. Mr. Rheinheimer stood with his head bowed, waiting a full minute before he moved us on to the next song.

After our performance, we choir members all trudged next door to the Hahn's parsonage to partake of the refreshments Myrna and several other church women had prepared for us. The parsonage was a well-kept ranch house whose exterior matched the tidy brick church. It was dark outside, but the welcoming porch light illuminated the perfectly manicured shrubs on either side of the front door.

As I stepped through the door into the Hahns' spacious living room, I gasped in amazement. The room was immaculate, beautifully decorated in warm earth-tones. The massive bookshelves and tables, all with the same smooth maple finish, held objects that piqued my interest: bowls, vases, masks, and figurines that appeared to be artwork from foreign countries. Lush houseplants in macramé holders hung in several of the windows. Decorative pillows with bold, bright prints provided the perfect color accent to the leather sofa and matching recliners. All the furnishings appeared new, and rather expensive.

I felt a rush of shame when I thought about my own shabby home with the scuffed flooring, the second-hand kitchen table, the sagging, twenty-year-old sofa, and my father's ragged armchair.

Myrna and the other ladies busied themselves in the kitchen while Reverend Hahn sat like a benevolent king on his throne of a recliner, holding court with his young subjects. I noticed a cane leaning against his chair, something I'd never before seen the debonair minister use.

Smiling broadly, Reverend Hahn engaged the choir members in jovial conversation, asking our names and where we were from. Pointing out the various art objects sitting around the room, he told us stories about acquiring them on his mission trips to other countries.

Presently, his wife stepped into the living room and informed us in a faint little voice that the refreshments were ready. With the aid of his cane, Reverend Hahn struggled to his feet.

"Let us bow our heads in prayer," he said. His sonorous voice thanked the Lord for the blessing of our performance, and for all of the wonderful young people who'd chosen the path of righteousness. Then he instructed the choir members to proceed into the kitchen.

Because I'd spent a few moments hunting for my misplaced purse, I ended up bringing up the rear of the line. As I stepped forward to accept my hot chocolate and cookies, Myrna laid a trembling hand on my arm. "Victoria, that was such a beautiful solo," she said, her eyes brimming with tears again. "You touched my heart. You're such a lovely girl."

"Thank you," I said, smiling at her with genuine affection.

Then I heard footsteps and the tap-tap of a cane on the tile kitchen floor. I turned to see Reverend Hahn walking up behind me.

"You are a beautiful young woman, Victoria," he said, echoing his wife's compliment. "And very talented."

As I gazed at Reverend Hahn at close range, I noticed the sagging skin of his face and the deep creases around his eyes and mouth. I realized that the minister who was once known for his dashing good looks was now an old man, wrinkled and jowly, his lanky frame hunched over a cane.

Suddenly, Reverend Hahn seemed to lose his composure. "You're so pretty," he blurted out. "I bet you have all the boys chasing after you. A girl like you should be really careful." Shifting his cane from his right hand to his left, he reached out and took my hand, a strange, hungry look in his eyes.

{On a Saturday morning in November 1959, the telephone rings in the California residence of Harry and Myrna Hahn. Expecting a call from a parishioner in need, Reverend Hahn strides into the living room and picks up the receiver.

"Harry," says the plaintive voice on the other end of the line, "this is Ada Unruh."

Harry contorts his handsome features into a grimace. He fears Mrs. Unruh has misunderstood the nature of their brief connection at the mission station in Mexico. He'd picked up on that when they were parting ways. Women had such an unfortunate tendency to cling. He's glad Myrna has gone out shopping. This call might be difficult to deal with.

"I'm sorry to bother you," Ada says, "but I have to tell you something."

He forces himself to speak kindly. "Yes, Ada."

She remains silent, as if suddenly at a loss for words.

"Go ahead, Ada," he says, careful to keep the irritation out of his voice.

"Harry, I'm going to have a baby."

At first, he doesn't catch the import of her announcement. So what if she and her husband are going to have another child? What business is that of his?

A moment later, the reason for her call hits him full force, and he sinks into a nearby armchair. "I see," he says.

"It's yours, Harry."

Stunned by the blow of her words, he grasps at ways to ward off the inevitable. "Are you sure?"

"Absolutely sure. You're the only one I've been with."

"How about your husband? Isn't it possible the child is his?"

"Harry, I haven't been with Herman for more than a year."

"I see," Harry says again. He feels the life force draining out of him, leaving him weak and shaky. "What are you going to do?"

"I don't know, Harry." Ada's voice sounds desperate. "I don't know what to do."

"Does your husband know about this?"

"Yes. I told him."

"How did he take it?"

"He was angry, of course. But don't worry. Herman's not the kind of man to make trouble for you."

Just then, Harry hears Myrna's car pull into their driveway. "Ada," he says hurriedly, "I'm sorry to cut you off, but I need to go now. This has been a lot to take in. Surely, you understand that I'll need time to think about this. But I'll call you back. Don't worry, I'm not going to dodge my responsibility. I'm giving you my word on that. Let me have your phone number."

He reaches for a notepad lying beside the phone and jots down the Indiana number as Ada tells it to him. "I'll call you soon," he says.

He hangs up the phone. Just as he is stuffing the slip of folded paper into his shirt pocket, his wife walks through the front door, her arms laden with shopping bags.

"I'm home," she announces offhandedly.

Harry forces himself to smile at her. "Looks like you bought out the store, honey," he says. "I hope you got something nice for yourself."

Myrna walks past him into the kitchen, deposits a bag of groceries on the counter, and then carries the remainder of her purchases into their bedroom in the back of the house.

Harry slumps forward in his chair, hanging his head, staring at his hands resting on his knees. He's never before seen his own hands tremble like this. His chest feels so tight that he can hardly breathe.

"Oh, God!" he gasps. "What have I done? What have I done?"

He's long ago admitted to himself that his greatest human weakness is his vulnerability to the temptations of the flesh. There have been times when he's fallen to his knees and begged the Lord for forgiveness. He's always been confident of that forgiveness. But nothing like this has ever happened to him. He's forty-eight years old, facing a dilemma usually encountered by a young man.

"This can't be true," he whispers. "This can't possibly be true."

But even while his body trembles with fear, his shrewd mind races ahead. He's had to work through other sticky problems, and he'll manage this one as well. Ada and her husband will raise the child, of course. What other alternative would there be? They'll keep quiet about their child's paternity. They'll want to avoid the shame of others knowing. And surely, they'll respect his position, his reputation.

He'll do his part. He knows the Unruhs aren't people of means, and he'll compensate them financially for raising his child. He'll have a talk with them to get everything straightened out. Myrna will never need to know. He'll spare her that pain.

Suddenly, through the murk of his shame comes a feeble ray of light, a wave of joy. He's going to have a child, the son or daughter that Myrna could never give him. He will have offspring after all, his own flesh and blood living on in the world after he's gone.

"My child may never know me," he whispers to himself. "But that doesn't matter, because somehow, some way, I will know him or her. I'll make sure of that."}

As Reverend Hahn held my hand, a shudder of revulsion swept through my body, and it was all I could do to keep from flinging his gnarled old hand away from me. *Oh my God!* I thought. *He's hitting on me! What an old creep! It's no wonder Mrs. Hahn is so sad. Her husband makes passes at young girls, right in front of her. How can she stand to be with him?*

I forced myself to smile at the minister while extricating my hand from his desperate clutch. Then I picked up my refreshments and carried them into the living room, where I went to stand beside Daniel. "Reverend Hahn's a pervert," I whispered into my boyfriend's ear. "He held my hand and told me I was beautiful."

Just then, Reverend Hahn emerged from the kitchen, slowly making his way back to his recliner, smiling, ready to engage his young subjects again. Daniel eyed the tottering preacher, then looked at me and grinned.

"If that old coot ever bothers you again," he whispered, "tell me, and I'll knock him over with my little finger."

CHAPTER 18

*"For he hath not despised nor abhorred the affliction
of the afflicted; neither hath he hid his face from [her]; but
when [she] cried unto him, he heard." Psalm 22:24*

It seems that life never goes smoothly for more than a
short stretch of time, and before I knew it, the years of
peace and stability in our household came to an abrupt halt.

It happened in July, during the summer vacation
between my sophomore and junior years of high school.
As I always did during the summer, I spent long hours
reading in my bedroom or watching TV. From time to
time, I'd grudgingly rouse myself to help my mother, who
was also on break from her job at the college, with some
household chore.

Now that I was sixteen, my mother allowed Daniel to
come to the house to spend time with me once or twice a
week. Although I complained about it, I didn't mind too
much that the two of us were forbidden to be alone in my
bedroom. As far as I was concerned, life was good.

If I'd been paying attention, I could have read the signs
that trouble was brewing. My father's mysterious evening
excursions became more and more frequent, until he was
leaving the house almost every night. His craggy face
looked heavier, the lines of sorrow etched more deeply.
My mother would glance at him and shake her head in
disgust, as if discounting whatever concern was weighing
down on him.

Then one night, I awoke around midnight to the sound
of voices in the kitchen. When I heard footsteps on the

stairs, I opened my door to see what was going on. I found myself face to face with the sister I hadn't laid eyes on in three years.

She stood there in ragged sweatpants and a filthy tee shirt, holding a garbage bag that presumably contained her meager belongings. Her long red hair was straggly and matted. Her face looked expressionless, her blue eyes vacant.

"Lucy!" I exclaimed.

She said nothing, but turned and walked into her former bedroom, slamming the door behind her.

I slipped downstairs to eavesdrop on the heated conversation my parents were holding. My mother was pacing around the kitchen wearing a white nightgown, her gray hair hanging like a shawl around her shoulders. I'd rarely seen my mother looking so odd and off-kilter, and I knew she'd been roused out of a sound sleep.

"How could you do this?" she snarled at my father, who looked as if he was ready to drop from exhaustion. "You know this is going to throw our household into an uproar again."

"I know that," my father said wearily. "I don't expect this to be easy, Ada. But our daughter needs our help. We're still Lucy's parents."

"She made her own choices," my mother retorted, "and she needs to live with the consequence of those choices. Bailing her out isn't going to help her. She'll just go right back to doing what she's always done."

My father looked at her pointedly. "Sometimes when people make mistakes, they need mercy, not punishment. You of all people should know that."

My mother turned away from him, her face ashen. "That's not fair, Herman."

Lucy quickly fell back into her old patterns of lounging around her room all day, coming downstairs only to use the bathroom. However, she no longer left the house at night, not even to go to work. She refused to shower, and every time she walked past me, I was greeted with a nauseating blast of the worst body odor I'd ever smelled. The first few days she was home, my mother barked at her to clean herself up. But Lucy glared at her in such a way that made my mother back off without a fight.

Lucy never joined the rest of the family for meals, but at night, she came downstairs to raid the pantry and refrigerator, no doubt carrying a stash of food up to her room. Items my mother had planned to use for meals came up missing: a block of cheese, a bag of walnuts, chocolate chips she was going to use for cookies.

Every morning, the kitchen would be a mess, and my mother would set about cleaning it up. Muttering to herself, she'd screw the lid back onto the jar of peanut butter, transfer the contents of a mangled box of raisins into a *Tupperware* container, throw half a piece of chocolate cake into the trash, pour down the drain the remainders of a gallon of milk Lucy had left out all night. Then she'd wipe down the table and countertops with sudsy water, trying in vain to eradicate the blight from our home.

I could tell my mother felt hopeless, utterly defeated. She no longer bothered to complain to my father about Lucy's behavior. Each day, she seemed to grow smaller, weaker, a shrinking shadow of her former self.

For the remainder of the summer, I stayed downstairs as much as possible. My bedroom had ceased to be my haven, as every time I went up there, I had to contend with the unpleasantness emanating from the room across the hall. Sometimes, I'd hear incoherent mumbling, punctuated by weird laughter. Other times, I'd hear heart-wrenching sobs. I'd feel conflicted, wanting to shut out the disturbing sounds, yet compelled to do something to help my sister.

One day when I heard a sudden piercing scream coming from Lucy's room, I opened her door to check on her. She was sitting up in bed, her eyes wide with terror.

"What wrong, Lucy?" I asked.

"I'm so scared, Tori Grace," she whimpered.

"You're safe here," I reassured her. "Nothing's going to hurt you."

She shuddered, contorting her face into a grimace. "The devil is in this house. I see him in every room."

I laughed. "That's not true, Lucy. You're being silly."

"It's not silly," she protested. "He's here for Mom."

"Why would the devil be here for Mom?"

"Because she's like him. She's evil."

"No, she's not, Lucy," I said. "Mom's a good Christian woman. She loves God and hates the devil."

"She's evil," Lucy persisted. "He's going to kill her. Then he'll kill the rest of us."

"That's not true. You need to stop thinking that way."

"It is true," she insisted. "I know he's here because I see him every day. I hear him laughing."

I suddenly realized she wasn't making up this nonsense, that her disturbing thoughts were real to her and were causing her genuine distress. Drawing on my religious indoctrination, I said, "God is more powerful than the devil, Lucy. When you get scared like this, you should pray to God for help."

Her face softened, and she looked at me imploringly. "Will you help me pray, Tori Grace?"

"Of course," I said. Braving my sister's overwhelming body odor, I sat down on the edge of the bed and took her grimy hand. "Dear God," I prayed, "Lucy is feeling scared. Please watch over her and don't let anything bad happen to her. Watch over our whole family and keep us all safe from harm."

When I opened my eyes, I saw Lucy smiling in gratitude. "Thank you, Tori Grace," she said, more rational than she'd sounded minutes earlier. "I feel better now."

Sensing that she might be in a cooperative mood, I decided to capitalize on the moment. "Lucy, why don't you get up and take a shower? Then put on some clean clothes. That will help you feel even better."

"Okay, Tori Grace," she murmured sweetly.

While she was in the shower, I stripped the filthy sheets off her bed. Then I carried them, along with an armload of her dirty clothing, down to the washing machine in the mudroom, hoping that my mother would be kind enough to launder them. Then I took some clean sheets from the linen closet and carried them upstairs. When Lucy walked back into her room, her hair wet from her shower, I was just tucking in the corners of the top sheet.

"Tori Grace!" she exclaimed. "You made my bed for me. Thank you."

As I left her room, I congratulated myself on

discovering a strategy for dealing with my sister. Surely, things would be better now.

Three days later, when I heard another anguished cry emanating from Lucy's room, I opened the door and stepped inside, ready to calm her with prayer again.

"Lucy? What's wrong, Lucy?" I called to the body huddled under the covers.

She sat up, brushing her tousled hair out of her face. "Lucy, Lucinda, Luella, Lavilla. I wish you'd stop calling me that."

"I didn't call you all those names," I said. "I only called you Lucy."

"You were thinking them. I heard you."

"No I wasn't. I've never thought of those names. You're just being silly."

She turned her eyes away from me, staring into the corner of her room. Then she emitted a loud cackle, pointing a finger into empty space. "It was you, you twisted little red devil!"

"What are you talking about, Lucy?" I asked.

She turned back to me. "This house is full of fakers."

"No, it's not. Mom and Dad and I aren't fakers."

"Fakers and farkers."

"What the heck is a farker?"

"I don't know. They haven't told me yet."

"Who hasn't told you?"

"The farkers." Her vacant eyes drifted up to the ceiling. "Fakers, farkers, folkers, fuh . . . . I could say more, but I won't." Then she looked down at her arm, furrowing her brow in concern. "Road kill."

By that time, irritation had replaced my compassion for my frightened sister. "Road kill! What on earth are you talking about?"

"I'm road kill." She held up her arm, pointing to a sticky smudge of dirt. "See? I have tire tracks all over me."

Then she lay back down and pulled the covers over her shoulders. "I'm tired, Tori Grace. Get out of here and let me sleep."

I'd had my fill of her nonsense. "You sleep too much, Lucy," I barked at her. "All you do is sleep. Why aren't you going to work at the Dairy Queen anymore?"

"They threw me out."

"Why?"

"Because I'm road kill. They threw me back out on the road."

"Cut the crap, Lucy," I snapped.

"Fuck you!" she screamed, grabbing her pillow and throwing it at me. "Get out of here, you bastard child! Get out of here and close that door! See what you've done? Every time you open that goddamn door, you let more of them in!"

Her blue eyes suddenly looked black, glinting with something that didn't seem human. She made a move to get out of bed. I knew if I stayed a moment longer, she'd come at me. Slamming the door behind me, I rushed down the stairs, nearly colliding with my mother as she was heading upstairs.

"What's going on?" she asked.

I spread out my arms to block her passage. "Don't go up there."

She attempted to push past me, but I stood my ground. "Don't! I'm not kidding you, Mom. You can't go up there. Not until Dad gets home."

"Why not?"

"It's not safe. Lucy's gone nuts. She's completely out of her head."

The next few hours seemed interminably long. Even though I knew my father wasn't due to come home until 3:30 or 4:00 p.m., I spent most of the afternoon waiting on the porch swing, desperately hoping that his old white Chevy would miraculously appear in the driveway.

From time to time, I got up and went inside to check on my mother and Lucy. I'd stand at the bottom of the stairs, trying to detect any sound coming from my sister's bedroom. All was quiet, and I assumed she'd fallen asleep.

My mother spent most of the day in the kitchen, working up a bushel of fresh peaches she'd purchased at Kercher's Orchard. Methodically, she peeled the peaches, sliced them, packed them in plastic bags, and added the sugar. Periodically, she carried a load of bags to our freezer in the mudroom.

I was glad she had something to do to distract herself during those fretful hours of waiting. I found this feeling to be odd, as I'd never before worried about how my parents occupied themselves. Every hour or so, I'd poke my head into the kitchen and say, "Are you okay, Mom?"

She'd shoot me a grim look, give a quick nod, and then nervously pick up her pace of peeling and slicing. Once, she said, "I don't know why you think you need to worry, Victoria. Your father and I will handle this."

In spite of her reassurance, I knew this problem was beyond what my parents could handle on their own. They'd had no experience with a crisis of this nature. I'd never felt like I needed to be in charge of my family's wellbeing, but that day, I knew my parents needed my help. As I faced the most difficult dilemma of my young life, I felt a heaviness that I'd never experienced before.

When my father finally pulled into the driveway, I jumped off the swing and walked to the edge of the porch to wait for him. As he trudged up the steps, his face reflected the concern that was undoubtedly present on mine. "What's going on, Vickie?" he asked.

"Lucy's gone crazy, Dad," I blurted out. "She's saying all kinds of weird things, and this morning, she almost attacked me. We've got to do something about her."

"Where is she now?" he asked, panic in his voice.

"Upstairs in her room. I think she's sleeping."

He slumped down on the porch swing, his head hanging in dejection. I sat down beside him.

"I was afraid of this," he said. "I'd been picking up on the signs myself. That's why I brought her back home. I knew she couldn't make it out there on her own anymore. It looked to me like she was losing her mind, but all along, I was hoping it wasn't true. A parent never wants to believe something like that is happening to their child."

"We have to do something," I repeated.

He raised his head to look at me, confusion and helplessness in his eyes. "Should we call Reverend Schrock and ask him to come over?"

"No," I said. "Reverend Schrock won't be able to help

Lucy. He'll just want to pray, and that won't be enough. We need to do something else."

"Like what?"

I bit my lip, thinking. Then my mind alighted on the memory of one of my Conrad Grebel classmates, Jimmy Jansen. The odd little fellow had always been an outsider, keeping to himself. Then one day, he abruptly stopped coming to school. A rumor circulated among the students that Jimmy had suffered a mental breakdown, and that his parents had taken him to Oaklawn Community Mental Health Center for treatment.

"Let's call Oaklawn," I said.

My father looked dumbfounded. "Oaklawn?"

"Yes. I'm pretty sure that's the place that handles things like this."

Just then, my mother stepped out on the porch. "She's right, Herman. We need to call Oaklawn."

I jumped up, ran into the house, and grabbed the phone book from a drawer in the kitchen. Scanning the yellow pages, I finally found the number we needed. "Here it is," I said to my father, who'd followed me into the kitchen. He stood there, looking dazed and disoriented, so I dialed the number and thrust the receiver into his hand.

"I-I think my daughter's having a problem," he stammered to the person who answered the call. After responding to a series of questions, he hung up the phone and turned to my mother and me. "We're supposed to take Lucy over to Elkhart."

"When?" my mother asked.

"Right now," he said. "I'm just hoping she'll cooperate with us."

My mother walked over to the foot of the stairs, as if ready to go up and rouse Lucy, but my father grabbed her arm. "I think you'd better keep out of this, Ada. You know how Lucy is with you. You'll get her too worked up. We don't want her to take off and run away."

"Fine," my mother said. At first, I thought she was angry, but then I saw the tears pooling in her eyes. She disappeared into her bedroom, closing the door behind her.

My father trudged up the stairs, and I followed. He hesitated a moment with his hand on Lucy's doorknob, then tentatively opened it and stepped inside her room. "Lucy, sweetheart," he called softly.

She rolled over in her bed. "Huh?" she mumbled sleepily.

"Lucy, it's your daddy." He sat down on the edge of her bed and patted her shoulder.

"What's going on?" she muttered.

I stood in the doorway, marveling at my father's skill in dealing with Lucy, observing a depth in their relationship that I hadn't known existed.

"I know you've been having a hard time of it, sweetie," he said tenderly. "I've been worried about you. Vickie and I have found a place to help you. We're ready to go there now."

"I don't want to go anywhere," she whined.

"I know, I know," he said. "You're scared. But you're not going there alone. Vickie and I are coming with you." He held out his hand. "Come on, let's get up now."

As Lucy grabbed onto his hand, I realized that she trusted my father just as much as I did. I knew that trust had been maintained, even strengthened, by the years of his faithfully going out to check on her when she was living away from our home.

Gently, he helped her to a sitting position. Eyeing her disheveled appearance, he said, "Why don't you let Vickie help you put on some clean clothes? I'll step out in the hall and wait for you."

Although I knew my father was on the other side of the door ready to help in an emergency, I realized that, for a few minutes, it was up to me to keep Lucy calm and cooperative. Rummaging through the piles of clothing on the floor, I found a relatively clean tee shirt and pair of jeans. "Here, Lucy," I said, imitating the soothing tone of my father's voice. "Let's put this on."

Obligingly, she held up her arms and allowed me to slip off her soiled shirt and replace it with the clean one. When she was dressed, I picked up a hairbrush from her dresser and ran it through her long locks.

"There," I said. "You look better now." Taking her by the hand, I led her out the bedroom door, and we followed my father down the stairs.

"Are you hungry, Lucy?" my dad asked as I helped my sister into the front passenger seat of the car. "I bet you haven't eaten all day. Let's stop at Burger Chef and get you and Vickie some hamburgers."

Again, I marveled at his brilliance in making this fateful trip seem like a normal family outing. By the time Lucy had finished her cheeseburger and fries, we'd arrived at our destination.

At the Oaklawn Center, a kindly Mr. Cramer ushered the three of us into his office. I held my breath as I watched Lucy survey her strange surroundings. I could see her agitation rising. She began pacing around the small room, muttering to herself. I caught smatterings of the weird talk I'd been privy to that morning, bits and pieces about fakers and the devil that lived in our house.

At times, Mr. Cramer's questions angered her, and she gave him menacing looks. I was afraid that, at any moment, she'd break out into a full-blown rage. While I knew my father was in emotional turmoil, outwardly he remained perfectly calm. Every few minutes, he got up and coaxed his disoriented daughter back to her seat.

When Mr. Cramer asked Lucy whether she'd been hearing voices, she shot him a scornful look and said, "Of course I hear voices. Don't you?"

"I mean hearing the voices of people who aren't really there," he said. But Lucy was back in her own little world, and refused to respond to him.

Mr. Cramer looked questioningly at my father. "Do you think she's hearing voices?"

My father shrugged. "Couldn't tell you. I don't know anything about that kind of problem." He glanced at me. "What do you think, Vickie?"

I took a deep breath, turning to face Mr. Cramer. "I think she is. Her bedroom is across the hall from mine, and I hear her in there talking and laughing, sometimes crying. A few days ago, I went in to check on her, and she was talking about the devil, saying he was going to kill our mother. This morning, she was talking so weird that I couldn't make sense of anything she was saying."

Mr. Cramer scribbled furiously on his notepad while I talked. Then he looked up and asked, "How long do you think this has been going on?"

"Couldn't rightly tell you," my father said, wringing his hands in his lap. "Lucy had been living on her own for a few years. From time to time, I'd go out to check on her, to see how she was doing. She'd been working at the Dairy Queen. But then she lost her job. I'm not sure why. She seemed to be slipping really bad, not doing much of anything, not taking care of herself. She was living with some people who weren't any good for her, and I could see they weren't going to do anything to help her. So I brought her back home."

"She's fortunate to have family support," Mr. Cramer observed. "That can make all the difference in a case like this."

"I've tried," my father said, his voice catching. "But to tell you the truth, I just don't know what else to do for my daughter. It's getting really difficult at home."

"You did what you needed to do by bringing her here," Mr. Cramer said. He scribbled a few more notes on his pad, and then looked up at my father again. "Lucy is experiencing a psychotic break. She's exhibiting symptoms of schizophrenia: delusions, hallucinations, and disorganized thought."

"What causes something like this?" my father asked.

"I really don't have a good answer for that," Mr. Cramer responded. "We don't know all the factors that contribute to the onset of mental illness."

My father looked at Lucy, who at that point was slumped in her chair, almost asleep. "The poor girl has had to face some things that are pretty tough to deal with."

"Like what?" Mr. Cramer asked.

My father just shook his head.

Mr. Cramer looked at him questioningly. Then he said, "Lucy is going to need a period of hospitalization so that we can get her stabilized on psychotropic medication."

My father looked bewildered. "What kind of medication?"

"Medication for her mental illness," Mr. Cramer explained. "It's something she'll need to stay on if she wants to have any kind of a normal life. We'll send her to the psychiatric ward at Elkhart General Hospital. Are you on board with this plan?"

My father nodded. "I'm willing to do whatever we need to do." Although my consent wasn't needed, I found myself nodding, too.

Mr. Cramer stood up. "I need a few minutes to arrange for a bed, and to get our psychiatrist to approve the admission."

After Mr. Cramer left the room, my father scooted his chair close to Lucy's and put his arm around her shoulders. Drawing her close, he murmured, "It's going to be okay, little girl. Your daddy's going to do everything he can for you."

CHAPTER 19

"The beginning of strife is as when one letteth out water: therefore leave off contention, before it be meddled with." Proverbs 17:14

"If it be possible, as much as lieth in you, live peaceably with all . . . ." Romans 12:18

After Lucy's hospitalization, a sigh of relief settled over our household. She remained on Elkhart General's psychiatric ward for more than two months, and was still there when I returned to Conrad Grebel Christian High for my junior year.

My mother resumed her secretarial work and her evening college classes, although I could tell there wasn't much wind left in her sails. She plodded along, a haggard automaton. She rarely spoke to me, not even to utter words of caution about immoral behavior with my boyfriend.

Always the rock of stability in our household, my father carried on his usual routine. While he undoubtedly lost many a night's sleep during our crisis with Lucy, he never missed a day of work. Three evenings a week, I helped him with the animal care chores after supper so that he could finish in time to visit Lucy at the hospital. And once a week, I went along with him.

"I know it does Lucy good to see you, Vickie," he said. "But you don't have to go with me every time. It's a lot on you, and you have school to deal with."

During some of our visits, Lucy appeared drowsy, barely capable of conversing with my father and me. Other times, she seemed cheerful and nearly normal, chatting away about what she got off the hospital's snack cart, showing us the craft projects she made in her occupational therapy class, and regaling us with stories about the outrageous behavior of the other patients.

My mother visited Lucy twice while she was in the hospital. The first time, Lucy became agitated when she saw her, and started ranting and swearing. My mother came home shaking like a leaf.

To her credit, she tried a second visit. After that, the hospital staff discouraged her from coming. "Lucy was upset for days after seeing her mother," one of the nurses informed my father. "Both times, she had a setback."

The day after Lucy's hospital admission, my father called Reverend Schrock. That evening, the pastor came to our home, and my parents and I sat with him around our kitchen table. We held hands while Reverend Schrock prayed for us: "Dear Lord, we know that you promise to be with us during our times of trial. We pray that Lucy feels the touch of your healing hand. And may your grace sustain this family through the difficult days that lie ahead."

Then, for the first time in my memory, my family was placed on the church's prayer chain. Thus, the news of Lucy's mental breakdown quickly spread throughout the congregation. While the support of other church members felt comforting, I was a bit uneasy about having our family problems exposed for the entire world to see.

Two days after Lucy's hospitalization, I called Daniel to tell him about it. "She has paranoid schizophrenia," I told him, demonstrating my newly acquired knowledge on the subject. "She has hallucinations and delusions.

Sometimes, she talks nonsense because her thoughts are disorganized." Then I described in detail some of the bizarre behavior I had witnessed.

Daniel was strangely quiet, and I suddenly wondered whether I'd told him too much. When he finally spoke, he asked, "Does this kind of thing run in the family?"

For the first time since I'd known Daniel, I felt furious with him. "I can't believe you just said that to me!" I shouted over the phone. "Don't worry. I don't plan on going crazy any time soon." With that, I hung up on him.

I went upstairs and lay on my bed, staring at the ceiling, trying to wrap my mind around the fact that Lucy's mental illness wasn't something she carried alone. It felt like her sickness had been inflicted on the entire family.

That evening, Daniel called me back, apologizing profusely for his insensitivity. "What I said came out sounding really stupid. I want you to know that I haven't stopped caring about you just because your sister has a problem. I care about you even more, because you're going through a rough time and you need me."

At the end of our conversation, Daniel told me for the first time that he loved me. I whispered the same words back to him. I went to bed feeling as if I was wrapped in a blanket of my boyfriend's affection.

Around the end of September, one of the hospital nurses informed my father that the doctor was ready to discharge Lucy.

The news seemed to both please and distress my father. "I'm glad my daughter's doing better," he said. "But we can't have her back at the house. Just as sure as

I'm standing here, the minute we get her home, she'll be fighting with her mother again. My wife's on her last nerve. She can't take any more. I can't be having everybody in the household breaking down."

Then he gestured toward me. "My other daughter can't be living in a mess like that, because she has to concentrate in school."

"We've discussed all that," the nurse responded. "We don't think sending Lucy back home is a viable discharge plan. She'd destabilize very quickly, and would end up coming right back here. Her doctor suggested that we look into a foster care placement. If Lucy does well enough in the foster home, she can eventually be set up in her own apartment."

Stabilized on antipsychotic medication and set up with disability benefits and a case manager, Lucy was released from the hospital one week later. My father and I helped her move her things into the foster home of Ruth Davis, who lived in a large Victorian house near downtown Goshen.

The hospital staff had told us that Mrs. Davis was one of the best adult foster care providers in the county, and that Lucy would be well-cared for in her home. I was relieved to hear this. After all the unlucky breaks Lucy had had in life, I was glad she'd at least landed in a top-of-the-line foster home.

"Lucy will probably never be able to hold down a job," the doctor informed my father on the day of Lucy's hospital discharged. "She'll be doing good just to take care of herself."

Three days after her release from the hospital, I was heading out the front door when I saw my sister riding up our driveway on an old, battered bicycle. Caught off guard, I exclaimed, "Lucy, what are you doing here? You're supposed to be in you foster home."

A second later, I kicked myself for speaking too harshly, but Lucy responded in a lighthearted manner. "Well, I don't have to be there every minute of the day. It's not like they chain me to my bed. I'm allowed to go out every now and then."

"Where did you get the bicycle?" I asked.

"One of the other residents loaned it to me. She said I could use it any time I wanted to."

My mother heard us talking and came to the door. When she saw Lucy, she looked dismayed, and I jumped in to ward off an unpleasant confrontation. "Lucy's just dropping by," I explained. "Her foster mother allows her to get out once in awhile. She can't stay long."

Lucy eyed my mother, a smirk on her face. "Don't worry. I'm not hanging around. Mrs. Davis is serving supper in half an hour. I think we're having spaghetti. I don't want to miss that!"

"Oh, dear God," my mother sighed as she watched Lucy ride away. "What are we in for now?"

Like a homing pigeon, Lucy rode her borrowed bicycle to our house two or three times a week for the next couple of months. Her visits kept all of us on edge, as we never knew what was going to happen.

Most of the time, she was in a good mood. She'd pace around the house, talking nonstop, laughing loudly. Her behavior got on my nerves, as I couldn't concentrate on anything while she was around, and it nearly drove my mother out of her mind. But she made every effort to respond to Lucy in a pleasant manner. She seemed to understand that her window of opportunity for shaping her daughter's life had passed, and she stopped confronting Lucy about her shortcomings.

As long as Lucy called her foster home to report on where she was, my mother allowed her to stay for supper. Afterwards, Lucy would volunteer to help with dishes, something she'd never done when she lived with us. I could tell she desperately wanted to be included in our family circle. During her best moments, it felt like we were more of a cohesive family than we'd ever been.

However, Lucy sometimes became edgy, especially if the visit had gone on too long. Perhaps her mood change was due to fatigue, or maybe it had to do with needing another dose of medication. At such times, the slightest trigger would make her turn on my mother.

One evening when my mother was drying the dishes Lucy was washing, she calmly pointed out a pan that Lucy hadn't gotten clean. Lucy blew up and began slamming dishes on the kitchen counter, saying she was sick and tired of my mother criticizing every move she made.

My father intervened, taking the dishtowel out of my bewildered mother's hand and leading her to the safety of her bedroom. Then he said, "It's getting late, Lucy. You need to get back to the foster home before it gets too dark. You don't want Mrs. Davis to be worrying about you."

Lucy slammed out the front door, and my father and I stood in the living room, looking at each other in dismay.

"Vickie," he said, rubbing a tired hand over his face, "I worry day and night about what goes on in this house. If things ever get out of hand when I'm not around, don't hesitate to call the police. I can't have anyone getting hurt."

At that moment, I recognized the depths of my father's concern. People in my church didn't ordinarily address interpersonal problems by involving the police. He had moved beyond worry into desperation.

After two similar episodes, my father stopped by the foster home and asked Mrs. Davis to keep Lucy from coming to our home for a while.

"I had no idea anything was wrong," Mrs. Davis said. She promptly reported my father's concern to Lucy's case manager, Mrs. Wade, who came to our house to discuss the matter.

While Mrs. Wade seemed like a reasonable person, I could tell she wasn't one to tolerate nonsense. I suspected she'd been toughened by years of dealing with unruly clients like my sister. "Lucy shouldn't be allowed to tyrannize your household," she told us after hearing my parents' account of Lucy's behavior in our home. "But she needs family relationships. Family support will make all the difference in terms of her getting better. I'm recommending that all of you go to family therapy to see if you can get this problem worked out. I'll let Lucy know she can't visit your home until her therapist tells me it's safe."

"I'm not doing this," my mother declared as soon as Mrs. Wade walked out the door. "I don't have time for this nonsense. I've got enough to deal with right now."

I knew what she was thinking. Her refusal to cooperate with Mrs. Wade's recommendation would keep Lucy away from our home indefinitely.

"Ada," my father chided. "How can you be so mean-spirited? We need to do this for our daughter's sake."

So my father, my mother, and I joined Lucy in family therapy sessions at Oaklawn, meeting with the same Mr. Cramer who'd arranged for Lucy's hospitalization. He helped us set up strategies to make Lucy's visits more successful. To start with, Lucy would stay at the house for no more than two hours at a time. If a visit of that length went okay, we could increase the time to three hours. No matter what time Lucy arrived, she had to get back to her foster home in time for dinner and her evening medication.

Most importantly, if there was any hint of friction between my mother and Lucy, they were to take space from each other in order to prevent escalation of the conflict. My mother would go to the safety of her bedroom, and Lucy would immediately leave our home. Mr. Cramer taught us all to use *I statements* when we needed to express upset feelings, so that no one would end up feeling attacked.

The cold winter months kept Lucy's bicycle trips to our home at a minimum. On Christmas Day, my father picked her up and brought her to our house so that she could be included in our holiday celebration.

On the occasional balmy day in March and April, I'd hear the crunch of bicycle tires on our gravel driveway. I'd sigh with exasperation, knowing that my sister had arrived.

My mother did her best to abide by our therapy agreements, using gentle *I statements* when Lucy started getting out of hand. While Lucy never left the house on her own, it took only two or three prompts to get her to go.

On a beautiful Saturday afternoon in early May, eight days before my seventeenth birthday and a month away from the end of my junior year, Lucy came for a visit. My mother was doing laundry, and had asked me to hang up a load of towels. I was lugging the basket out to the clothesline when Lucy rode up on her borrowed bicycle.

"Oh, crap!" I whispered to myself. I had an important paper to finish for my English class, an analysis of a modern American classic novel. My teacher, Mrs. Zuercher, had given us a list to choose from, and I'd selected *To Kill a Mockingbird* as the subject for my paper. The assignment was going to carry a great deal of weight in determining my final grade for the class.

I knew I wouldn't get anything done while Lucy was there. I wouldn't be able to concentrate, and I'd need to keep an eye out for any problems between her and my mother. My evening would be taken up by my date with Daniel. He and I were going to a Mennonite Youth Fellowship party at church that evening, an event I wasn't about to miss.

Sighing, I promised myself that I'd get in a few hours of studying after my father came home from work late that afternoon. Then, on Sunday after church, I'd barricade myself in my room, and I wouldn't come out until my *To Kill a Mockingbird* analysis was finished.

In spite of my irritation, I forced myself to greet my

sister cheerfully. "Hi, Lucy!"

"Hey, Tori Grace!" she called. Dropping the bike on the driveway with a clatter, she sauntered over to the clothesline. I could tell she was in an exuberant mood. Not wanting to annoy her, I allowed her to grab towels from my basket and pin them haphazardly to the clothesline. I cringed as I watched her, knowing the towels would dry crookedly. Then it would be difficult to fold them neatly, the way my mother liked them.

After we finished hanging the towels, Lucy strolled into the house through the back door, whistling loudly. As I followed her in, I saw my mother standing in the kitchen, dismay on her face. I knew she was thinking about her own class assignments that wouldn't get done that afternoon. But she forced herself to smile at Lucy and offered her a piece of pie left over from the previous night's supper. Then Lucy and I settled in to watch TV in the living room, while my mother disappeared into her bedroom.

Two hours later, my mother poked her head out the door. "Victoria, would you get those towels off the line? I want to get them put away before I start supper."

I jumped up and brought in the basket of towels, then dumped them on the kitchen table where we usually folded laundry. "What on earth did you do to these?" my mother asked me as she picked up the first towel. "They're all crooked."

I glanced at her and shook my head. I knew she caught the drift of what I was trying to communicate: that the crooked towels were Lucy's handiwork, and that it was best to drop the subject.

Lucy eyed my mother suspiciously as she walked into the kitchen. "What's wrong?"

"Nothing's wrong," I said hurriedly.

My mother picked up a towel, and smoothing it out the best she could, began folding it. From years of helping my mother do laundry, I knew the way she liked her towels folded: first, in half the long way, then in thirds. That way, they fit perfectly in a neat stack on the linen closet shelf.

Lucy picked up a towel and carelessly folded it in half the short way, then in half again. "Do it like this, Lucy," my mother said, demonstrating her technique with a second towel.

And that innocuous little request was all it took to set my sister off on a tirade. Grabbing the towel by one end, she slapped it violently against the table. "I can't do anything the way you want me to," she screamed. "I can't even fold a goddamn towel!"

I could see my mother tensing up, struggling to maintain her composure. Keeping her eyes on the towel she was folding, she said, "Just fold them anyway you want to, Lucy. I don't care."

Lucy jabbed the air with an angry forefinger. "You got that right!" she screamed. "You don't care! You've never cared about me!"

My mom glanced up at her, and the fear in her eyes seemed to fuel Lucy's outrage. "Why do you look at me like that? You think I'm some kind of a monster! You think I'm gonna tear your house down, don't you? Why don't you report me to my case manager like you did the other time? Go ahead! You might as well make it so I can't come over here anymore. You don't want me here, anyway. Don't think I don't know that."

On and on she ranted, accusing my mother of every unloving intention she could think of.

"Stop it, Lucy!" I shouted.

"Shut up, Tori Grace!" she snapped. Then she turned back to my mother, resuming her tirade. "I know I'm not good enough for you. I'm not perfect like your precious sons Michael and Robert. You know why those boys don't come to visit you? Because they know who you are!"

I glanced at the kitchen clock and saw that it was 3:45 PM. My father would be home any minute. *Oh, please, please, Dad,* I mentally begged him. *Come home right now!*

I could tell that Lucy's words were rapidly reducing my mother to a pile of emotional rubble. She made the mistake of collapsing onto a kitchen chair, and Lucy stood over her, continuing her menacing speech. Grabbing my mother by the arm, I pulled her to her feet. "Go to your room, Mom," I whispered.

Obligingly, she walked the short distance to her bedroom and closed the door behind her. I could hear the click of the deadbolt my father had installed to use in case of just such an emergency.

Enraged by the disappearance of her target, Lucy stood outside the closed door. "You coward!" she shouted. "You can't face up to anything, can you? You should have to go to therapy like I do! Then maybe you'd learn to tell the truth!"

"That's enough, Lucy!" I commanded. "You need to go. If you don't get out of here right now, I'm going to call the police!"

Lucy glanced sideways at me, and I saw the dark, inhuman glint in her eyes. "How about your little bastard child?" she yelled at the closed door. "She thinks she's so perfect. She's out here trying to order me around. Why don't you tell her who she really is?"

My mother burst out of the bedroom. "Shut up, Lucy!" she screamed. "Just shut up and get out of here!"

Apparently, getting my mother that riled up satisfied something in Lucy, as she suddenly became strangely calm. Grinning evilly, she said, "Maybe if I had a different father like Tori Grace does, you'd love me more."

I stared at my sister, unable to fathom what she'd just said. "What the heck are you talking about?"

"Tell her, Mom," Lucy demanded.

"Don't listen to her, Victoria!" my mother cried. "She's delusional! She's crazy! You can't believe anything a crazy person says."

"Tell her." Lucy's voice was low and sinister. "Tell her the truth, or I will."

"Tell me what?" I yelled.

"No!" my mother screamed.

Lucy turned to look at me. Her eyes softened as she searched my face, and thoughtfulness seemed to overtake her disordered mind. She opened her mouth to say something, and then shook her head. "Just forget it. Forget all that bullshit I just said. I'm leaving." She walked through the kitchen, heading toward the back door

Suddenly, something broke loose inside of me, and I rushed at my sister, pinning her shoulders against the kitchen wall. "Tell me what?" I snarled, glaring down at her.

Fear flickered in Lucy's eyes as she struggled to get free. "I'm sorry, Tori Grace," she whimpered. "I shouldn't have brought it up. Just let me go."

The adrenalin pumping through my body gave me the strength of three or four people, and even though my sister outweighed me by a hundred pounds, I kept her pinned and immobilized. "What is it you have to tell me?" I hissed, bringing my face close to hers.

Then I moved my hands from her shoulders and wrapped them around her neck, squeezing ever so slightly. "Say it now, you big fat bully, or I'll choke the goddamn life right out of you!"

"Dad's not your real father," she gasped.

"Who is it, then?" I tightened my grip on her throat. "Tell me who, or I swear I'm going to kill you!"

Suddenly, I felt strong hands gripping my wrists, pulling my hands away from my sister's throat. "It's Reverend Hahn," my father said. "Your real father is Reverend Harry Hahn."

CHAPTER 20

*"Hear, O Lord, when I cry with my voice: have mercy
also upon me, and answer me." Psalm 27:7*

I stared at the trio of family members standing in front
of me, my mouth hanging open in shock, my lungs
struggling to draw in air. Their three sets of eyes were
riveted on me, awaiting my response to the terrible news
that had just been dumped on me. My father's blue eyes
looked utterly weary, as if one more burden had been laid
on his overloaded shoulders. My mother's dark eyes
reflected an unspeakable anguish I'd never before seen in
them. And Lucy's eyes held an unusual clarity, as if the
events of the last few moments had jolted her into lucidity.

"Dad, you're lying!" I gasped when I finally managed
to get a word out of my mouth.

He shook his head. "No, Vickie, I'm not."

I turned to my mother. "Mom, is he telling the truth?"

She took a step toward me, reaching out a trembling
hand. "Victoria . . . "

"Don't touch me," I hissed at her. She stepped back,
tears pooling in her eyes.

Then I looked at my sister. "What the hell, Lucy?"

She made a motion of zipping her lips. "I'm not
saying anything else."

"Oh my God!" I screamed. "Oh my God!"

"Vickie," my father pleaded. "Try to calm down a
little bit, and then we'll talk all of this over. Your mom and
I will explain everything."

"No!" I shouted at him. "I don't want to calm down!"

Nausea churned in my stomach and rose up into my throat. I turned and bolted through the kitchen and the mudroom and out the back door, where the contents of my stomach spewed out on the ground by the back steps.

Unable to handle the frenzy of my emotion, I circled around and around the backyard, trying to discharge the frenetic energy. Everything I looked at seemed blurry and unreal. Lucy's psychotic words played over and over in my mind: "This house is full of fakers."

She hadn't been delusional; she'd spoken the truth. My parents were fakers, liars. Everything about my life was a lie.

I circled around my mother's vegetable garden. It was a lie. I passed the barn and the goat pen. The barn was a lie. The bleating goats were a lie. The birdhouse was a lie. The flower pots were a lie. The clothesline was a lie. Nothing in the backyard had anything to do with me. Even my name had nothing to do with me. I was no longer Victoria Unruh. I never had been.

I was vaguely aware of my father standing on the back steps. "Vickie, Vickie," he called, his voice sounding distant and surreal. "Come here, Vickie."

Suddenly, I spotted Lucy's borrowed bicycle lying on its side in the driveway. On impulse, I picked it up and jumped on it. As fast as I could, I rode down the driveway and turned onto the road, away from the sound of my father's voice, away from the house of lies.

As I pedaled furiously past the Hooleys' farm, I saw Daniel standing beside the barn. Waving, he called out to me, but I couldn't hear what he was saying. I didn't care.

"I'm going crazy, Daniel," I screamed into the wind.

"I'm going crazy like Lucy! Just like you thought I would!"

I heard a car behind me, and when I turned to glance over my shoulder, I saw my father approaching in his old white Chevy. He pulled alongside me, slowing down to keep pace with me. "Vickie, come back home," he pleaded through his open window. "Come back home, and we'll sort this all out."

For the first time in my life, I shouted curse words at my father. "Go to hell, Dad! Go to hell and leave me alone!"

He responded calmly to my fury. "You have every right to be upset, Vickie. Just come back home so we can talk about this."

"No!" I screamed.

For a moment, I thought he was going to get out and grab me and force me into the car, and I braced myself for a fight. But he said, "Just be careful, then. Come home when you're ready. Just don't be gone too long."

Indifferent to his words, I pedaled on. I heard him make a U-turn on the road and head back toward our house.

I rode up and down the county roads for more than an hour, with no destination in mind, scarcely aware of where I was going. The wind blowing against my face swept the unbearable thoughts out of my mind, keeping my new, horrifying reality from settling down and lodging in my awareness. I didn't dare stop.

All of a sudden, I realized that I'd come to Plymouth Avenue on the south side of Goshen. I paused for a moment to survey my surroundings. By then, it was early evening, and a voice of reason in my mind told me to turn around and go home before it got dark.

But my emotional turmoil overpowered any common sense. "To hell with it," I muttered. "To hell with everything."

Throwing all caution to the wind, I turned east onto Plymouth Avenue and headed toward Shanklin Park, located on the north side of the road. I paused in the entrance to the park for a minute, exhausted and winded. But standing still allowed the horrifying thoughts to overwhelm my mind, so I crossed the street to the head of the hiking trail that ran alongside the Millrace Canal and led to the dam at the Millrace Park.

As I pedaled along the familiar trail, an occasional hiker stepped aside to allow me to pass. I wondered if they could all spot me as the imposter that I was. *I don't belong here,* I thought. *This trail is part of Victoria Unruh's life. I'm not her.*

When I arrived at the dam, I encountered a small crowd of people milling around, some gazing at the water, some strolling along the trails in the woods. I felt unbearably vulnerable in the presence of others, certain they all could see my shame. For the first time in my life, I wished that I could be invisible.

I climbed around on the rugged rocks beside the dam, taking risks I shouldn't have taken. But I didn't care if I fell and broke a few bones. I didn't care if I plunged headlong into the churning water, dashing my head against a rock and breaking my neck. My life didn't matter anymore.

Finally, I found a sheltered niche in which to huddle. The roar of the water rushing over the dam soothed my agitated brain, giving me a safe place to pull out my thoughts and look at them.

How is it that I am not my father's daughter? I asked myself as I watched the water bubbling and spraying off the rocks at the foot of the dam. *Am I the child of Harry and Myrna Hahn? That old pervert of a preacher and his pitiful little wife? Did Herman and Ada Unruh adopt me? Why didn't Harry and Myrna want to raise me?*

No, I reasoned. *That can't be the way it was. Lucy referred to me as my mother's bastard child. So I am my mother's daughter. Somehow, she and Reverend Hahn got together and produced me.*

And how could that ridiculous idea be true? How did the two of them ever manage to have sex? Did they run off into the woods behind the church after the Sunday morning service? Hole up in one of the basement Sunday-School classrooms? Carry on an illicit love affair in a room at the Holiday Inn?

As those revolting images flitted through my mind, I realized that none of those scenarios were possible. According to what I'd heard, Reverend Hahn hadn't moved to Indiana until after I was born. He'd lived several thousand miles away in California. I was completely baffled. Nothing made sense.

Why had I never been told about my true identity? How was it that Lucy knew the truth about my paternity, but no one bothered to let me know? Did everyone in my church know? Did the Hooleys know? Was everyone talking about me, the poor little bastard child, behind my back?

The sky was rapidly darkening, and the other people in

the park were leaving. Suddenly, I remembered the youth party at church. *Had Daniel gone to my house to pick me up? What had my parents told him about why I wasn't there? That I'd run away because I'd just found out about my illegitimate birth?*

Then I thought about the English paper that was due on Monday morning. I'd never get it done now. But that didn't matter. I'd never go back to Conrad Grebel High School anyway. That was where Victoria Unruh had attended. I had no idea where the real me belonged.

My rocky perch beside the roaring water had grown chilly. Shivering, I stood up and climbed over the rocks. While I searched in the darkness for the bicycle I'd stolen from Lucy, the thought of my petty theft gave me pleasure. Victoria Unruh never would have stolen anything. Poor, stupid, unsuspecting Victoria Unruh.

I rode back along the hiking trail, a solitary figure in the darkness that was closing in around me. I began to whimper. The whimpering escalated into a rhythmic wailing that matched the cadence of my pedaling.

Suddenly, I was jolted out of my miserable trance when I lost control of my steering and fell off the bike. I lay there on the dirt trail, stunned and utterly humiliated. It felt as if God, offended by my sinful origins, had reached out an angry hand to topple me over, to let me know what he really thought of me.

When I picked myself up and tried to pedal again, I realized that the bike's front tire had gone flat. Swearing, I got off the bicycle and heaved it into the canal. Victoria Unruh would never engage in such vandalism. Who knew what the real me was capable of?

My loss of transportation played in perfectly with my pitiful plight. Now I could never go home. I'd wander around the streets of Goshen until I collapsed and died.

I stumbled along the trail without the slightest idea of where I wanted to go. I knew I was putting myself at a terrible risk, a young girl walking alone in the dark. But I didn't care. If some thug jumped out of the woods and clubbed me over the head, he'd be doing me a favor.

When I reached Plymouth Avenue, I walked across the street and into Shanklin Park. By that time, the adrenalin had left my system, and I felt weak, exhausted, and very cold. Imagining that I was near death, I lay down on a picnic table, hugging myself to keep warm. I longed for the comfort of my bed in the upstairs room of my family's ramshackle farmhouse. But that bed was no longer mine. The home was no longer mine. It had belonged to Victoria Unruh.

The clear night sky was filled with more stars than I'd ever seen in my entire life. *How do they have a right to be so beautiful?* I wondered. *How can they shine so brilliantly when such a horrible thing has happened to me?*

I am a child of sin. I shouldn't exist. My being born was against God's will. If my mother hadn't committed a vile sin, I wouldn't be alive. Lucy was right. The devil does live in our house. I am a child of that devil.

A moan escaped my lips. I moaned again and again, the sound bursting out of me. Each moan grew louder, until they became ear-piercing cries. I lay there on the picnic table, wailing until my voice lost its strength, until I could only whisper my pain.

I awoke to a flashlight shining in my face. When I opened my eyes, I saw two police officers standing there in the darkness. "Are you Victoria Unruh?" one of them asked.

"Where am I?" I asked, disoriented. "What's going on?"

"You're in Shanklin Park," the officer said. "Are you Victoria Unruh?"

Suddenly, the events of the recent hours flooded into my memory. "Yes," I said to the officer, even though I knew I was lying to him.

"Come on," he said. "We're taking you home. Your parents are worried about you." He held out his hand to help me off the picnic table.

Obligingly, I walked to the waiting vehicle and allowed the officer to help me into the back seat. Never before had I been inside a police car. The experience seemed to fit with my new identity. Perhaps the real me was a criminal.

As we drove home, dawn began to break through the darkness. I resented the fact that the sun had the nerve to rise in the face of the havoc that had just been wreaked on my life.

When the police car pulled into our driveway, I saw my father standing on the porch. "Oh, here's Vickie!" he exclaimed when the officer helped me out of the car.

"Do you want to file runaway charges?" the officer asked him.

"No," my father replied. "I'll handle it from here. Vickie's a good girl. She had every reason to be upset."

As I walked into the house, I saw Lucy sitting on the

living room sofa. "What the hell did you think you were doing, Tori Grace?" she scolded. "Running away like an idiot."

"You've done worse things," I snapped.

"You're not me," she said.

Feeling dead inside, I trudged up the stairs to my room. My father followed me. The pages of my *To Kill a Mockingbird* analysis were spread out on my bed. The assignment now meant nothing to me. I brushed the papers aside and sat down on the bed. My father sat down beside me, pulling me into the comfort of his arms.

"Vickie, Vickie, Vickie," he crooned. "You gave me such a scare." He stroked my tangled hair. "If I could, I'd take all of this hurt from you and bear it myself. I'm old and used to that sort of thing, but you're still so young and tender."

"Do you hate me, Daddy?" I whimpered as I pressed my face against his shoulder. "Do you hate me because I'm not yours?"

"Never," he said, his voice catching. "Never could I hate you, Vickie. I don't care who the man was that gave you life. You're my little girl, and I'm ready to take on anyone who says anything different than that."

CHAPTER 21

"In the day of my trouble I will call upon thee: for thou wilt answer me." Psalm 86:7

I must have slept for a few hours, because when I awoke, the midday sun was shining through my bedroom window. Momentarily, I felt confused. *What day was it? Sunday? Why was I still in bed? Had I missed church? Where were my parents? Why hadn't they gotten me up?*

Propping myself up on one elbow, I glanced around my room, taking in the pile of school books on my dresser, the basket of clean laundry I hadn't yet put away, the boom-box sitting on my nightstand along with several cassette tapes, the poster of the bearded, bushy-haired Cat Stevens that I'd taped on my wall just last week. Then I saw my blue jeans, dirty from my frantic bike ride, lying crumpled at the foot of my bed, and the memory of the previous day's events washed over me in a wave of desolation. Life as I'd known it was over.

I heard a tap on my bedroom door. "What?" I mumbled.

The door opened, and my father stepped into the room, carrying a sandwich on a plate and a glass of milk. "How are you doing, Vickie?" he asked as he approached my bed. "You're mother fixed some food for you."

I turned away from him, burrowing under the covers. "Tell her I don't want it."

"Vickie!" My father's voice was stern. "I need you to be sensible. You'll never start feeling better if you don't keep your strength up. Now sit up and try to eat."

Obligingly, I pulled myself to a sitting position.

"That's a good girl," he said, his voice softening. He placed the food on my bedside stand. "How are you doing, sweetheart?"

"What do you expect?" I muttered. "I feel like crap."

"You gave us quite a scare."

I shrugged indifferently, and then reached for the ham sandwich my mother had made for me. Although it was fresh and tasty, chewing and swallowing felt like overwhelming chores. After two bites, I set the sandwich down and lay back on my pillow.

My father sat down on the edge of the bed, looking as if he wasn't sure what else to say to me.

"So what's going on?" I asked him.

"Nothing, really," he said. "After you got home this morning, I took Lucy back to her foster home. By the way, she wants to know what you did with the bike."

"I threw it in the Millrace Canal."

He looked perplexed. "Why did you do that?"

"It had a flat tire."

"Okay." He seemed to be making a mental note to himself. "That wasn't Lucy's bicycle, so I'll have to replace it."

I wondered if he was expecting an apology from me. I had none to give him. The new me could muster no remorse for bad behavior.

"Your mother just got home from church," he continued. "I told her to go this morning. I thought it might help her feel better. I stayed home to make sure someone was here if you woke up." He paused, searching my face. "Your mom wants to come up and talk to you."

"No!" I protested. "I don't want to see her."

"I understand that," he said. "I figured you'd be pretty upset with her. I told her she might have to wait a little bit, until you're ready."

I sat up again, looking intently into his eyes. "Were you ever going to tell me, Dad? Or were you and Mom going to keep on lying to me for the rest of my life?"

He looked startled by the bluntness of my words. Then his face reddened, and he dropped his head. "Vickie, I know we've screwed this whole thing up, and I'm really sorry about that. But it's awful hard for a parent to know what to do in a situation like this. I guess your mom and me thought it was best to keep things quiet, just raise you like we did the other kids. We wanted to protect you from all the ugliness, and give you a fair chance in life."

He exhaled deeply, running his hand over the top of his bald head. "But I suppose the truth is always bound to come out. Maybe Lucy did us a favor by spilling the beans. Telling the truth takes down all the walls we have to build to keep things hidden."

When my only response was an unrelenting stare, he said, "If you have any questions, Vickie, I'll answer them as honestly as I can. You deserve honest answers."

"I want to know how it happened," I said. "How in the world did Reverend Hahn get Mom pregnant?"

Pain flickered in my father's eyes, and he averted his gaze. "It happened when they were in Mexico."

"Mexico? Why were they in Mexico?"

"Well, back in 1959, the year before you were born, Reverend Hahn came to preach at our church. He was getting everybody all fired up about his missionary project in Mexico, and was asking for people's help."

Bitterness crept into his voice. "Your mother wanted to go. She didn't tell me that, but I knew how she felt. She'd always wanted to go to some foreign country to do missionary work, but she'd never had the chance. So I said, 'Ada, why don't you take this opportunity and go down there and help Reverend Hahn?'

"Maybe I shouldn't have done that. Maybe this whole thing was my fault. God knows I wouldn't have encouraged her to go if I'd known what kind of a man Reverend Hahn was."

Then he lifted a palm and shook his head, as if canceling out what he'd just told me. "I hate saying it like that, Vickie. Because if your mother hadn't done what she did, we never would've had you. Having you wasn't a mistake. So maybe what your mom did wasn't a mistake. I can't seem to sort out what's right and wrong anymore. It gets an old man confused sometimes."

He stood up, and with considerable effort, bent his rotund body over and began picking up the pages of my English paper that were scattered across my bedroom floor. Laying the stack of papers on the bed next to me, he said. "You'll be needing these."

"No," I said, pushing them away. "I'm not going back to school."

He obligingly moved the stack of paper to the top of my dresser. "Vickie, I know this has got you turned upside down. It's going to take some time for you to get things figured out and start feeling normal again. I want you to know I'm going to be here. I'm going to see you through this, every step of the way.

"I've been thinking about this all morning. I know you won't be up for going to school tomorrow, not after a shock like this. So before I go to work, I'll call Conrad Grebel High School. I'll tell them you're not feeling well, and that you won't be there for a few days. That'll give you some time to get your mind settled."

"The office won't be open when you leave for work," I pointed out.

"I know," he said. "I'll leave a message on their answering machine. Then I'll stop by the school after work to make sure everything's in order."

"You're not going to tell them what happened, are you?" I asked, panicked.

"Of course not," he said. "This is your business, not mine, and I've got no right to tell anybody. If there's ever a time in your life when you want to tell somebody, then that's up to you."

Then he looked at me with pleading eyes. "Vickie, you've got to promise me something."

"What?"

"Promise me that you're not going let this ruin your life. Promise me that you'll do everything you can to sort this out and get back on track. I've already had one daughter fall apart. You're stronger than Lucy is. You're so smart and so capable. If there's one thing I could never live with, it's you ruining your life over this. That would kill me, Vickie."

His jarring words resonated with a sensible portion of my brain. "Okay, Dad. I promise."

"Here's the thing," he said. "Tomorrow, your mom and I will both be going back to work. You'll be here alone. That worries me. I need you to promise that you won't do anything stupid. I don't want you running off somewhere or doing something to hurt yourself. Every day when I come home, I want to find you right here, safe and sound. Promise me that?"

"Yes, Dad, I promise."

"You'll be thinking a lot, and you'll have questions. So when I get home from work, we'll just sit and have a talk. I'll do my best to answer any question you come up with. We'll get you through this, Vickie. I know you're hurting now, but I have all the confidence in the world in you. You're going to make it.

"Now, why don't you get up and do something normal this afternoon? Take a shower. Then come down and watch a little TV. You can't start doing like Lucy did, wasting your life lying around in your room."

"I'll shower," I said. "But I'm not going to hang out downstairs. I don't want to be around Mom."

"I understand that," he said. "But at some point, you're going to have to face her. You're going to have to get everything you feel about her off your chest. People in this family can't keep holding things back from each other."

As my father headed out the door, I asked, "Did Daniel come by last night?"

He stopped and turned to face me. "Yes, he did."

"What did you tell him?"

"I told him the truth, that Lucy said something that got you really upset. He knows how she is. He called just a little while ago. He was worried because you weren't in church this morning. I told him you'd come home, but that you weren't feeling well. He wants you to call him back."

I shook my head. How to deal with my boyfriend on this messy issue was something I couldn't begin to figure out.

My father seemed to catch my unspoken thought. "Call him when you're ready, Vickie," he said. "There's no rush."

After a long, hot shower, I spent a few minutes trying to tidy up my room. No matter how terrible I felt, I was determined not to sink into a world of squalor and indolence like Lucy had. I managed to toss the shirt and jeans from the previous day's bike ride into my clothes hamper. But the activity exhausted me, and I gave up and collapsed into bed.

I tried to slip back into the escape of sleep, but couldn't. So I rounded up a stack of my favorite cassette tapes: John Lennon, Cat Stevens, and Crosby, Stills, and Nash. I shoved one tape after another into my boom-box, allowing the soulful music to rescue me from drowning in my pain.

Several hours later, my father trudged up the stairs to my room again, this time carrying a grease-stained bag from Burger Chef. "I brought you a burger and some fries, Vickie. And a chocolate shake. I figured you'd be hungry by now."

"I'm starving," I said, reaching for the bag.

He held it behind his back, humor twinkling in his eyes. "You've gotta come downstairs to eat. It's a beautiful day. Let's go out on the porch."

"Dad!" I protested.

"You heard me, Vickie," he said. "Let's go."

"I have questions," I said as I munched French fries on the porch swing. "I want to know more about how Mom and Reverend Hahn got together. What did they do, have an affair down there in Mexico?"

My father's face darkened. "Something like that. I never pressed her for the details. I never wanted to know. All I know is that when she came home, she was pregnant with you."

I shook my head, shuddering. "How could you stay with her after she cheated on you? Why didn't you divorce her?"

Abruptly, he got off the swing and walked to the edge of the porch, looking out over the front yard. "This is just between me and you," he said, speaking with his back to me. "I can't have you repeating what I'm telling you."

Then he stopped, standing silent and motionless for so long that I finally prompted him. "What, Dad?"

When he resumed speaking, I could tell he was struggling not to break down. "I've never been what your mother wanted, Vickie. I'm just a fat old bumble-head. She needed someone smarter than me, more educated. She needed a husband with more class."

Although I hated hearing my father talk about himself in such a derogatory manner, I knew he was representing my mother's feelings with one-hundred percent accuracy.

"Why did the two of you get married?" I asked.

He shrugged. "I guess for a little while, she thought I was someone that I wasn't. I was trying to go to seminary, and that impressed her. When she realized I wasn't cut out for that kind of thing, it was too late. So we just had to make the best of things.

"She wasn't happy, Vickie, and sooner or later, she was bound to stray a little bit. I can't blame her too much. She had to get a taste of what she thought she wanted."

"I can't believe it," I said bitterly. "She preaches to me about morality all the time. She's always on me about how I act around guys, and I haven't even done anything wrong. And she's been on Lucy's case every day of her life. She's such a hypocrite. How could she be so hard on her daughters when she's done something so terrible? I feel like going out there and having sex with every boy I see. She wouldn't have the right to do anything to me."

"Vickie!" My father swung around to face me. "Don't be talking like that about yourself!" He walked back to join me on the swing. "Don't you see? Your mother is hard on you because she doesn't want you to make the same mistake she made. She doesn't want you to get hurt like she did."

"Get hurt?"

"Yes," he said, a haunted look in his eyes. "Your mother suffered over her mistake. I've never seen anybody suffer like she did. I don't think she's ever gotten over it."

{Herman Unruh stands beside the bed, hesitating to climb in next to his wife. She's turned away from him, lying on her side to accommodate her swollen belly. She's just three weeks away from delivering her child, and Herman knows she's uncomfortable in any position.

He gets into bed and lies with his back pressed up

against hers. Then he reaches his hand back and momentarily rests it on her hip. Ada doesn't move, doesn't even flinch, doesn't acknowledge his touch in any way.

For the first month after she came home from Mexico, his wife had been in emotional turmoil, her pain raw and palpable. Then the molten anguish had hardened into granite, hopelessness and joylessness solidified in the core of her being.

Herman rolls over and props himself up on his elbow. Laying a hand on his wife's arm, he says, as he's said a dozen times before, "I want you to know that I forgive you, Ada."

He wishes she would roll over, throw herself into his arms, and sob out her pain. He longs to be her hero, the man who stands beside her in the aftermath of another man's betrayal.

Gently, he shakes her arm. "I wish you'd accept that, Ada."

"How can I accept your forgiveness," she says, her voice cold and flat, "when I can't forgive myself?"}

CHAPTER 22

"Let all bitterness, and wrath, and anger, and
clamour, and evil speaking, be put away from you . . . ."
Ephesians 4:31

When I awoke on Monday morning, the house was silent, and I knew my parents were already gone. I lay in bed for a while, listening to the sounds outside: the quacking and clucking of the ducks and chickens, the bleating of the goats, the occasional vehicle driving past on our county road. In the distance, I could hear the cows mooing on the Hooley farm.

Then the rumble of Wendell's bus reminded me that I was missing school. It had been my mother's turn to drive the carpool. An hour ago, she would have driven around to pick up the other Conrad Grebel students who lived on the west side of Goshen.

"Where's Victoria?" they would have asked.

"She's not feeling well," my mother would have responded, the grim set of her mouth discouraging them from asking any more questions.

In my mind's eye, I pictured carloads of kids from all over town heading toward Conrad Grebel High. None of the students would have greater concerns on their minds than what grades they were getting on their English papers and science tests. Never again would I be that naïve. The innocent era of my life had ended when Lucy divulged our family's dark secret during her psychotic rant.

Mindful of my father's insistence that I not lie in bed all day, I decided to go downstairs and fix myself a bowl of cereal. When I got up, I saw that a scrap of paper had been shoved under my bedroom door. I picked it up. It was a note, scrawled in my father's barely legible handwriting.

Good morning, Vickie. I'm leaving for work now. I'll be thinking about you all day. Try to have a good day, and remember the promise you made to me. When I get home, we'll talk. Don't forget that I love you.

After my shower, I stood in front of my dresser mirror examining my reflection. I stared at myself straight on, and then picked up my hand mirror, using it as an aid to look at myself from different angles. I'd long been aware of the fact that I bore no resemblance to my stocky, red-headed father. I'd always assumed that I'd taken after the slender, dark-haired people on my mother's side of the family. Now, as I studied my features in the mirror, I realized that I HAD inherited some of my father's traits. Not my father Herman Unruh. My father Harry Hahn.

All my life, I'd been told I was pretty. Now, I could see Reverend Hahn's contribution to my good looks, his genetic endowment mixed in with my mother's. I'd inherited the shape of his nose and his jaw-line. I had his dark, intense eyes.

And, of course, there was my height. Now I understood why I towered over my petite mother and stood half an inch taller than my dad.

I recalled images of Reverend Hahn standing regally behind the pulpit, perfectly at ease in front of a crowd, feeding off the admiration of those who watched his performance. *Did my love of the spotlight come from him?*

I continued to gaze at my reflection, fascinated by the genetic endowment I'd never been aware of before. *What else might I have inherited from my biological father?*

All of a sudden, I felt repulsed. I turned away from the mirror and threw myself face down on my bed, thinking about the illicit act that had forever intertwined the DNA of my mother and Reverend Hahn in the person of me.

I'd never given any thought to my parents' sex life. I'd always assumed they were too old for such an activity. The way Herman and Ada Unruh lived together suggested no intimacy in their private life. There were no kisses, no tender touches, nothing that would indicate they were physically drawn to each other.

But now, my mind was full of lurid pictures that I couldn't eradicate: images of my mother and Reverend Hahn locked in a passionate embrace somewhere in sunny Mexico, oblivious to the feelings of my father and Myrna Hahn, unconcerned about the fact that they were committing adultery. Imagining my stern mother surrendering to the pleasures of the flesh made me want to vomit.

At that moment, I hated the idea of sex. I was glad that Daniel and I had never given in to the temptation of going all the way. I was determined to remain chaste for the rest of my life.

Mindful of my father's admonition, I told myself I could either lie there in my misery, or I could get up and do something. So I wandered downstairs and out the back door to the barn.

The goats bleated excitedly when they saw me coming, trying to convince me that my father hadn't already fed them that morning. Frederick, Bertha, Agnes, and Annabelle were long gone, and the goat pen now held their children and grandchildren. I patted the head of Annabelle's daughter Miranda, telling her what a good girl she was. But as I turned to walk away, she grabbed the back of my shirt with her naughty teeth, holding me captive. For a moment, the familiarity of the goat's mischief made me feel as if things were the same as they'd always been.

When my father came home that afternoon, he found me stretched out on the sofa watching a soap opera on television. I'd decided to distract myself with a story more sordid than the one about my mother, her illicit lover, and their illegitimate child.

My father didn't scold me for violating my mother's TV watching rules. "Good, Vickie," he said. "You're up."

Then he turned off the television and settled into his armchair. "How are you doing?"

"Not too good," I said.

"What've you been thinking about?"

"Dad," I blurted out. "I'm a child of sin. If Mom hadn't done something terrible, then I wouldn't be alive. God never wanted me to be born."

Giving voice to the thought that had been tormenting me all day took me down as low as I could go. I lay there on the sofa, my head buried in my arms, feeling like the most unworthy person on the face of the earth.

"I guess I understand how you feel, Vickie," my father said, drawing out his words. "Like I told you yesterday, things get confusing for me. Yes, your mother did wrong.

No one can argue that point. But I can't believe for a minute that you weren't meant to be. If you'd never been born, I would've missed out on a whole lot of joy."

I turned my head so I could peer at him with one eye, and I saw the tender look on his face.

"When you were just a tiny tot," he said, "you'd climb up on my lap and chatter away in your sweet baby talk. And I'd tell myself that I was so blessed. Even if you came into the world in a way that I didn't like, I wouldn't have given you up for anything."

I thought about the closeness my dad and I had shared over the years, the bond that had infused me with feelings of security. I'd always known he cherished me, and had taken that for granted. Looking at our relationship in the light of the information I'd received two days ago, I wondered how he'd come to love me so deeply.

"Vickie, I've always known you were a special child," my father continued. "I've thought that maybe God intended you to be special all along. Maybe you needed to have Reverend Hahn as your father in order to be who God wanted you to be.

"Face it, sweetheart, if I'd been your real dad, you wouldn't have turned out like you did. You wouldn't be so smart and capable and pretty. Maybe God wanted you to have two fathers: one to give you a good inheritance, and the other one to raise you with a whole lot of love."

His words landed dead center in my heart, nearly taking my breath away. Still, I wasn't ready to let go of my self-loathing. "I'm not special," I protested. "I hate myself. I'm the child of two cheaters. That makes me a horrible person."

Then my father uttered the words that would sustain me during the difficult months to come, words that carried me through times of confusion and self-doubt. "Listen to me, Vickie. This is something I want you to keep in mind. You are not your mother. You are not Reverend Hahn. What they did doesn't reflect on you. Not the least bit. What you do with your life has nothing to do with either one of them."

"Do you really mean that, Dad?" I asked.

"Yes, Vickie, I mean that."

I sat up on the sofa, brushing my hair out of my face. "Dad, you act like you weren't even upset about Mom cheating on you."

"Of course I was upset," he said. "I had a real hard time with it at first. It shook me to the core. Made me feel worthless. But then I had to set aside my self-pity and start worrying about the baby that was about to be born. I was afraid I wouldn't be able to love you, Vickie. Every child needs to be loved, no matter how they come into the world, and I was afraid you wouldn't get what you needed.

"The day your mother went to the hospital to have you, I went into the little chapel there in Goshen General Hospital. I fell down on my knees and cried, and I asked the Lord to give me the strength to love you as much as I loved my own children. As I knelt there praying, I decided I was going to make a point of loving you a little bit extra."

Then his voice choked, and a tear slid down one craggy cheek. "And you know what I found out? It wasn't hard to love you at all. As a matter of fact, I couldn't help but love you. The first time I held you, it didn't matter to me who had planted the seed that gave you life. I got to be the one to watch over you and tend to you while you grew. And I counted myself lucky, Vickie. I counted myself downright lucky."

I buried my face in my hands, sobbing quietly. My father reached over and laid a gentle hand on my shoulder before he got up and ambled out to the kitchen.

When my father came home from work the following afternoon, he said, "Your mother has class tonight. Let's go out to eat."

"I don't want to," I said.

"Why not?"

"I don't want to see anybody, and I don't want anybody to see me."

"I know what you're scared of, Vickie," he said. "You're thinking the whole world knows about this, and that they're all talking about it. I felt that way right after I found out your mom was expecting you. I felt too ashamed to walk out my front door. But I knew I had to make myself do it, and you know what? My life just kept on going like it always had.

"And yours will, too, Vickie. No matter what's happened these past few days, you still have a life here in Goshen, Indiana. It's a good life, and I'm not going to let you cut yourself off from it and hide. You have nothing to be ashamed of."

The look on his face told me he wasn't going to relent. I gave an exasperated sigh. "Okay."

"Let's drive over to Penguin Point," he said. "You won't even have to go inside. I'll bring the food out, and we can eat in the car."

Twenty minutes later, while we were sitting in Penguin Point's parking lot munching tenderloin sandwiches, I blurted out a question I hadn't thought to ask before. "Dad, does Reverend Hahn know about me?"

"Yes, he knows about you, Vickie," my father said. "I'm sorry. I don't know why I didn't think to tell you that."

"How did he find out?"

"Your mother told him after she found out she was expecting you."

"Did she tell him in Mexico?"

"No. She didn't know for sure that she was pregnant until after she came home. Reverend Hahn had gone back to California, and she called to tell him."

"Why did she think he had to know?"

My father wadded up his sandwich wrapper and shoved it in the empty food bag. "Well, Vickie, I had to ask the same question. I told her I'd just as soon handle this on our own and not let Reverend Hahn in on it. But I suppose the man had a right to know he was going to have a child. And I think your mom was hoping for the best."

"What do you mean, hoping for the best?"

My father suddenly looked uncomfortable. "I shouldn't be saying these things, Vickie."

"Dad!" I protested. "I have a right to know!"

For a long moment, he stared out over the parking lot. Finally, he said, "I might be stepping out of line in telling you this. But I think your mother was hoping Reverend Hahn would do the right thing by her, that he'd leave his wife and be with her so the two of them could raise their child together. She never told me that, but I sensed it.

"But that's not what happened. Reverend Hahn came out here to Indiana and met with your mother and me. We all sat down and talked about what we needed to do."

I contorted my face in disgust. "How could you stand to talk to him, Dad? Didn't you feel like beating him up?"

My father laughed. "Well, I wasn't happy to see him, that's for sure. I had to bite my tongue a lot. Right off the bat, he apologized to me. I can't say he was humble about it. He kept his head held high. He said that in unusual circumstances, like him and your mom being together in Mexico, it's easy to be overcome by the temptations of the flesh. When he said that, I felt bad, like it was my fault, like I shouldn't have let my wife go off and be alone with a bunch of strange men. Anyway, we shook hands like we understood each other, and then we got down to business."

"Got down to business?" I said sarcastically. "That's what it was for him, business? Didn't he act like he cared that he was going to have a child?"

My father reached over and took my sandwich wrapper and my empty cup and stuffed them into the bag. Then he got out of the car and tossed the bag into the restaurant's trash can. When he got back into the car, he put the key in the ignition, and I thought he was going to drive me home without answering the question I'd just asked him.

But then he turned to me and said, "Yes, Vickie, Reverend Hahn cared that he was going to have a child, and he cared about you. I never had a bit of respect for him, acting like such a mighty man of God, standing up there behind the pulpit preaching about sinners, all the while taking advantage of some other man's wife. Reverend Hahn might be a scoundrel, but he did care about you. I could tell it was hard on him not to be able to step up and be a real father to you."

{Herman Unruh stands outside the nursery on the second floor of Goshen General Hospital. Ada and the baby girl will be coming home today. Herman knows what he's committed to, and he's unwavering in his resolve. Still, he feels at loose ends. This isn't the same as when Ada came home with Michael, Robert, and Lucy.

He looks up when he hears a familiar voice addressing a nurse in the hallway, a voice he's grown to despise. "I'm Reverend Harry Hahn. I've come to see the Unruh baby."

"Certainly, Reverend Hahn," the nurse says cheerfully. Clearly, she thinks he's making a pastoral call. Herman marvels at how the man can use a few smooth words to manage an awkward situation, to protect his impeccable image.

"Here's the father now," Reverend Hahn says as he strides toward Herman, the nurse at his side. She smiles coyly at the minister before heading into the nursery.

Herman has known Reverend Hahn would be coming. He understands the need for that. He'd called him when Ada went into labor three days ago. But his nerves are shot from the strain of the past few days, and he doesn't feel prepared to deal with this unwelcome presence. He wonders what story the California minister fabricated for his unsuspecting wife when he suddenly needed to fly to Indiana for the birth of his illegitimate child.

"God, give me strength," Herman whispers.

Reverend Hahn steps up to Herman's side. Herman can see their reflection in the nursery window, his own heavy-set, flannel-shirted form next to the suave, lanky minister in his expensive black suit.   Suddenly, he understands why Ada did what she did, and he despises himself. He despises his wife and the man she fornicated with.   He despises all three of them for the mess they've gotten themselves into.

"God, help me," he pleads silently.

Reverend Hahn clears his throat.   "How is she?"

"You mean Ada?" Herman asks.

"The baby," Reverend Hahn clarifies.

"Of course," Herman tells himself.   Reverend Hahn might have lusted after Ada at one point in time, but he doesn't give two hoots about her now.

"The baby's fine," he says.   "Strong and healthy." He hesitates, then adds with a twist of ill-humor, "Ada's fine, too.   Came through it like a trooper."

"That's good," Reverend Hahn says.

The nurse pokes her head out the nursery door.   "The baby is in with Mrs. Unruh right now.   You can go see her there."

Herman leads the way to Ada's room.   His wife looks startled when Reverend Hahn follows him through the door.   She knew he was coming, but Herman can tell she isn't ready to handle the awkward situation.

She's holding the baby, who has fallen asleep after nursing.   She fumbles awkwardly with her gown, making sure her breasts are discretely covered.

Reverend Hahn approaches the bed.   "May I hold her?"

Without a word, Ada lifts the baby into his outstretched arms.   The baby wakens for a moment, squirms, and then falls asleep again.

Reverend Hahn gazes raptly at his infant daughter, oblivious to the presence of the others in the room. He holds her tenderly as he slowly paces back and forth in the room's small floor space.

"My child," he whispers. "My sweet, sweet child." He bends down to kiss the baby's forehead. "Have a wonderful life." Sighing, he reluctantly hands the sleeping bundle to Herman. "Take good care of her for me."

Herman sees tears in the minister's eyes. "I will," he says. He looks down at the baby in his arms. Her dark eyes flicker open, and she gazes at him as if she recognizes him. Then she sleeps again.

As he watches Reverend Hahn stride out the door of the hospital room, he whispers, "I'm the lucky one."

"Goodbye, Reverend Hahn," he hears the nurse gush in the hallway.

He can't make out Reverend Hahn's muffled response, but it is followed by lighthearted laughter.

Herman glances at Ada. Her eyes are closed, her face contorted in pain. He feels a rush of pity for his wife.}

"Yes, Vickie," my father said as he turned the key in the ignition. "Reverend Hahn did care about you, and he never backed out of the agreement he made with your mother and me."

"What agreement?" I asked.

My father eased the car out onto U.S. 33, heading for home. "Reverend Hahn said it would be best for everyone if your mother and I raised you. He said he'd provide financial support. He told me he'd never expect me to foot the bill of raising a child that wasn't mine. So he sent us checks a couple of times a year. I have to give him credit for that. He was faithful in sending money. He always sent us more than what we expected from him."

The mystery money! The thought stunned me. *So that's where it came from. Reverend Hahn's child support.*

"Given the circumstances," my father continued, "he's done everything he could for you. The money's still coming in. We got a check just a month ago. And if he thought you needed something special, he'd send a separate check for that."

"Like for what?" I asked.

"Like school clothes. He wanted you to be well dressed. If he ever thought your mother was neglecting you in any way, he'd be on the phone telling her about it."

My father chuckled, shaking his head. "Yup, the man was quick to speak up if he thought something wasn't up to snuff. It got to be pretty hard on your mother. She felt like she couldn't do anything right in his eyes. Reverend Hahn is a powerful man, and to tell you the truth, your mom has always been a little bit scared of him.

"Many a time, she wished he'd disappear and leave her alone. Many a time, I would've gladly done without the money and raised you on my own income. But I have to say, what Reverend Hahn has provided has really helped."

My father looked sideways at me. "Reverend Hahn is paying for your tuition to Conrad Grebel High, you know. He thinks it's important for you to attend a Christian high school. Your mother and I never could've swung that on our own."

I sat there staring at him, my mind blown into a million pieces. Never had I imagined that another party had been involved in my parents' decision to send me to Conrad Grebel High School.

As if that wasn't enough to take in, my father hit me with another overwhelming piece of information. "Do you know you're the reason Reverend Hahn moved from California to Indiana? He wanted to be close enough to watch you grow up."

I blew my breath forcefully through my lips. "You've got to be kidding me!" For the first time, I recognized the enormous impact my birth had made on my biological father's life. He'd left his home and his work in California, just to be near me.

"No, I'm not kidding, Vickie," my dad responded. "That's why he preached at our church so many times, so he could have a chance to see you. I never went to church the Sundays he was going to preach. I didn't care to see his face. But your mom always went, because she had to take you. And remember when you did that play at Towncrest and you saw Reverend Hahn in the audience? He went to more of your school activities than you'll ever know."

I felt weird and confused as I tried to sort out a tangle of emotions: unrelenting hatred for the man with whom my mother had committed adultery, yet a tinge of affection for the second father who'd cared so much about me.

As my dad pulled the car into our driveway, I asked, "Does Myrna Hahn know about all this?"

He turned off the ignition. "Not to my knowledge. Reverend Hahn has a way of doing everything so secretly. He's told your mom exactly when and where she can call him. He's told her never to call him at home. I'm sure that when he moved his wife to Indiana, he made up another reason for why he was doing it."

"Does anyone else know? Do the people at church know? Couldn't they figure out that Mom got pregnant while she was in Mexico?"

"If anyone's figured it out," my father said, "I haven't heard a word about it. You were born almost three weeks late. I think your mom was determined to hang on as long as she could so that it would look like she'd gotten pregnant after she came home. It's amazing how a person's mind can have power over their body."

"How did Lucy know?"

My father sighed heavily, his shoulders sagging. "When Lucy was a little girl, she overheard a conversation between your mom and me. I was hoping she hadn't caught on to what we were talking about. Evidently, she put the pieces together when she got older. I guess I always knew she was a ticking time bomb on this subject, but I was hoping that wasn't the case. I was hoping she could keep quiet and spare you all this pain."

He stared out the car window, his voice thick with emotion. "As far as I can tell, keeping this secret is what drove your sister out of her mind. It wasn't fair to her. Not fair at all. I should've talked to her, let her get it off her chest. I should've helped her sort it out. I feel like I've never done right by Lucy."

"I hate Reverend Hahn," I blurted out. "He's such a jerk. He ruined everybody's life."

My father sighed again. "You don't need to hate him, Vickie. I'm not telling you all these things just to make you hate him. Hatred never does anybody any good. It just hurts the one that's doing the hating.

"There was a time when I hated Reverend Hahn so bad that I wanted to expose him for what he'd done. I wanted to blab it all over the place. Everybody thinks so highly of him, and I wanted to bring him down. Then I had to think about all the people who'd be hurt if I did that: your mother, the rest of the family, Myrna Hahn. And all the people in the church would've been shook up, and some of them might've lost their faith over this. So I kept my mouth shut."

He opened the car door and put one leg out. Then he turned back to look at me. "Hatred is like poison, Vickie, and if you let it, it can take over your life. I don't want that to happen to you."

CHAPTER 23

"For all have sinned, and come short of the glory of God." Romans 3:23

The first three days after the blowup in our household, I avoided my mother as much as possible. Whenever I came downstairs to use the bathroom or to get something to eat, I'd brush past her without speaking. But every time I saw her, she was crying.

Tears streamed down her face as she mopped the kitchen floor or peeled potatoes at the sink. She sobbed openly as she swept the carpet in the living room, the sounds of her distress drowned out by the roar of the vacuum cleaner. Her face was perpetually red, her eyes swollen.

The tears seemed to wash the starchy sternness right out of her, leaving her wilted and feeble. I'd seen her in a weakened state before, but never reduced to such a pitiful condition. Seeing her like that was almost more than I could stand.

I knew she wanted to talk to me, to reestablish some sort of connection. Late Tuesday evening, when I came downstairs to brush my teeth, she suddenly appeared in the bathroom doorway. "Victoria," she said in a timid voice, "do you have any dirty clothes you want me to wash?"

"I'll do my own laundry," I growled through a mouthful of toothpaste.

But I knew that whether or not I was ready, I needed to listen to what my mother had to say to me. I had to make a gesture of receptivity in order to relieve the unbearable tension in our household. It was time to restore some normality.

So on Wednesday evening, after my parents were finished with supper, I came downstairs and sat at the table while my weeping mother washed up the dishes.

"I know you want to talk to me, Mom," I said gruffly. "Go ahead. I'll listen to you."

She swung around, surprised. Although she wasn't finished with her task, she dried her hands on the dishtowel and came to sit with me at the table.

We stared at each other for a minute, and then she lowered her eyes and said, "I know your dad has talked with you about all this. He's better at that kind of thing than I am."

I was shocked to hear her admit that my father possessed a particular strength. All of my growing-up years, I'd known that she regarded him as little more than a bumbling fool.

"Yes," I said, "we've talked."

She seemed to be at a loss for what to say next, so I took charge of the conversation. "Why didn't you tell me I wasn't Dad's daughter? Why did you lie to me all these years?"

I already knew how she'd answer, but I needed her to be accountable to the same question I'd asked my father.

Fresh tears sprang to her swollen eyes. "I wanted to protect you, Victoria. I never wanted this to be a burden on you."

Then she buried her face in her hands, and her words gushed out along with her tears. "I'm so sorry, Victoria. I can't tell you how sorry I am. Every day, I asked the Lord to forgive me for the terrible thing I did. I've tried so hard to live a good life, to make it up to Him. I've tried to follow His will."

"Mom!" I said, wanting to stop the tide of her self-condemnation. "I know you love God. I know you try to live right."

But she continued, anguish and desperation rising in her voice. "It just kills me, Victoria, to see you hurting because of this. You shouldn't have to suffer because of the sin I committed. You don't deserve that."

"It's okay, Mom. I forgive you." I uttered those words knowing I wasn't anywhere near the point of true forgiveness. But I had to do something to rescue her from her misery.

"You don't hate me?" she whimpered.

"Of course not," I said, lying a little bit. Part of me despised her, but mostly, I pitied her. For the first time in my life, I saw my mother for who she really was. Under all that rigidity and righteous anger was a lonely and disheartened woman.

My reassuring words stopped the flow of her tears, and she looked at me imploringly. Suddenly, I felt like the strong one, as if it was up to me to give her the courage she needed to keep on living.

"Can I ask you some questions?" I said.

She winced, but nodded. "Go ahead. You deserve answers."

"Why did you do it? Why did you have an affair with Reverend Hahn?"

"We were in Mexico . . . ."

"I know that. Dad told me."

"We were working together, and we got close. I . . . I guess I lost my good judgment. It seemed right at the time, but later, I realized how wrong it had been."

"Who started it? Whose idea was it to have sex?"

I could tell my bluntness made my prudish mother extremely uncomfortable. I'd never even heard her utter the word *sex*, let alone admit to indulging in it. Averting her gaze, she said, "I'd have to say it was his idea. Honestly, Victoria, I never would've thought to start something like that. I . . . I thought highly of Reverend Hahn . . . and I guess I wanted him to feel the same way about me. We had such nice talks, and I enjoyed that so much. He was such an interesting man. I'd never met anyone like him before. But I never would've taken it as far as . . . as having sex."

Her frail body started shaking violently, sobs ripping up from her abdomen. Without thinking, I reached out and covered one of her hands with mine, my anger melting in the face of her suffering.

"I guess I went along with it because he was a minister," she blurted out. "I trusted him to know right from wrong."

I knew my mother was telling me the truth. I knew she'd never play the role of the temptress. She'd been seduced and misled by a man she trusted, a man she held in high esteem. I suddenly understood why she seemed to fear and despise all things male, and why she'd tried to instill the same feelings in me.

"Did you love him?" I asked.

She stared down at the table. "At the time, I thought I did," she whispered. "I thought he cared about me, too."

"How long were the two of you together?"

"Not long. Just a month or so. It all ended when we left Mexico."

"Do you still talk to him?"

"Every now and then. I have to, Victoria. But it's all business. If you're wondering whether there's anything between us now, absolutely not." She raised her head, her swollen eyes glinting with anger. "If it was up to me, I wouldn't have anything to do with that man. I would've washed my hands of him a long time ago."

{It's a Sunday morning in July 1968, and the congregation at Westside Mennonite is finishing up the potluck meal that followed Reverend Hahn's sermon. Little Beth Schrock has just informed Ada that Victoria was chasing a boy around the church and fell down and hurt herself in the gravel parking lot.

Fuming, Ada goes outside to corral her eight-year-old, who seems unperturbed by her mishap. "You need to come in and sit with me," she commands. Grabbing Victoria by the arm, she marches her toward the church.

At that moment, Reverend Hahn steps out of the building and meets the two of them in the parking lot. "Hello, Mrs. Unruh," he says. "Hello, Victoria."

Ada manages a grim smile. Victoria shoots the visiting minister a disinterested glance and tries to squirm away from her mother. Ada keeps a firm grip on her daughter's arm.

Reverend Hahn's eyes flicker down to inspect the condition of his child. Then he looks up at Ada again. She winces when she sees the disapproval on his face.

She desperately wishes she hadn't put Victoria in Lucy's hand-me-down dress that day. When Victoria fell on the gravel, she'd stepped on the hem of the skirt, ripping it away from the bodice of the dress. The child looks ragged and pathetic. She has a smudge on her cheek and a bloody scrape on one elbow. Her hair looks a mess, as if Ada hadn't carefully combed and braided it that morning.

Reverend Hahn turns abruptly and heads back toward the church, indignation in his stride. Ada dreads the call that she knows is coming.

Sure enough, the phone rings the next morning. "Ada," Reverend Hahn says, "if you and Herman are short on money, you should let me know. Victoria looked a little shabby yesterday. I'm going to send you an extra fifty dollars. Please buy the poor child some decent clothing."}

"Have you talked with Reverend Hahn recently?" I asked.

My mother looked at me warily. "What do you mean?"

"Have you told him? Does he know that I know?"

She nodded, looking guilty. "Yes, I told him, Victoria. I called him yesterday."

{Ada pulls her car into the Kroger parking lot. She's exhausted, completely spent from the turmoil in the household the past two days. The task of grocery shopping seems overwhelming to her. But she must continue to feed her family. She cannot add irresponsibility to the list of sins she's committed.

And the outing gives her the opportunity to do

something else she needs to do. Instead of heading straight for the store entrance, she slips around the side of the building to an empty phone booth. She can't make this call from the house. She doesn't want Herman or Victoria to overhear her conversation.

She knows she isn't supposed to call the Hahns' home. She's already decided that if Myrna answers the phone, she'll hang up and call another time. But the voice on the other end of the line is Reverend Hahn's.

"This is Ada Unruh," she says.

"How can I help you, Ada?" His official pastor's voice doesn't mask his irritation with her.

Her own anger flares. "Why do you always treat me like I'm one of your pesky parishioners?" she thinks. "I'm the mother of your only child. You can acknowledge that I once meant something to you, even if I was nothing more than a passing fancy."

"Harry," she says, "Victoria found out."

The silence on the other end of the line seems to go on forever. She tells herself it was foolish to make this call. She'd hoped that for at least one minute of his precious time, Reverend Harry Hahn would share the burden she's been carrying alone for the past seventeen years.

"How is she responding to the news?" he finally asks.

Ada knows where his question is coming from. He's thinking along the lines of self-protection. He's thinking about how to prevent his misstep from being exposed to the world.

She forces herself to speak evenly. "Not well. She was really upset at first. But she's calming down now. I think she's coming to terms with it."

"Good," he says.

"Okay," she says. "I just thought you should know."

She can hear Myrna Hahn's plaintive voice in the background, calling for her husband. She knows she needs to hang up the phone, but suddenly, she blurts out, "Harry, do you want to see her?"

"Ada, I've seen Victoria dozens of times."

"I mean, do you want to talk to her? Explain things to her?"

He remains silent for another long moment. "Someday, I'll want to speak with her. But now is not the right time."

Ada knows what he means. She's heard the news that Myrna Hahn has been diagnosed with terminal breast cancer. She knows Harry doesn't want to open this can of worms while his wife is still living.

Rage rumbles inside her. She has no choice but to deal with the fallout from her affair with Harry Hahn on a daily basis. But Harry has always insisted on handling things on his own terms, in his own timing.

"Does she want to see me?" he asks.

Ada knows if she says anything else, her feelings will erupt in a torrent of hateful words. She hangs up on Reverend Hahn without answering his question, without even saying goodbye.}

My mother looked at me with fear in her eyes. "Were you . . . were you wanting to talk with him?"

"Hell, no!" I exclaimed as I shoved my chair away from the table. "I don't want anything to do with that son-of-a-bitch!"

My mother didn't scold me for my bad language. The faint smirk on her face suggested that she agreed with my choice of words.

CHAPTER 24

"A friend loveth at all times . . . ." Proverbs 17:17

By Thursday, I was beginning to feel bored and restless from being at home all week. In the late afternoon, I went out to sit on the porch swing, waiting for my father to come home from work.

Suddenly, an old, rusted car pulled into our driveway, rousing me out of my lethargy. I leaned forward, squinting, trying to make out the identity of the driver, but I couldn't even tell whether it was male or female. Then a tall, lean figure got out of the car, wearing faded blue jeans, a Goshen Redskins tee shirt, and a baseball cap that partially covered short, dark hair.

The figure moved toward the porch with a long-legged stride. Within seconds, I saw that it was my old friend Judy Prentiss, looking every bit the tomboy I'd known her to be during our growing-up years.

Judy and her brothers had long since stopped attending Westside Mennonite Church. While Judy and I had been best buddies in elementary school, we'd drifted apart during our middle school years at Towncrest. I hadn't seen her for three years, not since I'd started attending Conrad Grebel High and she'd gone on to Goshen High School.

I had, however, seen her picture on the sports page of *The Goshen News*. As the star pitcher on the Goshen Redskins girls' softball team, Judy was known for her speed-of-light fast pitch, her curveball, and her screwball.

"Hey, Victoria!" she called out in a husky voice as she stepped onto the porch.

I returned her greeting. "Hey, Judy!"

"Long time no see," she said.

Suddenly, she looked ill at ease. She stood in front of me, shifting her weight from one foot to the other. Then she spoke apologetically, as if needing to justify her intrusion into my life. "I just saw Beth Schrock down at Hooks' Drugstore, and I asked about you. She told me you were sick, and that you'd been out of school all week."

Then she stepped toward me and handed me a pale blue envelope.

"Thanks," I said as I pulled the card from the envelope. On the front was a lovely seascape and the words, *Get Well Soon.* I opened the card and saw that she'd written in her familiar crimped handwriting, *from your old pal Judy.* Evidently, she'd purchased the card after hearing Beth's news about me.

I felt sheepish sitting there on the porch swing, obviously able-bodied. "I'm not really sick," I admitted to her. "Just . . . just not feeling well."

Her dark eyes searched my face. Something flickered in them, and I knew she'd hit upon the truth, that my problem was an emotional one. "Going through a rough time?" she asked.

I nodded, tears springing into my eyes.

"I'm sorry to hear that." She sat down on the swing next to me. "I want you to know that even though we haven't been close for a while, I still care about you. I think about you a lot, and I miss you."

A tear slid down my cheek. "Thanks, Judy."

She braced one sneaker-clad foot against the porch floor and gently moved the swing by flexing and extending her long leg. "So what's going on?" she asked.

"Just a whole bunch of bullshit," I muttered.

"Wanna tell me about it?"

I looked into her kind brown eyes, and suddenly, I felt the urge to unburden myself to my old friend. Next to my father, she was just about the most trustworthy person I'd ever known. During junior high, the awkward, acne-faced Judy Prentiss had never taken part in the gossip and petty bickering typical of the popular girls I'd hung around with. Judy had known too much of life's pain, and she'd known better than to hurt others by treating them unkindly.

"If I told you something," I said, "would you keep it a secret?"

"Of course," she said. "You have my word on that."

"Well, I just found out . . . ." Then I stopped myself. Judy had known my family for years, and she'd always looked up to my father and mother. There was no way I could divulge a secret that would so drastically alter her perception of people she loved and respected. She needed to believe in the idea of a well-functioning family with parents of stellar character.

"I just can't tell you," I said. "I can't tell anyone."

"That's okay," she replied. "You don't need to say anything. Whatever it is, I want you to know I'm here for you." She scooted over and encircled my shoulders with her sinewy pitching arm. I leaned my head against her shoulder.

"Victoria," she said, "you and your parents were there for me during a time when my life was a living hell. My dad was drinking all the time, and he was mean as a snake. My mom was at her wit's end. When your father would come by with the mail, she'd go out to the car and talk to him for a few minutes. He'd say something encouraging to her, something to help her get through her day."

I turned to look at Judy, and she smiled. "But you know what? Three years ago, my mom finally got the nerve to kick my dad out of her life. It took a little bit. She had to call the cops on him a few times when he came slinking around trying to get her to take him back. Sometimes, he'd be bawling like a baby. Other times, he'd be threatening her. Once, she found him lying on her doorstep in a puddle of his own vomit. But she never gave in to him, and things are a lot better now. She's working at Goshen Rubber and doing okay. We still don't have much money, but at least we have some peace and quiet."

"That's good," I said. "I'm really glad for you."

She squeezed my shoulders. "Now it seems like you're the one whose life is turned upside down."

Her kindness burrowed its way down to the pain lodged in the core of my heart, and I began to sob.

"Whatever it is," Judy said, "I'm sorry you're going through it. Whatever it is, I'm here for you."

We sat without talking for a few minutes, as Judy's long leg continued to propel the swing. Then she said, "I'm sorry, Victoria. I have to leave. I've gotta get back to the school for softball practice." She stood up, then took my hand and pulled me to my feet. "But I want us to do something first."

Still sniffling, I followed her out to her beat-up car. She opened the door and reached into the back seat, bringing out two baseball gloves and a ball. Tossing one of the gloves to me, she said, "Let's play catch."

Smiling through my tears, I put my hand in the glove. Judy walked a dozen paces away from me, then turned and lobbed the ball toward me. I caught it and tossed it back to her. Back and forth we threw the ball, like we'd done when we were ten-year-olds, until the rhythmic activity lulled me into a state of peace.

All the while, Judy kept her concerned eyes on my face. It seemed that with her every pitch, she tossed me her sympathy and understanding. With every catch, she received my pain and held it for a moment before tossing me back a little more kindness.

After five minutes, she removed her glove, tucked it under her arm, and then walked toward me. "You're going to be all right, Victoria. Whatever it is that's bothering you, it's not going to take you down."

"How do you know that?" I asked.

"Because you're not the type of person that gets taken down," she said, confidence in her voice. "You're a winner. You're a star."

"You're the star," I said. "You're the one with your picture in the paper all the time."

She reached out for my glove, and I handed it to her. "It's just temporary," she said. "After I graduate next year, I'll be working at Goshen Rubber alongside my mom."

Opening her car door, she tossed the ball and the gloves into the back seat. "I'm just an ordinary person, Victoria. You're extraordinary. You're the one that's going places."

"I doubt it," I said.

She raised a prophetic index finger in the air. "Mark my words."

Then she got into the driver's seat, and through her open window, she said, "I'll pray for you, Victoria. I'll pray for you every night."

"Guess who came to visit me," I said to my father when he trudged up the porch steps fifteen minutes later. "Judy Prentiss!"

"Wonderful!" he exclaimed. "Did you have a nice time with her?"

"Yes. It was really good to see her."

He smiled, his eyes soft with pleasant memories. "I haven't seen that little girl in a long time. She and her mom moved a few years back, so they're not on my route anymore. They had such a rough time of it, and I always worried about them. How's Judy doing now?"

"She's fine. She and her mom are doing good."

"Well, I'm glad the two of you had the chance to spend some time together. I think you're getting back to your normal self, Vickie." He looked at me pointedly. "Sweetheart, you need to start thinking about going back to school on Monday."

I scowled at him. "I don't want to."

"You need to," he said. "You're going to have to make up your mind that you can do it."

When I went upstairs later that afternoon, my eyes fell on the pages of my *To Kill a Mockingbird* paper still piled on my dresser. Schoolwork had been the farthest thing from my mind that week. I picked up the stack of papers and leafed through them, arranging the pages in the proper order. One page was missing. I searched around the room, then got down and looked under my bed. Sure enough, it was there. I inserted the page where it belonged.

I sat on my bed, perusing what I'd already written. As I read, I drew a parallel between my own life and the life of the book's main character. *An ordinary life gets turned upside down. For a little while, all hell's breaking loose. Then life gets back to normal. But the person has learned something new that will never let her be the same again.*

I had three pages to go to complete the paper. I'd have to copy the whole thing over because the pages were stained and crumpled. But I had time to get all that done tomorrow.

I picked up my binder, which was sitting forlornly on top of my chemistry and geometry textbooks. Opening it, I saw the completed math and science assignments I'd tucked inside, assignments I'd finished the previous weekend before Lucy's fateful visit. I'd hand them in, along with my English paper, on Monday morning.

I thought about the week's worth of homework I'd have to make up. And I'd have to get busy and start studying for final exams.

I'll get it done, I told myself. *I'll catch up.*

CHAPTER 25

"A talebearer revealeth secrets: but [she] that is of a faithful spirit concealeth the matter." Proverbs 11:13

Daniel had called me three times on Sunday and twice after he got home from school on Monday. Each time, one of my parents answered the phone, promising to pass along the message that he'd called.

I kept postponing my return call, as I had no idea how to explain to Daniel the sudden upheaval in my life. I was normally an open book with my boyfriend, telling him any petty thing that bothered me. I'd carry on and on about someone at school who'd upset me, until his eyes would glaze over with boredom. But now, I had no idea what to say to him about the real crisis in my life.

I knew I had to face Daniel in church on Sunday, and then in school on Monday. I wanted to talk with him before I saw him in person. So I called him late Friday afternoon, when I knew he'd be home from school.

His mother Marilyn answered the phone. "Oh, it's you, Victoria!" she exclaimed. "How are you? Daniel's been so worried about you."

"I'm fine," I said. "Can I talk to Daniel?"

When he came to the phone a minute later, Daniel sounded petulant. "I thought you weren't going to call me back. I thought you were trying to give me the hint that you didn't want to go out with me anymore."

"I'm really sorry," I said. "I wasn't trying to break up with you."

"Are you mad at me?" he asked.

"Not at all," I responded. "I didn't call because I wasn't feeling well."

"Are you still upset about what your sister said?"

"I guess so. But I'm getting over it."

"What the heck did she say to you, anyway? It must've been really bad if you've been upset about it for a week."

"I can't tell you, Daniel," I said. "Not now, anyway. It's too complicated."

I could tell by the tone of his voice that my boyfriend was frustrated with me, and very hurt. We'd been together for a year and a half, and prior to that, we'd been good friends. I'd never shut him out like I had the past week.

I tried to rescue the moment by steering the conversation in a lighthearted direction. "So what's going on at school?"

He proceeded to tell me how Conrad Grebel's baseball team had edged out Fairfield High School by a single run in the last inning of Wednesday's game. "You should've been there," he said sulkily.

"I'll be there the next time," I said. "I promise."

"Are you coming to church Sunday?"

"Yes. And I'll be at school on Monday."

After hanging up the phone, I curled up in the corner of the sofa, thinking about how I was going to deal with my life-changing news in the context of my relationship with Daniel. When I imagined myself telling him about my real father, I pictured utter devastation on his face. He'd barely been able to handle the news of my sister's mental illness. How could he possibly accept the fact of my illegitimate birth?

He'd known and respected my parents all his life. They were his trustworthy neighbors. There was no way he could cope with such shocking news about them. He'd be unable to keep the secret from his own parents. How would Marilyn and Wendell Hooley ever recover from hearing such a disgraceful story about their longtime friends? No doubt, the story would spread throughout the church, throughout the community. How would my parents ever hold their heads up?

No matter which way I looked at the situation, I could see no benefit in letting Daniel know the truth about my paternity. There was nothing to do but to keep my secret.

When I met Daniel at church on Sunday morning, he wrapped his arms around me and held me like he never wanted to let me go. "Oh, Victoria," he murmured in my ear, "I was so scared I'd lost you."

Then he released his embrace and pulled a card from his pocket. "Happy birthday!" he said.

"Thank you," I murmured, resisting the temptation to say, "There's nothing happy about it."

The previous day, my mother had timidly observed, "Tomorrow's your birthday, Victoria. How would you like to celebrate it? Do you want me to fix you something special?"

In all the turmoil of the past week, I'd completely forgotten about my birthday. Now, marking the day of my illegitimate birth seemed like a scandalous thing to do. "I don't want to celebrate it," I snapped. "I'm not in the mood for a birthday."

"Don't you even want a cake?" she asked.

Scowling, I pointed a finger at her. "Don't you dare make a cake! If you do, I won't eat any."

Both of my parents knew I meant what I said, and they made no further mention of my birthday.

So my birthday went unrecognized that year, by everyone except Daniel. On the inside of his sentimental card, he'd written, "Happy birthday to the girl I love."

Oh, Daniel, I thought. *Would you feel this way if you knew the truth about me?*

During our Sunday-School hour, the two of us sat side by side in the youth classroom in the basement. We knew better than to hold hands in such a setting, so we allowed them to rest between us on the pew, inches away from each other. Every few minutes, Daniel reached out a furtive pinky finger to make contact with mine.

On Monday morning, my mother drove me to school, along with the other students in the carpool. When I walked through the doors of Conrad Grebel High, I felt weak and a little lightheaded, on the verge of passing out. I stared at the kids milling around in the hallway, kids who all looked like younger versions of their parents. I was sure that at any moment, they'd start nudging each other and pointing at me, whispering about the dissimilarity between me and my stocky, red-haired father.

I braced myself for having the entire student body pounce on me, demanding to know the reason for my week-long absence. But most of my friends simply said, "Victoria! You're back!"

When a few of them pressed me for details about my

absence, I said, "It was personal." They immediately backed off, apparently assuming my ailment was some kind of embarrassing female problem.

My teachers said little more than, "It's good to have you back, Victoria," before handing me the list of assignments I'd missed.

Daniel and I carried on as we had before, meeting by my locker between classes, eating lunch together. But I could feel the strain in our relationship. I knew Daniel was obsessed with the secret I was keeping from him, and that he was taking the matter personally.

From time to time, he'd say, "It seems like you're mad at me. What did I do to upset you?"

"Nothing," I'd tell him, my impatience rising. "I've told you that a hundred times. My problem had nothing to do with you."

"It would help if I knew what the problem was. Why won't you tell me?"

"Some things can't be told, Daniel. Just drop it."

He'd try to drop it, but the subject would come up again and again. He'd ask me if I'd told my friends: "Does Beth know? Does Jill know? Does Angela know?"

"No, they don't know," I'd snap.

Once, he began listing the names of my former boyfriends. "Did you tell Robbie Zook? Zach Gingerich? How about Brian Schertz?"

"Of course not!" I almost screamed at him. "Would you stop being such an idiot?"

I grew so tired of seeing his sad-sack expression that I had to suppress the urge to slap it off his face.

Before I knew it, school was over. My parents and I attended Daniel's graduation ceremonies. Afterwards, we went to the party Wendell and Marilyn hosted for him at their house. The presence of the other party guests rescued Daniel and me from the tension we invariably felt whenever we were alone together.

My dad had given me money for Daniel's gift, and I'd bought him cassette tapes of his favorite bands, Hall and Oates and The Moody Blues. Daniel thanked me, but when he hugged me, our embrace felt cold and dead. I could tell he had not recovered from the week in which I'd shut him out of my life without any explanation. He no longer trusted me. And I was completely fed up with his sulking.

I knew our relationship was coming to an end. But I was determined not to be the one to initiate the breakup. My perception of myself as a good and decent person was far too shaky to bear the guilt of breaking my boyfriend's heart. I'd wait it out until Daniel was ready to throw in the towel.

The weekend following his graduation party, Daniel took me to see *Star Wars* at the Concord Cinema in Elkhart, a movie every teenager in town was dying to see. My mother ordinarily didn't allow me to watch such shows. However, since the blowup in our household several weeks earlier, she hadn't objected to anything I wanted to do. I figured she thought she'd lost all rights to provide me with parental guidance.

Daniel and I held hands for a little while during the show, but passion no longer pulsated between our palms. Having his fingers interlaced with mine did nothing but irritate me. When I extricated my hand to brush a strand of hair out of my face, Daniel didn't reach over to re-establish contact. Clearly, we were both more interested in watching the show than we were in being with each other.

Afterwards, we sat in his car, waiting for our turn to pull out of the crowded parking lot. Instead of turning his key in the ignition, Daniel turned to me and said, "Vickie, we need to talk."

I knew what was coming. I felt sad, but mightily relieved. My boyfriend was ready to put our dying relationship out of its misery.

"Okay," I said. "Talk to me."

"I'm going to Purdue in the fall."

"I know that."

Daniel hung his head, and his voice sounded plaintive. "I was hoping we could stay together, Vickie. I was going to get you a promise ring before I left. I was thinking in terms of us getting married after I graduated from college."

He stopped talking. The silence between us seemed to go on for an eternity.

"What are you trying to tell me, Daniel?" I finally asked.

"I don't think it's going to work out between us."

Another long silence ensued.

"You're probably right," I said.

The light from the passing headlights illuminated the anguish on his face. Daniel was a thoughtful young man who'd never taken our relationship lightly, and I knew he'd invested a great deal in his plan for our future. I knew the dissolution of that plan hurt him deeply. He was hoping I'd do something to turn things around, like crying and throwing myself into his arms and begging for another chance. Such a dramatic response on my part would temporarily refuel our passion. We'd drive to some secluded spot and do some heavy petting, maybe even go all the way for the first time.

But I knew that such passion would die down again, and that our old problem would resurface. After increasing the level of our intimacy, Daniel would expect me to divulge the secret I'd been hiding from him.

"Well, I guess that's that," he mumbled as he started the car.

"We could stay friends, Daniel," I said, offering him a consolation prize.

He didn't respond, and we drove home in silence. When he pulled into our driveway, I leaned over and kissed his cheek, but he didn't return the gesture.

I got out of the car and ran into the house. Without a word to my bewildered parents, I ran up the stairs to my room. Throwing myself across my bed, I cried the obligatory breakup tears.

Then I got up and walked over to my bedroom window, where I stared out into the starry darkness. I felt empty and amorphous, as if all the structures that had given form to my previous existence had completely dissolved. In ending my relationship with Daniel, I'd let go of one more thing that belonged to my innocent past.

In the clarity of the stillness, I could see that Daniel and I never would have worked out in the long run. He'd graduate from Purdue with some type of agricultural degree, and then would come back to Goshen to farm with his father. That wasn't a world I'd be content to share.

I thought about my mother, trapped in a life that limited her potential and stifled her joy. She'd resorted to indulging in an illicit love affair in an attempt to escape her bleak reality. There was no reason for me to repeat her mistakes.

The rest of that summer crept by at a snail's pace. I had no boyfriend to go out with, and no enthusiasm for hanging out with my friends from Conrad Grebel High. But I did accomplish something noteworthy: I got my driver's license.

I'd taken driver's education during the second semester of my sophomore year. However, the summer following my sixteenth birthday, our family life had been overtaken by Lucy's problems, and my father had been too overwhelmed to take me out for driving practice.

But that summer, he seemed eager to take me out driving, as if wanting to make up for the rough time I'd just been put through. By August, I had my driver's license in hand.

This accomplishment, and the resulting independence it afforded me, felt like something that belonged to the new Victoria. Now, I could jump into one of my parents' vehicles and run an errand, driving to Kroger's or to Hook's Drugstore to pick up an item someone needed. With the money my mother allotted me, I drove on my own to the Concord Mall in Elkhart to purchase school clothing for my senior year.

The new Victoria was quieter and more contemplative than my old show-off, attention-grabbing self. I liked spending time alone, just thinking. I questioned things I'd previously considered to be immutable aspects of my existence: my church, my school, my friends, the community of Goshen. I allowed myself to visualize other possibilities for my future. With the shattering of my old self-concept came the realization that I could, and would, create new definitions of myself. Now, there were no limits on what I could do with my life.

On a Friday evening in late August, a week before school started, I decided to call Judy Prentiss. She seemed pleased to hear from me, and readily accepted my invitation to hang out. The following afternoon, I borrowed my mother's car and drove to the Prentiss home.

Judy's older brothers had all moved out of the household, and she and her mother now lived in a small trailer in Goshen's Twin Pines Mobile Home Park. When the haggard Mrs. Prentiss answered my knock on the door, she beamed and kissed my cheek. "It's so good to see you, Victoria!" she exclaimed. "Judy has missed you so much."

My old friend and I sat on the bed in her tiny bedroom. Although our quarters were cramped, I felt completely comfortable. Judy's imperfect life made me feel at ease with the problems in my own life. I knew she was alright with whoever I was.

"How are you doing?" she asked me.

"Much better," I assured her.

We talked about the kids both of us had known at Towncrest, most of whom had gone on with Judy to Goshen High School. When she asked about some of her former classmates who were attending Conrad Grebel High, I told her that Daniel and I had recently broken up.

"I didn't know you were dating Daniel Hooley," she said, a strange expression on her face. "I saw him in town last week. He was with a girl. I don't know who she was."

"What did she look like?" I asked.

"Real cute. Long blonde hair. She was really short. A little chubby, but not fat."

"That was Deanna Yordy," I muttered. "I should've known he'd start going out with her. It sure didn't take him long to move on."

"Are you dating anyone now?" Judy asked.

"No," I said. "I don't want to. Not for awhile. How about you?"

She shook her head. "I don't date. I'm not interested. After having a dad like mine, I'll never be able to trust a guy. I figure I'm better off on my own."

When Judy and I emerged from her bedroom, Mrs. Prentiss was sitting on the couch watching television. She smiled fondly at us, her eyes glistening with tears of tenderness. I knew she was grateful for my visit, for alleviating her daughter's loneliness.

Wearily, she got up and retrieved her shabby purse from the kitchen table, then pulled out two hard-earned dollar bills and handed them to Judy. "Why don't you girls go get some ice cream?"

"My sister used to work here," I said as we sat in the car in the Dairy Queen parking lot, eating our soft-serve ice cream cones. "But she came down with a mental illness, and she's not able to work anymore."

Judy looked at me with gentle eyes. "That's rough. I feel for her. Life can drive a person over the edge sometimes."

CHAPTER 26

". . . Am I my [sister's] keeper?" Genesis 4:9

After the blowup in our household, Lucy didn't visit our home for the rest of the summer. I wondered if she was ashamed of her behavior, whether she thought it best to keep her turbulent presence away from the rest of us for awhile. I also realized that I'd thrown away her borrowed bicycle, and that perhaps her failure to visit was simply a matter of lacking transportation.

But I was far more relieved than concerned by her absence. With all I was going through, I didn't have the mental energy to worry about my sister's problems.

A month after I started my senior year, my father informed me that Lucy had moved into her own place. He'd attended a meeting with her case manager Mrs. Wade, her foster mother Mrs. Davis, and her Oaklawn therapist Mr. Cramer. They'd all agreed that Lucy was ready to try living on her own. So she was set up in an efficiency apartment in Elkhart, where she was closely supervised by Mrs. Wade and a mental health technician from Oaklawn named Grace.

I wondered if the crisis in our family had jolted Lucy into trying to improve her life. Perhaps my physical assault on her had brought her to her senses. Or perhaps letting go of her big secret had relieved some of the pressure in her troubled mind.

Suddenly, I wanted to see my sister. Things had been left raw and jagged between us. After all, the last time she'd visited our home, I'd choked her and threatened to kill her. I needed to make amends. So on a Sunday afternoon in October, I asked my mother if I could borrow her car.

"Where are you going?" she asked.

"To see Lucy in her new apartment."

Fear flickered in her eyes. "Are you sure you want to do that?"

"Yes, I'm sure."

"Why don't you wait and go with your father next time he visits her?"

"No, Mom," I said. "I can do this by myself."

"I'm not comfortable with this," she protested. "You don't even know how to get there. And what if Lucy gets out of hand?"

Stubbornly, I held out my hand for her car keys. "Dad already gave me the directions. And Lucy knows I'm not going to take any crap from her. After I choked her, she's probably scared of me now."

I had to knock on Lucy's apartment door repeatedly before I heard a sleepy voice call out, "Who is it?"

"It's Tori Grace," I called back.

"Just a minute," she said.

The shuffling sounds I heard told me Lucy was getting out of bed and pulling on some clothing. When she opened the door a full three minutes later, I was taken aback, both by her appearance and by the condition of her apartment.

My sister's beautiful, long red curls had been cut off. Her new, short hairdo was in disarray, sticking up in a terrible case of bed-head. She looked as if she'd gained another fifty pounds in the five months since I'd last seen her. As we stood looking at each other, she must have seen the shock on my face, as she made a futile attempt at smoothing her hair down.

"Sorry, Tori Grace," she said, as if apologizing for the totality of her dreadful state. She pulled her ratty, too-tight tee shirt down over her round belly. "This medication they got me on makes me fat as a hog. All I wanna do is eat and sleep."

Her apartment was smaller than what I'd expected. The kitchen, living, and sleeping spaces comprised one room. A daybed, from which Lucy had just emerged, doubled as a sofa. Her kitchen furnishings consisted of a few cupboards, several feet of counter space, a tiny stove, and a dormitory-sized refrigerator. A single folding chair was pulled up to a battered card table.

I could tell the apartment had been refurbished before Lucy moved in, as the beige carpet was new and the walls had been freshly painted. But in the short time she'd lived there, Lucy's quarters had already deteriorated into an unbelievable state of disorder.

Several unpacked boxes of clothing sat against one wall, their contents spilling out onto the floor. Instead of storing the items in the old dresser standing in one corner of the room, Lucy apparently settled for rifling through the contents of the boxes to get whatever she needed. Dirty dishes sat on the kitchen counter, on the card table, and on the floor next to the daybed. The new carpet was already marred by a large pink stain. I suspected that Lucy had spilled something, and hadn't bothered to clean it up.

As I glanced around the apartment, my face must have

registered my revulsion. "I know, I know, I'm a pig," Lucy said, grinning. "I'm gonna have to get my act together. Mrs. Wade told me if I don't keep this place up, she'll send me back to foster care."

She gave the covers on her daybed a few yanks to straighten them out, and then said, "Sit down, Tori Grace."

I reluctantly settled myself onto the grungy bedcovers, and Lucy plunked herself down beside me. "Why did you come over?" she asked.

"I just wanted to see how you're doing," I replied. "And to apologize to you."

"What for? You haven't done anything to me."

"I choked you."

She threw back her head, laughing loudly. "Oh, that. Well, I had it coming. I was acting like a horse's ass."

"But I shouldn't have done that." My statement of remorse was weakened, as I couldn't help but smile in the face of her hilarity.

"I didn't think you had that in you, Tori Grace," she gasped when she finally got her laughter under control. "It was pretty damn funny. You're more of a bad-ass kid than I thought you were."

She stood up and ambled over to the kitchen. "I'm hungry. I just got up. Want something to drink?"

"Sure," I said.

She bent down to open her tiny refrigerator and took out a pitcher containing something that looked like strawberry Kool-Aid. She pulled a plastic tumbler out of her cupboard, and then grumbled in frustration as she searched among the dirty dishes on her countertop for a second one. As she poured the drink, her hands shook so badly that some of the Kool-Ade spilled on the floor. She seemed unconcerned about the mishap. I suddenly understood the reason for the pink stain by the daybed.

"These damn meds," she muttered. "They make me shake like an old woman. But I get in big trouble if I don't take them." She grabbed a bag of chips off the kitchen counter, tucked it under her arm, and then carried the drinks to the daybed.

"So what's up, Lucy?" I asked as she handed me the Kool-Ade. "What's going on with you these days?" I noted that she'd unthinkingly given me the dirty glass, but I decided not to point that out. Reluctantly, I tasted the drink and found it to be sickeningly sweet, apparently doused with twice the amount of sugar it needed.

Lucy sat down, then tore open the bag and reached in for a handful of chips. "Nothing much," she said as she crammed the chips into her mouth. "I go to day-treatment at Oaklawn three times a week, and that's about all I do."

"What's day-treatment?"

"Me and a bunch of other crazies go and hang out for a while. The staff has activities for us. We have group therapy." She snorted. "For all the good that does. And we play games and watch movies. That kind of stuff."

She munched noisily on a few more chips before continuing. "Mrs. Wade comes by here and checks on me twice a month. That witch is always on my case about something. And Gracie from Oaklawn comes out a couple of times week to help me with stuff. She takes me to the grocery store and the laundry mat.

"Do you like it here?" I asked.

She yawned sleepily. "I guess so. It's better than the

foster home. The other residents got on my nerves, the way they were always crying and hollering and carrying on. But I miss Mrs. Davis's cooking."

"Do you cook?"

She shook her head. "Not much. Gracie tries to help me plan menus. Mostly, I just eat something out of a can. Soup or spaghetti. Easy stuff like that."

I looked down, trying to hide my concern. My sister seemed content with the aimless life she was living. She'd mastered the art of indolence. She showed no inclination toward self-improvement, had no goals for her future. Her lack of self-respect made me unbearably sad.

"How about you, Tori Grace?" Lucy asked. "What are you up to these days?"

"Just going to school," I said. "I'm a senior now."

She smiled sweetly at me. "It's hard to believe my baby sister is that grown up. Are you still dating that Hooley kid?"

"No. We broke up four months ago."

She winced, as if she understood the reason. "That's too bad. You guys were good together."

I shrugged. "It just didn't work out. He's gone off to college."

"Did you tell him?"

"Tell him what?"

"You know what I mean."

I shook my head.

"Have you told anyone?"

"No," I said. "Whenever I think about telling somebody, it doesn't seem like a good idea. Too many people would get hurt."

"Yeah," she said, "it's a messy business."

"Dad told me how you found out. He said you overheard him and Mom talking."

Lucy's face darkened, and she lowered her eyes. "Yup, that was a fucked-up time. I was nine. They didn't think I'd catch on. Mom told me just to forget about what I heard them say. But how can a kid forget something like that? Later on, I figured it all out."

In my mind, I pictured nine-year-old Lucy, confused, unsupported, alone with a secret that was too heavy for a little girl to bear. Tears welled in my eyes, and I looked away from my sister until the wave of emotion passed.

"Do Michael and Robert know?" I asked when I turned back to her. "Is that why they hardly ever come around?"

Lucy shrugged. "I couldn't say for sure. We've never talked about it. But they're not stupid. They were teenagers. They could've done the math. And everyone can tell how different you look."

She cackled evilly. "You look just like Reverend Hahn, you know. Spittin' image of that son-of-a-bitch. You act like him, too."

Her provocative words riled me, and I bit my lip to keep from snapping at her. Then I said, "Lucy, how did you manage to keep the secret all these years? You're such a blabbermouth. How's come you didn't tell everybody?"

A thoughtful look crossed her face. "Probably for the same reason you don't tell anybody, Tori Grace. I might be fuckin' crazy, but I do have a little bit of sense. Mostly, I didn't want to hurt you. None of what happened was your fault, and I didn't want to screw up your life." She grinned. "Even if you were a little pain in the ass."

"What made you finally spill the beans?"

She shook her head. "I don't know. Maybe it was just time the truth came out."

"I'm glad it did," I said.

"Really?" She sounded incredulous. "You don't hate me for telling you?"

"No, I don't hate you. I would've found out, somehow, sooner or later. I might as well know now so I can deal with it and get on with my life."

"Yeah," she said, petulant. "You've got a life. Everything's always been so easy for you, Tori Grace. You're so smart and so pretty. I always hated you for that."

"You hated me?"

"Well, I don't mean I actually hated you. I loved you, I really did. But I didn't think it was fair that you got all the breaks. You're lucky you had a different dad. Did you ever think about that? Otherwise, you might've ended up like me."

She struck a pose like a pin-up girl, batting her eyes. "I take after Herman Unruh. I'm fat and stupid."

"Dad's not stupid," I protested. "Don't say things like that about him. He's been really good to you. He looks after you. He looks after me, too."

My sister looked at me pointedly. "Face it, Tori Grace. Herman Unruh is a loser. He let his wife crap all over him, and he didn't do a damn thing about it. He just took it. He should've walked out on her a long time ago."

Lucy's words hit me like a punch in the gut, taking my breath away. "You think Mom and Dad should've gotten divorced?"

"Yup," she said. "I would've gone to live with Dad.

And I never would've had a thing to do with Mom after that."

"You hate Mom, don't you, Lucy?"

She nodded. "Pretty much. She's such a hypocrite. All my life, she's hounded me about every mistake I've ever made, and I've never done anything half as bad as what she did. Cheating on her husband. Raising her illegitimate kid and acting like nothing was wrong."

I winced.

"Sorry, Tori Grace. I didn't mean anything against you. Like I said, it wasn't your fault."

"I don't hate Mom," I said. "But I can see where you're coming from."

Nodding, Lucy reached into the bag for more chips. "I was always her punching bag. The real problem was that she hated herself, and she took it out on me. She hated me because I knew her for what she was. A whore. A fuckin' whore who acted like she was a good Christian."

I shuddered at Lucy's crude assessment of our mother. "Don't you think you could ever forgive her?"

"Forgive her?" Lucy spat out the words derisively. "Maybe if she could forgive me for everything I've done to piss her off, I could forgive her. But forgiveness isn't a word she even knows. She never lets go of anything."

I stood up. "I gotta get going, Lucy. Gotta get home and finish my homework."

She yawned, stretching dramatically, then got up and walked me to the door. "Don't be a stranger, Tori Grace. Maybe the next time you come over, I'll have this place cleaned up. If I don't do something pretty soon, Mrs. Wade's gonna be all over my ass."

As I surveyed her dismal surroundings, I blurted out, "I'll help you, Lucy. If you want, I'll help you get your apartment organized. We could fix it up really cute."

"That's sweet of you," she murmured. "Maybe I'll take you up on that."

"Just call me when you want to work on it."

"Okay, Tori Grace. I'll let you know. You take care, now."

On impulse, I reached down and wrapped my arms around my sister, something I hadn't done in years. Her plump body felt soft as a pillow. She smelled sweaty, like she hadn't showered in days.

In that moment, I knew that no matter what kind of challenge my sister might pose for me, I would never turn my back on her. The circumstances surrounding my birth had caused her unbearable pain. My very existence had created an enormous amount of suffering for her. I had to make it up to her.

Right then and there, I made a decision. When my father grew too old and feeble to care for Lucy, she'd be mine to look after. I'd shoulder that load.

CHAPTER 27

". . . Commune with your own heart . . . and be still."
Psalm 4:4

". . . In quietness and in confidence shall be your
strength . . . ." Isaiah 30:15

My senior year was quieter than my previous three years at Conrad Grebel High. I spent little time socializing, and a great deal of time holed up in my bedroom, studying. While I didn't know where the new Victoria was headed in life, it seemed to me that stellar grades would help take her wherever she needed to go.

I didn't go on a single date my senior year. I had no desire to start another relationship unless I could be honest with the guy about who I really was. Clearly, that wasn't possible in the tight-knit community in which I'd spent my entire life. Dating would have to wait until a time when I could step out into a bigger world.

I allowed my classmates to presume that I was still maintaining a relationship with Daniel Hooley, so the boys, for the most part, left me alone. On the infrequent occasion when I was asked for a date, I rebuffed the overture by saying, "I'm sorry, I'm not available."

Initially, my peers were puzzled by my social reticence. "What's up with you, Victoria?" they'd ask on a Monday morning after I hadn't shown up at a party or a sporting event over the weekend. "You never do anything anymore."

However, the other popular girls seemed pleased that I'd bowed out of the competition for top diva. The tide of peer pressure and the struggle for social acceptance rushed on without me.

When Daniel came home from college over Thanksgiving weekend, I found myself face-to-face with him at church. "How are things at Purdue?" I asked him.

He seemed surprised by my question. We hadn't spoken to each other since our breakup five months earlier, except to say a polite "hi" to each other in passing. "Good," he said. "Everything's good."

"Glad to hear that," I said. Then a mean-spirited impulse overcame my resolve to maintain my dignity. "How are things going with you and Deanna Yordy?"

Daniel's face turned red, and he shook his head. "I'm not seeing her. We just went out a couple of times."

"Okay," I said. "That's not my business, anyway."

Daniel's earnest eyes searched my face, as if trying to detect any lingering feelings, any spark of interest that might be rekindled. But I knew that the passion between us had been completely extinguished. Daniel Hooley was a wonderful young man, but the circumstances of my life had destroyed any possibility for a future with him. As I walked away from him, I sincerely hoped he'd find an equally wonderful young woman who could be the partner he needed.

I'd resumed my old habit of sitting with my parents during church services. I felt too vulnerable, too transparent, to sit with the other youth. Having a parent on either side of me felt like a protection against the intrusive eyes of the rest of the congregation.

That Sunday after Thanksgiving, as I sat sandwiched between my mother and father, I was surprised when Alvin Troyer got up to lead the singing. Alvin hadn't led our congregational singing for several years, due to his declining health. I'd heard he was battling cancer, which was now considered to be terminal.

I suspected this was the last time he would ever lead the singing at Westside Mennonite Church. The former robust tenor now looked gaunt and frail, his body ravaged by disease and chemotherapy treatments. But his eyes glistened with the spirit of God.

"Please join me in my favorite hymn," he said. *"Come, Thou Fount of Every Blessing."* Then he raised his still magnificent but now quavering voice as we sang.

Come, thou Fount of every blessing,
Tune my heart to sing thy grace:
Streams of mercy, never ceasing,
Call for songs of loudest praise.
Teach me some melodious sonnet,
Sung by flaming tongues above;
Praise the mount—I'm fixed upon it—
Mount of thy redeeming love!

This time, instead of being the awe-inspiring performer, I was a member of the audience moved to tears by someone else's singing. Alvin Troyer, staring into the jaws of death, was still proclaiming an unwavering faith. My own trial paled in comparison to his. I struggled to sing the second stanza along with the rest of the congregation.

Here I raise my Ebenezer,
Hither by thine help I'm come;
And I hope, by thy good pleasure,
Safely to arrive at home.
Jesus sought me when a stranger,
Wandering from the fold of God,
He, to rescue me from danger,
Interposed his precious blood.

I'm the stranger in this song, I thought as tears rolled down my face. *I don't know who I am anymore. Others don't know me, either. Is God really seeking me out in my confused condition? Does He accept me with this messed-up identity? Am I okay with God just like I am?*

I lay my head against my father's shoulder. As always, he seemed to understand what was troubling me, and pulled me into the circle of his arm. I glanced at his face, and saw a tear on his cheek. We both cried as we sang the last stanza, my alto voice rising along with his errant tenor.

Oh, to grace how great a debtor
Daily I'm constrained to be!
Let that grace, now, like a fetter,
Bind my wandering heart to thee.
Prone to wander, Lord, I feel it;
Prone to leave the God I love--
Here's my heart, oh, take and seal it,
Seal it from thy courts above.

Throughout my senior year, I made a point of visiting my sister at least once a month. Lucy never took me up on my invitation to help her organize her apartment, and her living quarters remained in disarray. Every now and then, she'd clean up a portion of her mess, washing a pile of dishes or stashing some clothing away in her dresser drawers, doing just enough to keep Mrs. Wade at bay.

Sometimes, my father would hand me a few dollars and tell me to take Lucy out to eat. She particularly enjoyed going to Peddler's Village and the South Side Soda Shop. I'd have to prompt my sister to change her clothing and brush her hair before going out in public. When she was especially grungy, I'd insist that she take a shower.

Lucy's love of our outings generally rendered her compliant with my demand that she be clean and well-groomed. The first time she balked at my directives, I didn't bother to struggle with her. I simply walked out her door and went home. After that, she never challenged me, as she knew I meant business.

The one friend I didn't keep at arm's length that year was Judy Prentiss. The two of us spent time together almost every weekend. Occasionally, we went to the Concord Cinema to see a movie, but mostly, we hung out at either her house or mine.

She'd often be at my house on a Friday afternoon when my father came home from work. She'd sit on the sofa while he rested in his armchair, chatting with him about the people she knew on his mail route.

I could tell she trusted him deeply, and that she craved the fatherly attention she was getting from him.

Genetically speaking, Herman Unruh belonged no more to me than he did to her, and I was happy to share him with her.

"I wish I had a dad like yours," she said to me time and again.

It's not the way you think it is, I wanted to tell her. But I knew nothing would be gained by correcting the record for her.

"You're always welcome here," my dad often said to Judy. "You can come over any time."

The first time he uttered those words, I glanced at my mother. Her face registered no objection. Over time, I realized that having another party in the house created a buffer between her and my father and me, giving her more opportunity to retreat into the safety of solitude.

In the spring, I sat on the bleachers at Goshen High School's baseball diamond, watching Judy pitch. Surrounded by people who didn't know me, I felt free from the social pressures I would have felt if I'd been watching a Conrad Grebel sporting event. I'd cheer Judy on, marveling at her smoking-hot pitches, glad to be the fan instead of the one in the limelight.

Judy was an average student with no aspirations for higher education. She expected nothing more out of life than to work alongside her mother at Goshen Rubber after her high school graduation.

I knew that, from her point of view, excelling in softball was the only time she'd ever shine. I wanted that time to be as special as possible for her. So I attended every one of her games.

At the end of her team's winning season, my father and I celebrated with her by taking her out to eat at the Super Steer Steak House. We invited my mother and Mrs. Prentiss to come along with us. My mother declined.

"You sure it won't look funny, me being alone with Barbara Prentiss and the girls?" my dad asked her.

My mom waved her hand dismissively. "Don't worry about it. Just go out and have a good time."

"You two are like family to me," Judy said as we ate our steaks.

"We always will be," I said.

"Absolutely," my father chimed in.

Mrs. Prentiss put down her fork and dabbed at the grateful tears spilling from her eyes.

My only extracurricular activity my senior year was singing in the Conrad Grebel choir. I accepted a few solos, but for the most part, I declined the spotlight, telling Mr. Rheinheimer that the younger students should be given the opportunity to perform.

Since I had no boyfriend to make out with, I had no inclination to misbehave on the tour bus. I'd stare out the window, trying to shut out the childish commotion going on around me.

In November, our choir was once again scheduled to sing at the First Mennonite Church in Warsaw. Upon hearing this news, I had a few moments of panic.

"What should I do?" I asked my mother. "I can't handle seeing Reverend Hahn. Maybe I should call Mr. Rheinheimer that day and tell him I'm not feeling well."

"You don't have anything to worry about, Victoria," my mother quickly assured me. "Reverend Hahn isn't there anymore. He retired a couple of months ago."

"Really?" I said. "Where is he now?"

"He and his wife moved to one of the assisted living apartments at Greencroft, here in Goshen. Myrna is sick, and Harry can't get around well enough to take care of her on his own."

So the concert in Warsaw ended up being no cause for concern. The new pastor of the First Mennonite Church looked to be around thirty years of age, with a young wife and two small children. I sincerely hoped he was living an upstanding life, without the deception and intrigue that had marked the career of his predecessor.

I did sing a solo at the Warsaw church, an arrangement of *Precious Lord Take My Hand.* This time, my heartfelt emotion wasn't elicited by the tears of the audience. This time, I had my own experience to draw from.

One day in March of my senior year, as I sat on the sofa browsing through a copy of *The Goshen News,* a familiar face in the obituaries column caught my attention. It was Myrna Hahn.

I stared at the photo of the sad-faced woman, realizing that, technically speaking, she was my stepmother. I wondered whether she'd ever suspected that her husband had a child by another woman. Had his covert behavior ever made her question his faithfulness to her? Or had she learned to turn a blind eye to his exploits?

For a moment, I imagined what it would have been like if my parents and the Hahns had handled the circumstances around my birth with openness and honesty. I pictured myself spending time in my biological father's home on weekends and holidays, going on the occasional vacation with the well-to-do couple. How would Myrna Hahn have responded to me?

I was almost certain that, after grieving over her husband's infidelity, the tenderhearted woman would have been gracious and accepting of me, just as my father Herman Unruh had been. No doubt, she would have treated me like the daughter she never had. She probably would have offered me more affection than I received from my own mother.

Suddenly, I felt sad that I'd never gotten to know this woman who might have loved me. But mostly, I hoped that Myrna Hahn died without the heartache of knowing about her husband's dishonorable behavior.

I carefully folded the newspaper and laid it on the coffee table in front of me. A strange feeling crept over me. I sat motionless, scarcely breathing, sensing that once again my life was about to change.

CHAPTER 28

*". . . He that is without sin among you, let him first
cast a stone . . . ." John 8:7*

I finished the final exams of my senior year on a
Friday in late May. That afternoon, I came home feeling
both relieved and exhilarated, knowing that I'd just
completed the last few steps of my high school journey.
The future would bring more challenges, but for now, I was
looking forward to doing absolutely nothing. I had plenty
of time to relax before my graduation ceremonies the
following weekend.

I was exhausted, as I'd stayed up late the night before,
studying. As I headed upstairs, ready to collapse on my
bed for a late-afternoon nap, I heard my mother call out in a
timid voice, "Victoria?"

I paused on the stairs. "What do you want, Mom?"

"Can we talk for a little bit?"

Irritated, I walked back downstairs and followed her
into the kitchen.

As we sat facing each other at the table, her face
looked haggard and fearful, as if something had been
weighing heavily on her mind. "How . . . how did your
exams go?" she stammered.

"Fine," I said, bewildered by her unwarranted anxiety.
"They went fine. Were you afraid I was going to fail?"

She lowered her eyes, shaking her head slightly.

I waited for her to say something else, and when she
didn't, I pushed away from the table and stood up.

"Wait," she whispered.

"Mom," I said. "I'm dead tired, and I want to take a nap. Would you just spit out whatever it is you want to say?"

Without raising her eyes, she blurted out, "Reverend Hahn wants to see you."

My legs suddenly felt weak, and I sank back down on my chair. "What?"

"Reverend Hahn wants to see you," she repeated, still staring down at the table.

"You've got to be kidding me!"

"No, I'm not kidding." She looked up at me, and I noticed her eyes were bloodshot. I knew she'd been crying again.

"What the hell?" I exploded.

My mother sighed heavily. "Victoria, you had to know this was going to happen, sooner or later."

"But why does he want to see me now?"

"He thought this was the right time."

"He thought!" I shouted. "What about what I think? I've been stressed out all week, studying for my exams. I was looking forward to relaxing for a while. And then you spring this on me. I can't deal with this right now."

"I guess it's up to you," my mother said. "If you don't want to do this, then I'll call and tell him."

"I don't." I pointed to the phone hanging on the kitchen wall. "Go ahead and call him. Tell him I don't want to see him. Not now. Not ever. Tell him I don't want anything to do with him."

She winced, biting her lip. "Okay, then. I'll call him after supper." She stood up and walked over to the kitchen counter, resuming the preparation for our evening meal.

With her bare hands, she began squeezing together the ingredients for meatloaf. The task seemed to require more strength than she possessed, and I felt sorry for her. I knew that being the intermediary between my biological father and me had to be putting an enormous strain on her.

I remained at the table, still trying to digest the momentous news that had been dumped on me.

"When did he want to see me?" I asked. "Where? Was he going to come here?"

"He wanted to see you tomorrow." My mother spoke with her back to me as she formed the meat mixture into a loaf on a baking pan. "He said if that didn't suit you, then Sunday afternoon would be fine. He wanted you to come to his apartment at Greencroft."

Anger flared inside me, but I tried not to raise my voice again. "Just because he wants it that way doesn't mean it's going to happen. Who does he think he is, making plans for me like that?"

My mother put the meatloaf in the oven, and then turned around to face me. "Victoria," she said in a tired voice, "that's just the way he is. I learned a long time ago that Harry Hahn makes things happen when he wants them to happen. Everything takes place on his terms. I gave up trying to fight that."

I snorted in derision.

She continued, sounding as if she was defending him. "This wasn't a rash decision on his part. He puts a lot of thought into everything he does. He decided to wait until you were done with exams, because he knew that hearing from him would be a shock to you. But he wanted to see you before you graduate. He plans on attending the ceremonies. He wanted to talk to you ahead of time so that you'd know he was there to support you."

I pointed an accusing finger at her. "You've been talking to him about all this behind my back!"

My mother looked ashamed. Turning around again, she busied herself with wiping off the counter top. "Yes, Victoria. I told you before. Harry and I have talked about you all these years. He insists on being kept up to date, and he always wants to have his say about things. He's not one to sit back. He likes to be in charge."

I jumped up, shoving my chair back from the table with a clatter. "Well, I've got news for Reverend Harry Hahn. He's not in charge of me."

I was far too riled up for a nap, so I went to the living room to join my father, who was sitting in his armchair, looking dejected. I knew he'd overheard every word of the conversation between my mother and me.

"Can you believe this, Dad?" I fumed as I flung myself onto the sofa.

He raised his tired eyes to look at me. "One more thing for you to deal with, huh?"

"Yup," I said. "I'm so sick of this. It seems like I don't get a moment of peace before something else flies up and smacks me in the face."

"I know," he said. "You've had a rough year."

I curled up and laid my head on the arm of the sofa, resting in my father's understanding presence.

"Vickie," he said after a few minutes. "You might want to think about going tomorrow. Sooner or later, you're going to need to face that part of your life."

"Later," I mumbled. "I'll do it later."

"The man is growing older," my father observed. "And from what I hear, he isn't well. I'm thinking you might want to speak with him before it's too late."

"Why? Why should I ever speak to him?"

"You came from him. He's part of you. There are things you might want to know about him. He might be able to help you in ways that I can't."

"I sincerely doubt that," I retorted.

"Vickie," my father said. "I can't make up your mind for you. But I know what kind of a girl you are. You're not one to run away from things. You face life head-on. In the long run, you won't be happy with yourself unless you face this." He paused, and then added, "I want you to know that you don't have to hold back on my account."

I raised my head and looked at him questioningly.

"I really mean that," he said.

"Alright, then." The words seem to come out of my mouth on their own volition, even though I was far from ready for the commitment I was making. I got up, and before stomping up the stairs, I called to my mother in the kitchen, "Tell him I'll be there tomorrow afternoon."

I'd always been one to sleep soundly, even in the face of stress. But that night, I experienced my first episode of insomnia. My sleeplessness made me furious, as I'd counted on crashing for ten or twelve hours after the strain of my exams.

I kept picturing myself face-to-face with my biological father, trying to rehearse what I would say to him. I finally gave up and decided I'd let him do the talking.

"I have nothing to say to you," I muttered aloud.

Then I remembered what my mother had told me. Harry Hahn always managed to be in control, and he'd undoubtedly take charge of our meeting. Even though the idea galled me, I'd let him. This time, anyway.

I finally fell asleep in the wee hours of the morning. When I awoke around 11:00 A.M., the memory of the day's agenda washed over me in a sickening wave. I bolted out of bed and began rushing around to get ready.

Why are you doing this? I asked myself as I took extra care in blow-drying my hair after my shower. *You might as well go looking like a slob. You don't care what that jerk thinks about you.*

Muttering curse words under my breath, I rummaged through my closet and pulled out my best pair of blue jeans and a top that everyone thought looked nice on me. Although I hated to admit it, I wanted to make a good impression on Reverend Hahn. I despised him, but I still wanted him to be proud of me.

My mother had offered to drive me to Reverend Hahn's apartment. She told me she'd wait in the car while I talked with him. I knew she was trying to protect me, that she was afraid I'd find my meeting with my biological father to be overwhelming. Those days, I didn't look to my mother for much of anything, but I did appreciate this gesture. However, I told her I could manage the trip on my own.

At one o'clock that afternoon, I turned the key in the ignition of her car, knowing that I was just minutes away from a monumental event in my life. In spite of my recent shower and the coolness of the spring day, I was sweating profusely. My chest felt so tight, I could hardly breathe.

I drove the route I'd rehearsed in my mind, going south on our county road, turning east on Plymouth Avenue, heading south on Main Street down to the Goshen College campus, turning east on College Avenue, then traveling the short distance to the entrance of the Greencroft Center complex.

Following my mother's careful instructions, I wound my way around several buildings before I located the manor in which Reverend Harry Hahn resided.

I stood in front of his apartment door a full minute before I summoned the courage to knock. Within seconds of my first feeble tap, the door swung open, revealing my biological father seated in a wheelchair. In spite of his age and physical infirmity, he appeared as dapper as ever, wearing a pair of neatly pressed black trousers and a blue shirt that look crisp and new.

As I stared into his smiling face, I had an uncanny feeling of staring at my own reflection, an older version of my own visage. His eyes looked like the eyes I'd seen in the mirror every day of my life. As they gazed back at me, it seemed as if they were looking right into the heart of who I was. I felt myself cringing, drawing back. Whether or not I liked it, those eyes knew me, through and through.

"Victoria!" Reverend Hahn exclaimed. "I'm so glad you came!" He wheeled his chair away from the door so that I could enter.

I stepped inside, taking a moment to survey my surroundings. The apartment was hardly any bigger than Lucy's place, but it was immaculately kept. The front of the apartment, arranged as a living room, contained a sofa and a recliner. The coffee table was laden with a tidy row of magazines: *Newsweek, Time, The New Yorker,* and *Christian Living.* A console television set stood opposite the sofa. Massive bookshelves nearly covered one wall. At a quick glance, I saw volumes of classic literature, along with books on psychology, philosophy, and theology.

The back of the apartment consisted of a tiny kitchenette and a small dining table with two chairs. A sliding glass door on the back wall opened into a courtyard. I assumed the closed door to one side of the living space led to a bedroom or bathroom.

Just as in his Warsaw parsonage, the furnishings in Reverend Hahn's living quarters were of high quality and in pristine condition, matching his polished persona. I could tell he allowed nothing shabby to enter his world. I suddenly felt scruffy in my casual clothing, and I wished I had run a brush through my wind-blown hair before I'd entered the apartment.

"Have a seat, Victoria," Reverend Hahn said with a graceful sweep of his hand.

I seated myself on the sofa, and he wheeled his chair around to an angle where we could converse comfortably. "I'm so glad you came," he repeated. "For years, I've looked forward to the time when we could sit down together and get to know each other."

I tried to reciprocate his smile, but my face felt frozen. I could think of no response to his comment.

"I'm sure you understand," he said, "that there were many reasons why this meeting couldn't take place earlier in your childhood."

I managed to nod. I could tell that my silence made him feel awkward, and I took wicked delight in his discomfort. I could almost hear his mental wheels turning as he searched for a way to manage the difficult situation.

"I'm sure you have things you want to talk about," he said. "Perhaps some questions you want to ask me."

"My mom and dad have already explained everything to me," I said, my voice cold and flat.

Reverend Hahn winced when I used the term *dad*, but he made no comment. Clearly, he knew better than to demand an acknowledgment of his paternal role in my life.

"What have they told you?" he asked.

I wasn't in a mood to sugar-coat any facts. "They told me that you and my mom had an affair when you were together in Mexico, and that you got her pregnant."

He winced again. "I'm not sure you could call it an affair. But, yes, I did impregnate your mother."

Having gotten the first few awkward sentences out of the way, I suddenly felt bolder. "If it wasn't an affair, then what was it?"

Reverend Hahn looked away for a few seconds, as if my question had knocked him off balance. "Your mother and I found ourselves working together in difficult circumstances, far from the comfort and familiarity of our homes and daily routines. And we developed an attraction for each other. I'm not saying what we did was right, but such things happen in situations like that."

"Did you love my mother?" I blurted out.

He hesitated before shaking his head. "Victoria, I know you'd like to hear that I was in love with your mother, and I wish I could tell you that was true. But our

295

relationship didn't progress to that point. Your mother and I had a very brief . . . ." He stopped to search for the right word. "Association. When we left Mexico, it was all over and done with."

"Oh." I sat back, deflated. I knew I was conceived in sin. Still, I'd been hoping to hear that I was a child of two wrongdoers who cared deeply for each other. Now it seemed as if my life had been initiated in utterly meaningless circumstances.

Then anger began to smolder inside me. Sarcastic words spewed out of my mouth, even though I knew I was being unthinkably rude to someone who was treating me with impeccable graciousness. "You act like it was no big deal. You're a preacher. You're supposed to be an example to other people. And you cheated on your wife and got my mother pregnant."

My accusation apparently hit a sore spot, and I watched Reverend Hahn struggle to maintain his composure. "I'll be the first to admit to you, Victoria, that what I did was wrong. I want you to know that it WAS a big deal for me. I spent many sleepless nights, praying about what I'd done, asking the Lord for His forgiveness, pleading for His guidance."

Then he uttered words that echoed what my father had said to me a year earlier. "But something wonderful resulted from my mistake. You were born. And that is something I can never regret."

The sentiment in his last few sentences succeeded in creating a flicker of warmth in my chest. But I forced myself to harden my heart and push on with my accusing agenda. "You hurt my mother. Even if you didn't love her, she was probably in love with you." Sneering at him, I added, "All the church women are in love with you."

He lowered his gaze. "I don't know what to say to that point, Victoria."

I sat back on the sofa, crossing my arms in a huff.

Then he looked up at me and smiled. "Why don't you ask me if I loved you?"

"Did you love me?" I snapped.

"Unequivocally," he said. "From the moment you were born. Actually, from the moment I knew you were going to be born. I have loved you every minute of your life, Victoria."

I stared mutely at him, not at all ready to receive the abundance of affection he wanted to offer me.

"I know you can't fathom the fact that I love you," he continued. "How could you have known that, when you grew up oblivious to the fact that I was your father? But I did everything I possibly could for you, everything I could do without upsetting your life."

"I know, I know," I interrupted him. "You sent money. My mom and dad told me that."

He looked surprised, as if he'd expected to have to defend himself against my parents' vilification. "Yes, I sent money," he said. "I wanted to make sure your parents could afford to give you everything you needed. I tried to be involved with making decisions pertaining to your wellbeing. And every single day of your life, I've lifted you up to the Lord in prayer, asking Him to watch over you and keep you from harm."

He stopped speaking, looking at me with hopeful eyes. When I offered him no response, he continued. "I did everything I could to be near you, Victoria, to catch glimpses of you as you grew up. Do you know why I moved all the way from California to Indiana?"

"Yes," I said, "my parents told me."

"Good." After an awkward silence between us, he added, "I chose your name. Did you know that?"

"No, I didn't know that." The news warmed me another fraction of a degree, melting my icy guard a tiny bit. I sat up a little straighter on the sofa, looking at him with more interest.

"I wanted you to have the best I could offer you, starting with a beautiful name."

I could tell he was trying to make all my reservations about him disappear. He was ready for us to begin a relationship right then and there. But I was nowhere near that point.

"Why wasn't I told you were my father when I was a little child?" I asked, resuming my confrontational tone. "Why did everybody lie to me? If Lucy hadn't blurted out the truth, would all of you have gone on lying to me for the rest of my life?"

Slowly, Reverend Hahn shifted his position in the wheelchair. The effort seemed to cause him pain. "Victoria, you're raising some valid questions, and I respect that. Before you were born, your parents and I did a lot of talking, and we decided on the course of action that we thought was best for you. I knew there was a possibility that you'd someday learn that I was your biological father. Such things have a way of coming out. I honestly didn't know how I'd handle such a situation. That was a matter I turned over to God. A year ago, when your mother informed me that you'd found out about your paternity, I prayed fervently, asking that God's will might prevail. Now here we are, sitting together and talking for the first time. God has brought us to this point, and I trust that He will lead us forward."

All that had softened inside of me hardened into anger again. I was quite aware of the fact that Reverend Hahn was manipulating me. He was using tactics that were familiar to me, tactics I'd used with other people in order to get my way. He'd introduced the idea of God's will to sweep past my unresolved issues and to take me where he wanted me to go. While it seemed sacrilegious to shout at the man who'd just claimed to have surrendered all of his thorny problems to God, my rage erupted in words that pummeled him mercilessly.

"Have you told the truth to anyone?"

"No," he admitted. "This has been a private matter between Herman and Ada and myself."

"You're a cheat and a liar. All these years, you've acted like you've done nothing wrong. I've heard you preach, carrying on about sinners needing to repent. You're the biggest sinner of all. And you think you've gotten away with this."

Reverend Hahn seemed to shrink before my eyes. His gnarled hands clutched the arms of his wheelchair, as if he was trying to keep himself from collapsing and falling out of the chair and onto the floor. Tears glistened in his eyes.

Cool it, Victoria, I told myself. *He's a sick old man. You need to stop being so nasty to him.*

But a moment later, he straightened his lanky frame, resuming his dignified bearing. "Victoria, I haven't gotten away with anything. You have no idea how much I've suffered over what I've done. I've punished myself more cruelly than anyone else ever could have punished me."

In spite of my resolve to be kinder, I carried on. "How many other women did you have affairs with? How many other illegitimate kids do you have? Do I have brothers and sisters I don't know about?"

Reverend Hahn took a deep breath, trying to restore himself after another attack of my hateful words. "Victoria, I'm not the scoundrel you think I am." He looked at me intently. "And there's one thing I can say for certain. You are my only child."

"Are you sure?" I said sarcastically.

"Absolutely sure," he responded.

He reached out his arthritic hand to touch my arm and then pulled back, apparently sensing that I was not receptive to such a gesture. "Victoria, do you have any idea what it's like to have a child that you can't parent? A beautiful, brilliant child that you're so proud of? I would've given anything to be fully present in your life, but I had to be content to watch you from the sidelines. In order for you to have the life you deserved, I had to remain in the shadows."

Once again, I felt myself warming up to him, although I knew full well the secrecy during my childhood had served to protect him as well as me. Making myself sound cold again, I retorted, "And you have no idea what it was like to grow up thinking one thing about yourself, then having your world turned upside down."

The sympathy in his eyes unnerved me. "Tell me what it was like," he said.

Against my will, my words tumbled out. "I thought I was just a normal kid, growing up in a normal family. I never dreamed that I wasn't my father's child. I love my dad. He means the world to me. It hurts to know he's not really mine. It hurts a lot."

I buried my face in my hands to hide the tears that began streaming from my eyes. I felt Reverend Hahn's hand on my knee, and I didn't shrink from his touch.

"Herman Unruh is a good man," he said. "A remarkable man. If the tables were turned, I doubt that I could've done what he did. I'm truly grateful for everything he's done for you. And I envy him. He had the privilege of raising you. I envy the love you have for him."

"I hate the fact that my mom cheated on him," I sobbed. "He didn't deserve to have her treat him like that. I hate the fact that I'm a child of sin. The sin that you and my mother committed. Do you have any idea what that feels like?"

I waited a few moments for a response, and when none was forthcoming, I removed my hands from my face and looked at Reverend Hahn. His regal bearing had once again abandoned him, and he appeared withered and spent, an old man whose life was running out.

"My dear child," he said, his voice catching. "It nearly destroys me to know that you've been hurt so badly. This is exactly why I made the decision to have you raised by your mother and her husband. This is why I gave up all rights to you. I didn't want you to feel like an illegitimate child."

Suddenly, what he said made sense to me. For the first time, I fully understood the decision that my mother, my father, and Reverend Hahn had made to protect me. I found myself on the verge of forgiving the three of them for their deception when Reverend Hahn asked a question that turned my mind in a different direction.

"Victoria, do you like who you are?"

"No," I said. "I'm the child of two people who lied and cheated. How could I like that?"

"That's not what I mean. Do you like who you are as a person? You're beautiful. You're extraordinarily bright. You're superbly talented. You're a scholar. You're a singer. You're an actress. You're popular with your peers. You're a natural leader. You are a powerful young woman. Do you like those things about yourself?"

I stared at him, astounded. "I . . . I guess so."

He leaned forward, gazing intently into my eyes. "It's true that what your mother and I did was wrong. But our misguided action brought you into the world. And I can't think for a minute that it wasn't God's will that you were born. Your life has already blessed many people, and as you move forward into adulthood, you will be of great service to others. Your birth may have been the consequence of my transgression. But not an unfortunate consequence. There's nothing unfortunate about you, Victoria. How can your existence be anything other than a part of God's divine plan?"

As I stared at him, trying to absorb what he was saying, he sat back, a glint of self-satisfaction in his eyes. "If you'd been born under . . . different circumstances . . . you might not have been so fortunate. You could've turned out like your sister Lucy."

His words slapped me hard, sending me reeling. When

my mind finally stopped spinning, I came face to face with something I'd never wanted to admit to myself, that I always thought of myself as superior to my sister. Even as a tiny child, I'd counted myself lucky that I wasn't like Lucy. During my growing up years, I'd felt smug about the fact that I had a better life than she did. I was smarter, more capable, and more popular than she could ever hope to be. And now, every time I visited Lucy in her pitiful little apartment, I felt profoundly grateful that fate had spared me her lot in life.

I looked at the shelves of books on the wall behind Reverend Hahn, books that could be appreciated only by a brilliant mind. And I realized that I'd never seen Herman Unruh pick up a book other than the Bible. The level of his literacy took him no farther than the pages of the daily newspaper. Without question, Herman Unruh possessed a noble character and a heart of gold, but he was an intellectual dullard. In the arena of intelligence, I stood with the man who'd given me life, head and shoulders above the man who'd raised me.

Although Reverend Hahn was far too dignified to openly say something so arrogant, I knew he was suggesting that I was fortunate to have inherited his genetics. I hated him for making me face my own smugness, the self-satisfaction that was so like his own. I felt the urge to shove his wheelchair into the shelves behind him, burying his frail old body under a cascade of his books, walking out and leaving someone else to rescue him from the wreckage.

"You son-of-a-bitch!" I hissed. "How dare you insult my family like that?"

I jumped up to leave, but as I headed toward the door, Reverend Hahn's voice rang out, loud and strong. "Victoria! Stop!"

Unable to defy the powerful command, I halted my steps and turned to face him. "You can walk out on me now," he said, "but at some point, you'll need to come back and finish this conversation."

"I don't have anything else to say to you," I retorted. "You know what I feel like doing right now? Going out there and telling the whole world what you've done."

"You can do that," he said. "But you won't."

"How do you know that?"

"Because I know you. You have more class than that. You won't go out there and run your mouth and make a fool out of yourself. And you won't hurt the people you love."

I sneered at him. "How can you even say that?"

"Because I know you," he repeated.

I walked back to the sofa and sat down. Reverend Hahn was controlling the situation, controlling me. But I knew he was right.

"Okay," I said. "I'm not going to tell. But it's not for your sake. It's for my dad's sake. He didn't do anything wrong. I don't want to hurt him. He's been hurt enough."

"I understand that," Reverend Hahn said. "He's done right by you, and he deserves your loyalty and your protection. I know you think Herman Unruh is a better man than I am, and I can't argue with that. It's probably true."

Suddenly, I felt empty, exhausted, and deeply ashamed of my display of despicable behavior. I'd been unkind and disrespectful from the moment I'd set foot inside Reverend Hahn's apartment. "I'm sorry," I mumbled. "I'm really sorry."

Reverend Hahn smiled tenderly at me. "It's okay, Victoria. You're entitled to your feelings, and I appreciate your honesty with me. It's inevitable that we'll have to get through a few storms before we can establish a good relationship with each other."

I cringed at the word *relationship*, realizing that once again, my biological father was gently but persistently leading me to where he wanted me to go.

Not knowing what else to say to him, I gazed around at the furnishings in his small apartment. Then I surprised myself by asking, "Do you like it here?"

Reverend Hahn chuckled. "Yes. I love it. I feel blessed to be here. It's a wonderful place to spend my later years."

I got up and walked through the kitchenette to peer out the sliding glass door. The small patch of lawn in the little courtyard was manicured, the flowerbeds immaculately kept. A variety of irises were in bloom, along with recently planted coleus, marigolds, geraniums, and begonias. "It's really pretty," I said.

"Yes," he said. "I enjoy wheeling my chair out there. I'm looking forward to spending a lot of time out there this summer."

Surveying the tiny kitchenette, I asked, "Do you do your own cooking?"

He shook his head. "Not a lot. I don't do much more than make myself a cup of coffee. I take my meals in the community dining room." He gestured with his long arm.

"It's just down the hall from here. Sharing meals with others gives me an opportunity for fellowship."

I smiled, picturing the elderly gentleman charming the other residents of the manor with his charismatic personality. The old women would adore the handsome widower, and would clamor for his attention. He'd beam his affection on all of them, making each one of them feel special.

"There's a lot you don't know about me, Victoria," he said.

"I know," I replied.

"Any time you have questions, feel free to ask me."

I'd already taken in more than I could handle for the day, and I wanted to go home. "Maybe another time," I said. Then I realized I'd just given Reverend Hahn the impression that I'd be visiting him again.

"What are you doing this summer?" he asked.

"I'll be getting a job. Hopefully, waitressing. I've put in a lot of applications."

"Good for you," he said. "You're on the ball. And then you'll be going to Goshen College in the fall. You've been awarded a Menno Simons scholarship."

I looked at him, startled. "How did you know that?"

He smiled. "I keep on top of these things. I stay in touch with what's going on at the college. What are you planning to major in?"

"I don't know yet. Maybe psychology. Maybe communications or music."

"We can talk about it. I'll help you figure it out."

"Won't it look weird if I keep coming over here?" I asked. "Won't people suspect something?"

"Not at all," he said. "I counsel a lot of young people."

I stood up. "I need to go."

He stretched out his arms. "Can I have a hug?"

At that moment, I knew that if I wanted any kind of relationship with my biological father, I couldn't allow him to bowl me over. I had to assert a strength that could stand up to his. "I'm not ready for that," I said.

"I understand." The twinkle in his eyes told me that he was proud that I had the will to stand my ground. I allowed him to clutch my hand for a few seconds before I walked out the door of his apartment.

As I stepped through the front door of my home fifteen minutes later, I saw my dad sitting in his armchair. Apparently, he'd just gotten home from delivering his Saturday mail. He was sleeping, his head dropped forward. His broad chest and rotund belly rose and fell with the rhythm of his breathing.

I could hear thumping and swishing coming from upstairs, the sounds of my mother running her dust mop over the linoleum floor in Lucy's old bedroom. I knew that keeping busy was her way of dealing with her anxiety about my visit with Reverend Hahn.

I closed the door softly so as not to awaken my dad. But he roused when he heard my footsteps. As he raised his head, I saw the weariness in his eyes, the resignation in the lines of his craggy face. I knew full well that, in spite of what he'd told me the previous day, my visit with my other father had caused him pain. He felt like he'd lost me.

In that moment, I knew something with absolute certainty. As I would be stepping out into the world as a young adult, looking for opportunities to soar, my father would be winding down his ordinary life, a life filled with far more than his share of disappointment. And I knew that no matter where my life took me, I'd give Herman Unruh the very best that I had to offer. I'd make sure his last years were the most blessed years of his life. He'd given his best to me. I would do nothing less than return his abundant love.

As I approached his chair, he smiled at me. "How did it go, sweetheart?"

"Fine," I replied. "It went fine."

I got down on the floor and sat with my head resting against his knee.

"Daddy," I said.

"Vickie," he said as he reached out his beefy hand to stroke my head. "Vickie, Vickie, Vickie."

AUTHOR'S NOTE

In this novel, I have referred to a number of businesses and organizations that currently exist or have existed in the city of Goshen, Indiana, and the surrounding communities. I have used them fictitiously, and it is not my intention to accurately portray any activities, events, or people associated with those businesses and organizations. Westside Mennonite Church, First Mennonite Church of Warsaw, and Conrad Grebel Christian High School are entirely products of my imagination.

I have given a number of my characters surnames common in the Mennonite community. I have not used the full name of any person whom I have ever known. If any of my characters share your name or the name of someone you know, please understand that this is unintentional and purely coincidental.

OTHER BOOKS BY LOIS JEAN THOMAS

Me and You—We Are Who? (The Sambodh Society, Inc., 2006)

All the Happiness There Is (The Sambodh Society, Inc., 2006)

Johnny and Kris (The Sambodh Society, Inc., 2013)

Daughters of Seferina (Seventh Child Publishing/ CreateSpace, 2013)

Days of Daze: My Journey Through the World of Traumatic Brain Injury (Seventh Child Publishing/ CreateSpace, 2014)

Rachel's Song (Seventh Child Publishing/CreateSpace, 2014)

A.K.A. Suzette (Seventh Child Publishing/CreateSpace, 2014)